CURSE OF SILENCE

THE TRAGIC STORY OF REMPHELIA

VIOLA TEMPEST

CONTENTS

Curse of Silence

THE TRAGIC STORY OF REMPHELIA

Curse of Silence

The Tragic Story of Remphelia

© Copyright 2021 Viola Tempest

Cover Design by Ryn Katryn Digital Art
https://www.rynkatryn.com/

ISBN-13: 978-1-952716-20-1 (Ebook)
ISBN-13: 978-1-952716-19-5 (Print)

CHAPTER 1

THE FALL OF ACACIA

Far beneath the dark, heavy clouds, laid a beautiful kingdom, both powerful and majestic. Ruled by a magnificent king, the kingdom of Acacia dominated the Russian nation and surrounding countries. Known for its beauty and charm, tourists from all over the world traveled to Acacia to admire its wealthy estates and rich soil.

The people of Acacia lived a peaceful life, content with

the mundane routines they had and usually kept to themselves. Their children played amongst other children with no quarrels or jealousy, no animosity or hate. Adults helped each other out without expecting anything in return. No wars ever broke out in Acacia, not even a single fist fight. The kingdom of Acacia was a calm one, so calm that sounds were barely heard, and sometimes, neighboring towns forgot the kingdom even existed.

Nearly four thousand miles away from Acacia, laid the kingdom of Norfolk. Unlike Acacia, Norfolk did not boast a calm and peaceful lifestyle. A kingdom located in the south of France, Norfolk was hungry for power, and they would do anything, including murder, to seize it.

You see, Norfolk and Acacia used to be part of one kingdom, ruled by two brothers who worked side by side to create the most powerful realm in the entire world. However, with creative minds, also came creative differences. Soon, the two brothers found themselves tearing down the empire as they wanted to go their separate ways. Kilgert Norcia, the older of the two brothers, moved his half of the empire to northern Russia, while Prylar Norcia, the younger brother, stayed in France.

At first, things went as smoothly as planned, Kilgert ruling his docile kingdom while Prylar overtook the aggressive. However, soon, this divide began to create conflict. Kilgert slowly became the powerhouse, the respectable king, while Prylar was seen as a joke. Kilgert wore the crown of dominance over his head while Prylar was crushed under the weight of his, and the supremacy of Europe belonged to the East.

The Eastern part of Europe belonged to the Russians, a territory marked with wisdom and intelligence, and was considered to be the land of the rising sun. Their territory was surrounded by beautiful and lush green forests, magnificent blue lakes, and spectacularly high mountains. They were well-established; cities were built with underground drainage systems, houses were made of brick and stone, and their education was among the best in the world. It was also considered a global market for trade, with merchants traveling far and away from other countries, elevating the land with even more riches.

On the other side of the continent, lied the French, the side not so well off. Because of the failing kingdom of Prylar, France began to fall apart, with its people living in poor conditions on the streets, their homes made of mud and wet wood, and they were forced to eat whatever animals and rodents they found roaming the dirty streets. They had no clean water, resorting to only showering whenever it rained, and despite the beautiful mountains that used to surround them, now, they were just mountains of trash and hatred.

Their king had failed them, and the people of France became bitter and angry. Once hard-working peasants, they had now given up on life, waking up each morning and cursing to themselves that they were still alive. The French despised the Russians for claiming all the riches and wealth while they were left to eat dirt. They hated Kilgert and his people, yet they never did anything about it. Still, the barriers around Acacia were so strong and powerful that they couldn't even if they wanted to.

One depressing morning, Kilgert Norcia, the esteemed king of Acacia, fell ill. He was nearly ninety years old, and his body no longer had the strength it did before to handle the harsh cold winters of Siberia. He soon passed away, and his lovely wife, Racinda, took over his empire as the new ruler.

The people of Acacia were devastated about the passing of Kilgert, but they were hopeful that the kingdom would remain strong even under the new rule of Queen Racinda. However, life started to take a turn, and the once peaceful kingdom of Acacia fell weak at the hands of the new docile queen. Racinda didn't know how to rule a kingdom, not like her husband. She was more focused on immediate needs like hearty foods and large homes than she was on safety and security. She didn't know how to negotiate trade, and soon, merchants stopped coming, losing their main source of income.

Because of this, Racinda decided to make some cuts. She tore down the walls around the empire and removed the military guards so she would have enough money to continue feeding her people and allowing them to keep their lavish homes. Neither she nor the people of Acacia saw this as a problem. Never once in their lifetime had they ever faced an invasion. No one expected one to happen any time soon.

Far to the left, the bitter French were preparing for battle. Prylar Norcia had heard about the death of his brother and gathered his army for takeover, now that the barricades around the kingdom were down, allowing for easy access.

"It's time we take back what rightfully belongs to us!" he commanded as he prepared his army for battle.

While Kilgert always cared deeply for his brother, Prylar never batted an eye when it came to sabotage. He had always been jealous of Kilgert, seeing the injustice of his brother's successful kingdom while his was sentenced to a lifetime of misery and pain.

THE SILENCE OF THE NIGHT IN ACACIA WAS BROKEN down by the screaming, crying voices of the upper-class citizens and their families. The French were out for blood, with no one left unscathed, slaughtering everyone in sight. The rage had built up inside the French for so long that their murders became impulsive. They had become blinded to the actions that they were committing.

The Russians tried to fight back, but they were powerless against the army of the French, who trained for battle most of their lives while the Russians sat back and enjoyed life for what it was. And after Racinda had sold all their weapons and armory, they were no match. Even hiding inside their homes didn't work; the French simply tore down their doors and slaughtered them.

Four long and brutal years later, the French and Russians were still at war, the Russians trying to escape and keep themselves from being found while the French refused to quit until every single last one of the Russians were dead.

During the winter of 1841, the climate proved much more challenging for the dying Russians. Their lakes were frozen, and they were slowly running out of food. All the farmers and their land had been decimated, and the few remaining people were entering into famine. The French had taken over the kingdom of Acacia, with Prylar threatening Racinda into marriage and becoming their new leader, and the remaining Russians were forced out to fend for themselves.

Far off in the countryside, hidden in a tiny cabin covered by snow and rotting trees, was the Billings family. At the head of the household, was Richard Billings, a hard-working Russian trader who used to live a lavish lifestyle. He never had to deal with financial hardships, his family always living a comfortable life, until now.

Less than a year ago, the Billings family tried to hide in their cottage within the kingdom of Acacia. They thought it was a good idea, spending millions in attempts to seal the home from any of the French intruders. However, the French were much more powerful than they had thought, and several barged in, killed Richard's son, and kidnapped his wife. Luckily, he was able to grab his two daughters, Sable and Francesca, in time to escape before they were captured alongside her.

Month after month inside the broken-down cabin, Richard and his daughters found themselves starving, chewing on the burnt twigs they collected from the woods to curb their hunger pains.

"Daddy, will this be over soon? I'm hungry, and I miss home," Sable cried out, her stomach wrenching in pain.

Sable was seven years older than her little sister, Francesca, always eager to venture out and take on new challenges while Francesca liked to keep to herself, preferring peace and silence to keep a clear mind.

"Soon, honey, soon," Richard whispered back.

However, deep within his heart, he knew this nightmare wasn't going to end until the French had their blood as well.

One dark night, Richard gathered a couple of the other

remaining Russian survivors and made a plan to take back their land from the French.

"Sable, stay here with your little sister. Daddy needs to go take care of some things. I'll be back as soon as I can."

"Are you going to bring back some food?" Sable asked.

Richard smiled. "Don't you worry, Sable, I'm going to bring back more than just food."

And with that, he grabbed his hand-carved stake, threw on his coat, and walked out the door.

THEIR PLAN WAS SIMPLE. THEY WOULD DIVIDE themselves into two groups, the distractors and the terminators. The distractors would drive the French's attention toward their way while the terminators slashed their necks from behind. It was a risky plan, with a high chance of most, if not all, of the Russian tribe dying. But they knew they had to try. Even if some were to sacrifice themselves and perish, at least the others had a chance of surviving the brutal winter.

"Alright, it's now or never," Richard exclaimed. "Everyone ready?"

As the others nodded, the gang slowly began approaching Acacia. Under the moonlight, the empire looked more beautiful than ever, especially during a time when they missed it the most. Even with the shriveled corpses on the ground and half the village in ruins, Acacia still flaunted one of the most beautiful landscapes in the country.

They walked closer toward the gates of the kingdom, their plan in action. The distractors turned left toward the guards while the terminators turned right. Richard was part of the terminators, and he crept down behind the bushes beside the wall and waited, waited for the gates to open so he could quickly run in.

However, their plan took a turn for the worst. The distractors managed to pull the guards away from the gates, allowing it to open wide for the terminators, but it was all a trap, arrows and knives shooting straight toward Richard and his group, several men falling fatal on the spot.

"Run!" Richard shouted, hoping to grab the attention of at least a few men before the rest of them fell victim to the French.

"Fuck! How did they know we were coming?" Marlin, Richard's closest friend, shouted as they started running back to their base camp.

"I don't know, but just keep running. We can't let them take us. I have two daughters at home I need to get back to!" Richard shouted back

"Oh, you two won't make it very far, but I guess I'll at least give you a chance," a female voice ominously said behind them.

The entire Russian gang were men, so hearing a female voice caught Richard and Marlin by surprise. They quickly turned around while continuing to run and saw long black hair hanging over the woman's face. Screaming in terror, the two men pushed themselves harder and harder, their legs tearing as their boots jabbed into their shins. All they needed to do was reach their base camp, where they created a dugout they could crawl inside for safety.

"Only a few more feet," Marlin reassured his partner as their legs began to go numb.

Richard could see it, the entrance so close yet so out of

reach. He couldn't focus on anything other than getting himself to safety. The lives of his daughters depended on it.

"Gotcha!" The woman startled both Richard and Marlin when she grabbed them by the shoulders. "Not fast enough, boys."

"Sable? When's father coming home?" Francesca turned to her older sister and asked several days later.

"Soon, Frannie, soon."

However, Sable didn't know whether it would be soon or not. She hadn't heard anything from their father, and she was beginning to fear that something had happened to him.

Suddenly, there was a loud knock on the door.

"Who... who is it?" Francesca asked, backing away into the corner of the old cabin, hugging her blanket tight.

Sable was just as terrified as Francesca, but she knew she had to stay strong. She had to protect her little sister at all costs. Slowly, she crept closer toward the door, and she pulled it wide open.

A rush of snow blew in from the harsh wind, blinding both Sable and Francesca. Sable tried to hold on tight to the door, but she soon found herself falling over onto the ground. When she finally regained her vision, she saw Isabella, Marlin's wife, standing at the front door, her eyes filled with tears, and clutching onto the skirt of her dress.

"Isabella?" Sable asked.

"Girls, I... I..." Isabella started to choke as she spoke. "I need you to come with me."

Francesca interjected. "But we can't! We have to wait for father to come home!"

This triggered Isabella to cry even harder, causing Sable to walk closer and hug her just to keep her from going hysterical.

"Isabella, what happened? Is father okay?" Sable asked.

Shaking her head, Isabella quietly whispered. "No. They got him; they got them all. They're... they're all gone."

As Isabella mourned for the loss of her husband and all the fallen warriors, she fell to her knees.

On the foggy night of December 28, 1844, the French military made their way back toward the White Palace. The White Palace was considered to be the most sacred place in Acacia, the place where the royal family resided, where heroes and gods were worshipped, and where people peacefully said their prayers. The building was made of marble stones, and in the middle, laid a celestial fire, symbolizing the Great Russian Empire, constantly burning to protect the Russian people.

Lord Kilgert had been decapitated, and Prylar leaned back on his throne smugly as the celestial fire turned to smoke, the Russians no longer safe and protected under the new rule of the French army.

Instead, the White Palace now celebrated a new tradition, a tradition they had carried in the Norfolk Kingdom for decades, gathering every last woman and child from the Acacia Kingdom they still found alive and selling them to the wealthy Frenchmen.

Among them, was Francesca.

Three years ago, when Isabella arrived at the Billings' cabin to deliver the daughters the bad news, she didn't realize that she was being followed, followed by the same French guards who killed her husband and the girl's father. They stabbed Isabella in the neck and proceeded to go after the two girls. Sable, being the strong-willed girl that she was, tried everything she could to protect her little sister. Unfortunately, she sacrificed her life in the process, dying a hero.

As a result, Francesca was captured, thrown in a carriage, and brought to the White Palace, where she, among many other young girls, were held captive, awaiting their fate on who would be in the next auction. This year, Francesca Billings was the chosen one, the chosen one to be auctioned off to the high priest of Paris. She was the perfect choice for the priest. As someone who valued wisdom and tenacity, Francesca became the easy choice to take back to his abode.

All the French peasants gathered around for the ceremony, the union between two countries, France and Russia. The French peasants saw the Russian's devastation as a moment to be proud of. All those years of suffering while the Russians had it all gave them no sympathy whatsoever.

Francesca was groomed and cleaned before her summoning, dressed in a traditional red garment as she walked down the aisle of the palace, the celestial smoke now filled with gold coins. Everyone in town gathered in the palace. Many even traveled from far away just to observe a moment they never thought would come to fruition.

The crowd cheered as the high priest took Francesca by the hand and blessed it, claiming her as his. It was a great emotional moment for everyone present, but all Francesca adorned was a sad frown.

Know your worth, Frannie. You're stronger than people give you credit for. Know your worth. I'm proud of you. Francesca could hear her mother's voice inside her head, repeating the same phrase over and over until her body stopped trembling with fear.

And so, little Francesca Billings packed up the minimal belongings she had after the military set fire to her cabin, and she followed the priest to Paris.

Paris looked nothing like Francesca's hometown in Russia. The streets were much dirtier, the people were much ruder, and everybody stared at her like she was a sinner. Trash littered the roads, and there were more strays than there were people. Arriving at the priest's home, Francesca found herself facing a building even larger than the White Palace. It was as if the city existed just for his home, and everything around it was his backyard. The interior was decorated with gold-plated everything, so luxurious that she couldn't take her eyes away from it.

Still, Francesca found herself missing her old life, her parents, her sister, her life back home. She struggled trying to adapt to her new identity and her new life. She looked at herself in the mirror and barely recognized her face. She didn't resemble the straggly-haired girl she had been for the past several years. Instead, she saw herself wearing a sequined gown finished with ribbons of red and yellow, and her hair was tied and braided.

The high priest had everything anyone could ever want inside his lavish home, and everyone around him hated him for it.

One night, after Francesca finished her duties for the day, she cleaned herself up and tried to get some rest. However, her quiet mind was soon disturbed by the ruckus of noises outside.

"Burn it down! Burn it down!" was all she could hear.

Before waking up the priest, she rushed over to her own window and looked outside. There, she could see an entire mob of French peasants carrying torches and setting fire to the abode.

From here, the war began, the war between the French peasants and the upper class. The French peasants were a bitter and envious group, never satisfied with what they had. They not only hated the Russians, but they also hated the wealthier class of France, always flashing their riches and plump bellies while the peasants were forced to starve.

Although the wealthy had more weapons and military equipment, the peasants were far greater in number, exhibiting the angry wrath they had been hiding for nearly a century and wiping out the higher class in just several days. They were known as the vigilantes, claiming vengeance on those who had hurt them and reclaiming the power for their own kind. They broke into every home of the rich and brutally murdered them while claiming the buildings for themselves. The men were killed while the women and children were imprisoned, eventually turning the entire northern central region of France into a river of blood.

And Francesca, poor little Francesca, had to witness yet another manslaughter, this time, of the high priest, who tried to protect her from being taken and seized, but was decimated himself in the process. Upon seeing the body lying cold on the ground, her mind flashed back to the bodies of Isabella and Sable who also fell cold to the ground, a pool of blood spilling out of them as the air from their bodies escaped.

"No! I'm not going with you! You can't take me!" she shouted at the men who walked toward her, her body backing into her closer door as their dirt-covered hands reached for her.

However, the men could only laugh. "What did you say? Hey, Raphael, get a load of this. This *stupid* child here thinks she actually has a say in this."

"I mean it! Come any closer, and you will feel my wrath."

The men all laughed again and, at the same time, all reached for her, seizing her tight and tying her up. Francesca tried to fight back, but she was no match for the five burly men standing before her.

As the French peasants seized little Francesca and dragged her out the door, her eyes began to glow a tint of red.

Loud screams were heard several hours later, and Francesca, blindfolded, feared for what Raphael and the other men were going to do to her. They took off the blindfold, and Francesca found herself in front of a large warehouse made of strong steel roofs and brick walls. As Raphael opened the gate and pulled her inside, she noticed the words, Death to all Russians, scribbled in French on the front wall.

She then found herself standing in the dark, surrounded by an army of French peasants, and she heard another scream. She tried to pull herself back out toward the door to avoid any potential horrors coming her way, but Raphael grasped tightly onto her arm.

"You're not going anywhere, you little runt."

He dragged her farther into the warehouse, and soon, they found themselves staring at another door. He opened it, and when Francesca walked inside, she saw a mess of women and children lined up and chained. She later found out that they had been starving and beaten while waiting for their fate. Raphael quickly chained Francesca up along with the others before walking out.

"Don't worry. You're young and pretty. You probably won't stay here long," the woman beside her said softly when the men left.

She looked much older than Francesca, probably old enough to be her mother's age.

"Wha... what's going on? Where am I?" Francesca asked, her voice trembling as the chains pulled tighter on her wrists.

"My name's Vanya," she sighed. "I've been trapped here for months, unable to leave, unable to escape. They only want the younger girls, the healthier and livelier ones, while leaving the rest of us here to rot, beating us senseless every time we speak." Vanya paused for a moment and showed Francesca the bruises on her leg. "None of us know where they take them, but wherever it is, I sure hope it's better than this shithole."

Not before long, the door flew open again, and a young girl around Francesca's age was thrown onto the hard ground. She was covered in blood, and it seemed that the shrilling screams Francesca had heard earlier belonged to her. Spitting blood, the young girl crawled her way over to the shared bowl of filthy water as the door closed again. Everyone stared at her in horror. She looked like she would barely survive another day, her left leg paralyzed and half the hair on her head missing.

"Hey, you there. Are you alright? What's your name?" Vanya asked as she nodded her head toward the girl.

"B... B..."

However, the girl could barely mutter her own name, her voice and body so weak that she soon collapsed onto the cold ground.

Before Vanya could say another word, the door opened yet again, and Raphael walked in. Starting from the right corner of the room, he examined every girl carefully, from the way their hair parted to the way their lips pouted.

Finally, he arrived at Vanya, a smirk crossing his face as he glared down at her half-naked body. All the girls in the room were dressed in torn rags, but being much older than the rest, Vanya's body had fully developed, and it was a sight to see for many of the men. He reached a hand up and began stroking the side of her face while the other explored her body. Vanya winced and tried to pull away, but there was only so much she could do.

"Leave me alone! Leave me alone!" Vanya screamed as Raphael held her in place.

He leaned down and tried to kiss her, but Vanya managed to bite his lip instead, causing him to slap her across the face.

With blood dripping down his chin, he yelled, "You do *not* disrespect your authorities! You're slaves. Whatever we tell you to do, you do!" He reached his hand out again to grope her.

"Hey! She said, leave her alone!" Francesca shouted, forcing Raphael to turn his attention toward her.

"And who the hell do you think you are? You stupid, little runt!" He slapped Francesca hard across the face and started to unchain her from the wall. "I guess you just volunteered to take her place."

"No, father! Don't go! It's dangerous out there! Don't go outside," Sable screamed, holding on tightly to Francesca as their father put on his coat and hat.

He turned to them. "It's okay, Sable. I just need to go outside to get some more firewood. Otherwise, we're all going to freeze in here. I'll just be a minute, I promise."

Richard Billings proceeded out the door, his arms

wrapped tightly around his body as he shivered toward the forest. Mere seconds later, bullets came flying straight at him, knocking him over onto the snow in an instant, and several masked men started rushing to the cabin as Sable and Francesca screamed.

Francesca Billings woke up in bed, sweat pouring down her face, and her lungs out of breath. It was just a dream. It was all just a dream.

Ten years after the death of her father and sister, Francesca found herself sitting by her bedroom window, staring out into the countryside farm. After she was forced out of the warehouse by Raphael, she was put up for auction, a chance to become another slave to the highest bidder, with one lucky man, Lyon Beauchamp, outbidding all the rest. He saw promise in her, and he treated Francesca well, almost like she was his own daughter. Unfortunately, he died soon after from a heart attack, and his ancestors took her in.

Looking out from the window of the bedroom, she saw well-paved streets and horse carriages, all surrounded by beautiful trees and mountains. It resembled the picture-perfect wealth of the French's arrogance. She sighed, her breath floating in front of her from the cold air. The farm reminded her so much of home, of Acacia, how her mother used to bring her out into the backyard every morning and just breathe in the aromatic fragrance of their garden. Those were the days.

Her memories were distracted when she heard a knock on the door. She walked over to open it and saw a well-dressed man standing at the doorway to greet her.

"Good morning, Ms. Francesca. My name is Sir Lonergan, and I'm here to take you over to the main mansion. Follow me, please."

For the past seven years, Francesca had been living with the Beauchamps, working as their slave while they gave her a place to sleep and took her in after Lyon passed away. Many members of the family hated her, but they couldn't kick her out as they promised Lyon they would look after her as if she were part of the family.

"Some house rules have changed over the past several days. You are now required to work solely on the farm. There has been a high case of deaths lately. Probably something going around. We also had to make some cut backs on the budget. From now on, you will be given one bread roll twice a day, and that's it. If you even so much as to ask for more, you will have one taken away instead. Do you understand?" he asked, turning to Francesca.

She nodded.

"Good." He smiled, turning his head away. "I'm responsible for you, so anything you do that's out of bounds, it's my ass on the line." He turned to face Francesca again. "And one more thing, now that you are of age, you are to be married to Lucas Beauchamp, the son of the heiress. The ceremony shall take place in three months."

Francesca had met Lucas before. He was six years older than her and the most arrogant person she had ever spoken to. He constantly bragged about how wealthy he was, and how she had to wait on him hand and feet or else he would tell his mother. Francesca had met spoiled before, but this guy was on a whole new level.

ONE MORNING, WHILE SHUCKING CORN ON THE FARM, Francesca accidentally bumped into a body that was pulling weeds beside her.

"Oh, sorry, I didn't mean to do that," she quickly apologized.

When she looked up, she saw a young man about her age, handsome as the sun was bright. He smiled at her, and she blushed.

"It's okay, happens to all of us," he replied. "Hi, I'm Dmitry." He held out his hand.

Francesca extended hers back and shook it. "Hi, Dmitry. I'm Francesca. I haven't seen you around before."

"I'm new, just got here last night and put right to work, ha-ha. No surprise there. I was living with a nice family in Marseille before a group of men dressed in black gunned them all down and brought me here. Don't ask me why; I just know the woman in there, the head honcho, is a real bitch." He pointed at the main building as he spoke.

"Oh, that's Juliana. Yeah, she can be a real pain sometimes. I find it's best to just nod your head and compliment on how pretty she is. Then she'll go a little easier on you."

"Ha-ha, thanks for the tip." He smiled again.

As the days went by, Francesca and Dmitry grew closer and closer. Dmitry had the most affectionate smile Francesca had ever seen, and she felt feelings toward Dmitry that she had never felt for Lucas. Unlike Lucas, Dmitry was kind and soft-spoken. He was humble, and he never acted like he was better than Francesca.

After several weeks, Francesca found herself falling in love with him.

And Lucas noticed. Oh, did Lucas notice. And he was

not about to let some low-life Russian peasant just swoop in and take his woman. He was supposed to marry Francesca in less than two months, and he wasn't going to let anything, or anyone, get in the way.

He ordered his guards to seize both Francesca and Dmitry and throw them into the basement dungeon, in separate cells. The only way he would ever set them free was if Francesca promised to stop loving the Russian.

"I can't do that," Francesca insisted. "I can't change how I feel. You can't force someone to love you and marry you when they don't want to. I don't love you, Lucas. I never have, and I never will."

"Don't you *dare* say that again! You'll be sorry if you don't marry me. You belong to *me*! I *own* you."

"Do to me all you want. I don't care anymore. I'd rather *die* than be your wife, you disgusting, foul-mouthed, arrogant *brat*!" she yelled.

That was the straw that broke the camel's back. Lucas broke into Francesca's cell and tried to strangle the life out of her.

"You take that back! You take that back right now!"

Francesca felt powerless. Lucas wasn't only much older than her, but he was also much stronger. She felt her body slowly growing weaker and weaker, the breath leaving her lungs, until suddenly, Lucas flew back against the wall behind him.

"Wha... what did you do to me?" He stormed back toward her, his face fuming red, his fists balled up.

"Nothing. I swear, I didn't do anything!" Francesca backed away. "I don't know what happened."

"You better watch your back. Next time, you won't be so lucky. That goes for your little boyfriend, too."

Francesca didn't know what was going on, but as the

days passed, she found her body changing, her body tingling and her eyes twitching whenever she thought of Lucas and how much she hated him. Things got even worse when Lucas dragged Dmitry out from his cell one night and stabbed him right in front of Francesca.

"You still love him, huh, Francesca? Would you still love him if he were dead?" Lucas taunted her by holding a knife to Dmitry's neck.

"Even if you kill him, I'll still love him more than I'll ever love you," she sneered.

That enraged Lucas even more, and he sliced open Dmitry's throat. Francesca screamed in agonizing sorrow as her fingers began to glow. No one noticed, not even her.

"You ready to love me *now*?" Lucas demanded, turning his attention to her as Dmitry's lifeless body fell to the ground.

"No."

Fed up with her stubbornness, Lucas opened her cage and went inside. He grabbed Francesca and started to kiss her, refusing to let her go even as she struggled.

"You will love me. You will marry me."

"Lucas, no, stop!"

Her eyes turned bright red, and the next thing she knew, Lucas was levitating in the air.

He begged her to stop. He begged her to put him down, but the rage inside Francesca was so strong that she couldn't control it. Her fingers flamed, her eyes bright, and with one twist of the neck, Lucas fell lifeless.

Terrified by what she had just done, Francesca backed away from the body.

"Oh, no, what have I done?" she whispered to herself. "I have to get out of here. I have to leave." She rushed out the open cell and turned the corner, just to find Lonergan staring right at her, his eyes wide in shock. "I didn't do it! I don't know what happened!"

Silent for a moment, Lonergan soon spoke up, "Witch!"

Francesca quickly ran up the stairs and made her way to the front door. Lonergan was close behind, always on her tracks. She was fast, but he was much taller. She finally made it out the door when Lonergan shouted "witch" again, this time, to the crowd of residents and workers outside.

"Get her! She's a witch!"

Voices began whispering all at once, and everyone rushed toward their pitchforks and axes. Francesca pushed past several of them as the rest came charging after her. She ran and ran, trying to make her way into the woods so she could hide out in the trees.

"Almost there," she whispered to herself. "Just a few more steps."

But then her plan was thwarted. The adults around her were much quicker than she had thought, and she soon found herself completely surrounded.

"She's a murderer!"

"Look at her red eyes. She's possessed!"

"She's a witch!"

"Kill her! Kill her!" the crowd began to cheer as they marched toward her.

Francesca fell to her knees and began to cry. "I'm not a killer. I'm not!"

Suddenly, an explosion of power shot out of her, shattering the bodies of everyone within a hundred yards from where she was standing. She opened her eyes, but all she could see were decapitated bodies and an incinerated farm.

It happened again, the same thing that happened with Lucas.

She didn't know what was going on with her, but she sure as hell didn't want to stay and find out.

She started to make a run for it again, but given the tight-knit community and the number of people still in the mansion, she knew she didn't have much time before more people started coming after her. Lucas was Juliana's prized child, and once she heard of his death, she'd sent an entire army after Francesca. Blindly running down the streets in a town she didn't know was her only chance left for survival.

She eventually made her way to the outskirt slums, her body now so fragile and weak that she felt like she was going to break. Luckily, a couple of German nomads passing through on their way to Spain saw her calamitous condition and rushed over to help her.

THE NEXT MORNING WHEN FRANCESCA OPENED HER eyes, she fell back. The nomads were staring straight at her, mumbling words she strained to understand. Finally, the woman spoke up, introducing herself as Schala. They cleaned her up, gave her a set of clean clothes, and let her stay in their tent for a few days until she recovered.

"So, where are you headed, Francesca?" Schala asked the next night.

Francesca paused. She didn't know how to answer her. She didn't have a destination. She just wanted to get far away from the royal family.

"Um... nowhere, I guess. I've done some very bad things, and I just need refuge somewhere," she eventually spat out.

"Say no more," Nico, Schala's brother spoke up. "We

get it. The government was pretty shitty where we came from. Why do you think we're on the road? Tell you what, we're headed over to Bilbao, in Spain. Why don't you tag along with us? There's a port there, and if you can get on one of those ships to America, the French can't touch you. You're not safe staying in Europe. If you did something truly horrendous and word got out, the entire continent will come running after you in no time."

The news came like a miracle for her, overjoyed with happiness that she could soon stop running and just live. She was so excited to escape from her problems. What she didn't realize, however, was that her problems would never truly escape, the pain and darkness always residing in her mind.

When they arrived in Bilboa several weeks later, Schala and Nico pointed Francesca in the direction of the port and said their farewells.

"Stay safe, Francesca. Send us a letter when you get there. We'd love to see America one day." Nico waved and walked away.

There were several fishermen at the port, loading the ship with crates and nets. It was dark, and the dim oil lamps were just enough for Francesca to climb on without garnering too much attention. Once the ship was loaded, and the sound of the horns signified its departure, Francesca tried to camouflage herself as best she could as the fishermen made their hourly checks on the way to the Port of Boston.

After two long weeks of sailing, the fishermen on board

began to notice their food supply dwindling quicker than they expected. They had brought enough food on board to last an entire month, and now, they barely had enough to get through the week.

"Ah, gotcha, you little freeloader!" A man grabbed Francesca by the shoulder when he caught her nibbling on a roll of bread, hiding behind the crates. "You thought you could just climb onto our ship and steal our food, and we wouldn't notice you?"

She did. After two weeks of not getting caught, she thought she really had a chance of making it all the way to America problem-free.

"I'm... I'm sorry, sir. I didn't mean to cause any trouble. I just needed to get across this ocean. Please, please don't send me back."

He looked at her, his eyes suspicious. "Where are your parents, young lady? Do they know you're out here on a stranger's boat all alone?"

"I don't have parents, sir. They... they died; my sister; too. All the people I knew and loved are all gone."

That's when the fisherman began to feel sorry for little Francesca. He could relate to her. His entire family was killed by the Italian mafia when he was just a small child, and he had to learn to survive on his own ever since. His name was Santiago, she'd found out, and he'd been traveling to the states to sell his fish for nearly twenty-two years.

"Tell you what, I have a friend in Stockbridge. She owns an orphanage, an excellent one at that. Why don't I introduce you to her? I'm sure she'll be able to find a bed for you there until you're old enough to go out on your own."

Francesca nodded.

And that's how it all began. When Santiago introduced her to Headmaster Samantha Walden, the woman in charge of Baylor Orphanage, she immediately took a liking to Francesca. She saw her as a polite and well-mannered little girl who would serve as a great role model to the rest of the orphans.

Francesca was in poor shape, so upon arrival, Samantha Walden called the orphanage doctor, Doctor Montague, so he could inspect and treat her. She was especially concerned about the tint of red shining through her eyes and hoped that Naphazoline would help reduce the redness. That was usually effective whenever the children got sick, and since they had no idea what was causing the redness, they decided to give it a try. And it worked. Little did they know, the cure was only temporary.

Baylor Orphanage was the only orphanage within a hundred miles of town. There were many children left abandoned and alone from the Mexican-American War, and with limited space, Francesca was forced to share a room with another orphan, Charlotte Harpins. Charlotte was Queen Bee at Baylor, a constant troublemaker who always pulled pranks on the other children and demanded she got what she wanted. She hated the idea of sharing a room with another orphan, especially one who smelled like raw fish.

"Now, now, Charlotte. We have to learn to share. You've gone a long time without a roommate while others haven't, and it's about time you learn to be a little more cooperative." Headmaster Walden told Charlotte when she complained about Francesca.

And with that, Charlotte stormed off. She had a tendency of doing that whenever she didn't get what she wanted, throwing fits in hopes that someone would change their mind. But it never worked, leaving Charlotte perpetually angry.

CHAPTER 4
A KILLER AMONG US

On the foggy morning of November 16, 1953, a sharp scream came from outside the garden. The loud noise startled everyone, and Francesca, along with the other orphans, quickly got up.

She followed the heavy steps of people running down the stairs and across the halls, eventually reconvening with them out in the garden. She wasn't very tall and could barely see anything over the heads of the older boys, but she could hear murmurs and chatters in the crowd. She saw Doctor Montague rush in through the crowd with his first aid kit. Seeing this as her chance, Francesca squeezed in after him. When she got to the front, she saw a dead body hanging on the branch of a tree. The blood from the neck of the victim dripped and dripped down onto the grass, and the body was turning blue.

But that wasn't all. Below the hanging body, were at least ten other fatally-wounded bodies surrounding it. No one knew what had happened, or why someone was targeting the orphans like a plague.

"Alright, children, nothing to see here. Everyone go back to your rooms," Headmaster Walden ordered as she sensed the children beginning to grow fearful.

She respectfully buried the bodies, said her prayers, and convinced herself that this was just a one-time occurrence.

But it wasn't. From then on, every month, on the exact same day, a new body was found hanging from the tree, with even more orphans surrounding it. The children began living in fear, refusing to leave their rooms. They even began to blame others, calling each other *murderers*, their fingers pointed at Charlotte, especially. The trust between the orphans began to diminish, and hate filled every room at Baylor.

And because Francesca was Charlotte's roommate, they all thought they were in it together. All the orphans began bullying and insulting Francesca and Charlotte, throwing their trash at them and labeling them both as sinners and children of the Devil.

Then there was Travis, a new boy who entered the orphanage, and suddenly, everyone forgot why they were so angry. Travis Scott was a year older than Francesca and a gorgeous specimen, with his luscious brown locks and affectionate smile.

He took one look at Francesca and felt an instant attraction toward her, captivated by her untainted beauty. Her silent nature and peaceful aura attracted him from day one. He was the most educated and intelligent out of all of them, and everyone loved him. They spent every moment of every day together, holding hands and kissing whenever they had the chance.

But close by, was Marianne, another orphan who was also obsessed with Travis. Marianne was the daughter of Samantha Walden, and she felt like she was in charge of the other orphans. She was the one who usually controlled who was able to hang out with who, and it burned a scar in her heart knowing that the most popular boy at the orphanage was with someone other than her.

One day, while Marianne was sitting in Walden's office, filing her nails and sticking stamps onto envelopes, she saw Francesca and Travis out walking by the garden. The cold wind was blowing against their hair, and the beautiful sun rays were shining over them. When Travis pulled Francesca in close and planted a kiss on her, that set Marianne off.

"Travis! Can you come in here, please? I have a letter for you!" Marianne shouted from the window.

"Oh, really? Who's it from?" he asked.

"How the hell should I know? I'm not allowed to open it, remember? Confidentiality and all that?"

Travis looked back at Francesca. "I'll be right back, okay? Stay here, and wait for me."

Francesca nodded as Travis ran inside. However, the window was still wide open, and she could hear their entire conversation.

"Alright, where's the letter?" Travis asked Marianne when he got to the office.

"Right here, but what's the hurry? Why not stay and chat for a minute? You know, we never really got to know each other since you got here." Marianne held the envelope in her hand and walked toward Travis. "Mmm, you smell yummy."

"I mean it, Marianne. Just give me the letter."

"Why are you always hanging around that child anyway? Don't you think you need a more... mature woman in your life?" Marianne continued.

"Let me guess, you mean mature woman as in you?"

"Mmm, exactly."

As Marianne spoke, she grabbed Travis by the shoulder and leaned in to kiss him. Travis kissed back at first, startled by the gesture, but then he quickly pulled away.

"No, Marianne, I'm with Francesca." He reached behind her and grabbed the envelope. "And I believe this is for me."

"You're going to regret this, Travis. She's not good for you. I can feel it. She's not good for anyone. You're going to regret this!"

From that fateful day, the friendship between Travis and Marianne never felt the same again. Travis began to avoid her, and this only added fuel to the fire for Marianne. Everything she had hoped they would have together, all the nights she spent dreaming about him, about them together, vanished into thin air.

"How dare he?" Marianne fumed.

The feeling was incapacitating. As her rage built and built and built, more wrath consumed her every waking moment. Marianne decided she wouldn't stand for it. And so, she started to play tricks on Francesca! After all, what else could she do? But each time, Francesca was saved by the wisdom of Travis. Eventually, the pair realized in their wisdom that it was Marianne who was responsible for the devilish tricks. These hurdles the woman presented were real, of course, but nothing they couldn't handle.

BESIDES, BOTH OF THEM WERE LIVING THE BEST ERA OF their lives. Their relationship was filled with love, care, laughter, and intimate conversations that carried on deep into the night. When it came to Francesca, Travis was the only one left in her brutal world. Her shining star. The one she could call "hers."

Every single moment that she spent with him was imprinted on her memory, like a burn mark on a piece of wood. And yet... it seemed as though there would forever be a struggle. Each evening when she walked back to her bed, ready for a peaceful night filled with good memories, that's exactly when the nightmares would start. Awful, despairing, hopeless terrors that left her shivering in the sheets. The nightmare depicted the past — the one she yearned to be free from.

Still, the morning would eventually come. Francesca would wake up, shrug off the dark dreams, and go about her life. One day during class, all of the orphans gathered around. Rather brutally, they began to bully her under the influence of Marianne. Particularly about her relationship with Travis. Francesca tried her best to ignore them, to look away. To block out their incessantly cruel mimics and taunts. But the words cut deep.

"So, you and Travis, huh?" one of the orphans, Ashley, called out nastily.

She then began to make a series of abhorrent hand gestures. Francesca spun around on her heel. In that moment, the memories of the nightmares were still fresh on her mind. She was emotionally disturbed and couldn't withhold her anger a second longer!

"Shut up," she growled.

It wasn't like her to say something so malicious. But the mocking voices of the orphans sliced through her like razor blades. They were all so loud, their words so taunting and menacing that they echoed in her brain. Always talking far too much. Everywhere she went, the cruel gossip of her fellow orphans followed.

Francesca ground her teeth. The molars slid against each other, bone on bone.

Why can't they just all shut up for once? she thought with annoyance.

No matter where Francesca went or hid to try and find a moment of peace, their insulting words reverberated closely behind. Nowhere was safe. All she wanted was for them to be quiet. Silenced. For once in their pathetic lives, to stop talking and just zip their intolerable lips! Rage bubbled up inside her chest.

"Shut up," she repeated again, louder this time.

"Wh-what's wrong with her?" a second orphan, Raquel, stuttered.

He began to back away, but it was too late. Francesca's eyes burned blood red, throwing Raquel across the library before collapsing onto the ground. With her head lowered, Francesca gasped for air and tried to concentrate on herself, counting out loud, "one, two, three, four..."

Travis, who had only been a few feet away, immediately

rushed forward while several of the workers rushed to Raquel's aid.

"Get back!" he roared at the crowd of orphans.

The scolding worked. They shrank, their eyeballs white and round with fear.

"Leave us, now," he added. "If you know what's good for you."

The sound of clicking signaled the approach of the headmaster, Samantha Walden. She was tall and slim, like the reedy branches of a willow tree. Her normally gentle face was firm. The middle-aged wrinkles on her forehead made her look years older than she was — almost by a decade. Her blackish hair was streaked with silver. Stress, perhaps? Or the burden of knowing too much.

"Travis," the headmaster said tightly. "Please assist Francesca by helping her to her room."

Travis nodded. He wrapped his arms around the girl, careful not to hurt her, and as Francesca closed her weary eyes, she whispered a quiet, "Thank you." Little did they know, Marianne was watching from a distance. Her face curved into a crooked smile, almost as if she was enjoying the sight before her. As Travis and Francesca weaved through the corridors and toward the students' rooms, Marianne slithered behind them. Her ears perked up when she overheard the headmaster speaking in low tones. The words were broken up by the wind, but Marianne was still able to catch parts of the sentences.

"We must launch... investigation... very unusual... too many deaths..."

Ah, thought Marianne.

It seemed that the murders taking place within the orphanage and town were being noticed. She should talk to Agnes. If anyone knew about the murders, it would likely be that woman, the woman who seemed to know everything about everyone. The cabin in which Agnes lived wasn't far from the orphanage, and as such, she was able to regularly sneak around and gather intel about the orphans. For many months, the nosy woman had been watching Francesca. She was convinced that, somehow, the little girl was involved in the deaths.

Marianne smiled wickedly. *Yes,* she thought. *Agnes needs to know.*

After disciplining the impudent orphans for their brazen bullying, Samantha soon thought it wise to check in on Francesca. After all, the poor girl had been distraught. With a gentle knock on the door, the headmaster peeked her head in. Much to her surprise, Francesca's figure was blocked from her full view.

Instead of being alone on her bed, Travis sat there with his back to the doorway. The pair were no more than a few inches apart, their faces so close together, that the headmaster thought for sure they must be talking. But when Francesca suddenly bolted upright and smiled at her, her cheeks blushed pink as if she had just been caught mid-kiss.

"Ahem," coughed Samantha with a smile. "My apologies. It appears I am interrupting."

"Not at all," replied Travis casually.

However, his slightly tousled hair and knowing grin painted a different picture. Beside him, Francesca blushed a deeper shade of crimson.

"Yes, well..." The headmaster's eyes darted to where Francesca's hand was still touching Travis. "I just came to check on Francesca. Are you alright, my dear?"

Francesca blinked. The look on her face was a look of fear and pure terror. Something dark — something strange — had overtaken her in that moment. And yet, try as she might to figure out exactly what had occurred, the heat from Travis' body kept distracting her thoughts.

"I'm fine," she replied instead. She swallowed hard to contain the lie. "Totally fine."

"Good," nodded the headmaster.

The woman shuffled forward and patted Francesca on the shoulder. Before pivoting on her heel to leave the room, she smiled widely. Travis returned the look with a grin of his own but yet, he too was hiding something...

As the door to the room quietly closed, he sighed. Deep down, and despite Francesca's answer that she was feeling okay, there was most definitely *something* else going on. He could feel it in his bones. Francesca placed her head on his shoulder. She was light as a feather and cold as snow. Almost deathly. At the terrible thought, Travis frowned. He pulled her in closer against his chest and hoped that the warmth from his body would transfer onto her. When he glanced down to where the top of her hair rested under his chin, he was disappointed to see her eyes filled with tears.

"Francesca?" he uttered in concern.

When she said nothing, he hugged her even tighter. Big wet drops fell like rain, seeping through the fabric of his shirt. But Travis didn't question it. He knew Francesca. Knew her heart better than anyone, in fact. When it was the right time, he was sure that she would tell him everything, and all would be revealed. Still, the sound of her soft sniffling disturbed him. He hated seeing her cry.

Off in the distance, a bell rang. This signaled to the

orphans that it was time for dinner. Hearing it, a loud rumble thundered in Travis' stomach. Damn, he was hungry. When had he last eaten? He couldn't recall. All of the drama with Marianne, and now this... it felt like he'd lived three days in one.

"Go," Francesca whispered. The wisp of her voice caught him off guard. Travis looked down. "Go get some food," she said again. "You must be starving."

"What about you?" he asked. His eyebrows knitted together with concern. "I don't feel right leaving you alone. Would you like me to stay?"

"No," Francesca forced a weak smile. "Go. Eat. I'll be fine. I promise."

He wasn't completely convinced, but figured that if he left now, he'd be able to return quicker. Travis moved to stand up. He gave Francesca's shoulder a squeeze, then disappeared through the doorway and into the hall.

"I'll be back soon," he said. "Try and get some rest."

Sure enough, when he returned barely an hour later, Francesca was fast asleep. Her exhausted snores buzzed throughout the room. Travis smiled. Trying to be as silent as a mouse, he closed the door behind him and wandered over to a chair in the corner of the room. The scraps of meat and potato chunks had gone cold on the walk back to Francesca's room. Nonetheless, he dug into the meal. He was famished.

After a minute of filling his stomach so that it no longer ached, Travis readjusted his focus to the figure curled up in a ball on the bed. She hadn't awoken. As he continued to chew, he watched the love of his life, immersed in deep thought.

There was so much to adore about this girl. Her ideology. Her kindness. And not to mention, her strong opinions about equality in the world. Travis shook his head. She was something else. Incredible, really. Her dynamic views and the unique representation of her ideas were her best qualities that Travis couldn't stop admiring. She was like no one else he had ever known.

It was at that moment that Francesca suddenly began to shout. Shivers overtook her body. She flailed against the bedframe, one arm thrashing out and knocking a glass of water clean off the bedside table. The cup went crashing to the floor. A thousand shards of glass scattered in all directions.

Travis couldn't make out the words, but she was dreaming. Or more of a nightmare. Immediately, she woke up. The whites of her eyes showed... terrified. Francesca panted heavily, and Travis tossed his food aside as he rushed toward her. Luckily, he had brought back a cup of water. As she thirstily gulped down the clear liquid, the pair locked eyes. Travis' deep brown eyes were startled to see a faint red rim around Francesca's.

"What the...?" he muttered.

But it disappeared in an instant. Seeing the worried lines creasing his forehead, Francesca tried to steady her breathing. She was hot and cold at the same time. Odd. And yet, the nightmare was passing. She was okay. Alive. It had just been a bad dream. *Another one.*

"Okay. That's it," Travis said. He sat back on the bed. The mattress bulged. "Tomorrow morning, we are going to talk to the headmaster and get you looked at by a doctor. I'm beginning to think that there's something seriously wrong with you."

"No!" Francesca nearly shouted. She didn't know why, but somehow, she innately knew that there was nothing a traditional medical doctor could do to cure this malady —

whatever it was. "Please, don't fret, Travis. It's sweet of you, but I'm fine. Truly. I just want to be left alone for a while."

Travis nodded. With tender lips, he kissed her on the forehead. The smell of fear and sweat from the nightmare still lingered on her skin. But Francesca was tough, he knew. If she wanted to be by herself, he had to respect her wishes.

Francesca flopped back against the pillow when Travis got up to leave. Just like before, she practiced counting to ten. Slowly, her wildly racing heartbeat became normal again. In the dim light of her bedroom, her eyelids began to flutter. Soon, she had fallen back to sleep.

The dreams that followed weren't as awful. But still, Francesca was restless.

Samantha Walden wrung her hands together fretfully. She poured herself a cup of tea but had forgotten to remove the teabag. Now, the water was murky. Too strong to drink and yet, the headmaster drank anyway. She was far too lost in thought to care... the red eyes. They were just so potent, so peculiar, so bizarre. Though she had always been fond of the child, something was off.

Never in her life had she seen something like that before on a child, on anyone. There weren't any illnesses going around the village. The affliction could've been genetic. With her parents dead, there was no true way of finding out. But something as strange as red eyes, she was sure she would've heard about it if there were previous cases.

Finally, the headmaster decided that she needed to do more research. With the assistance of a doctor, she planned to secretly conduct research on the condition of Francesca. Every week, they would observe the orphan. Her habits. What she ate. Where she went. Nothing ever stood out. This doctor, who went by the name of Charles Stanza, one day made an astonishing declaration.

"Headmaster Walden," he began. "I do believe I know what ails the child."

Hearing this news, the headmaster's eyes lit up.

"Excellent!" she exclaimed. "Tell me — what have you concluded, doctor?"

Unfortunately, his diagnosis was far from comforting. Based upon their research, Francesca seemed to be some sort of supernatural being who held the tendency to kill anyone around her, with nothing but the snap of her fingers.

"Something called... Remphelia, I believe. A young woman had a similar condition, back in the 1700s. Practically destroyed the world."

Well, the headmaster nearly fainted! "Francesca? Really? That fragile, silent, and obedient little child... a potential murderer? Speak of this to no one," she hissed to the doctor.

For all she knew, if people found out what Francesca really was, they might try to kill her. And even worse, if Francesca found out in the wrong way or was threatened, well, there would be no telling what might happen.

As Samantha absorbed this revelation, her mind flashed back to similar incidents. Of course, everyone had suspected that there was something very different about Francesca Billings. Especially that strange old Agnes who had once told the headmaster that she believed Francesca was some sort of demonic witch. Or, at the very least, some supernatural creature with magical tendencies. She didn't believe her at the time, but now... now, she wasn't so sure anymore.

"What ever will I do?" the headmaster mumbled, mostly to herself, rubbing her fingers against her temples.

A headache was beginning to bloom.

But now, what can be done? she wondered.

The facts were the facts. Still, the doctor may be wrong. Mistakes do happen, even amongst professionals. Determined to get to the bottom of the matter, the headmaster decided to continue her research, eventually coming across an article about the Beauchamp family in France, an entire farm incinerated and destroyed. No survivors remained, except for one. When she saw the picture of the sole survivor, her jaw dropped.

It was none other than the sweet child, Francesca.

Could she have been the one who caused it?

CHAPTER 5
THE ANGEL OF DEATH

In her dream — or rather nightmare — the dead had come alive. Francesca subconsciously rolled and tossed with images from the most fearsome corners of her mind. She walked into a small cottage in the blackness of the night. People were lying on the floor. A chilling voice called out among the piles of the rotting dead.

"This is fate," it jeered.

Suddenly, the piles of the dead began to move toward

her. Their hands were covered with blood, decomposing flesh and bloody clothes. The scariest of eyes were following her. Francesca, a poor girl. No longer at the orphanage, but instead, trapped in this dark abyss. Off in the distance, a clattering of people startled her. Barely able, Francesca managed to tear her eyes away from the bodies and twisted her head toward the cottage window. There was a clattering of people that she could hear from a far distance. Their voices, loud and terrible. It was a cacophony, like crows about to feast.

"Execute this evil witch!" they roared.

With every step they made toward her, the voices began to rise. Louder. Angrier. Their eyes were directed straight into her own eyes, searching for any glint of red. The tell-tale sign of a witch. The faceless voices came closer toward her, and as they did, they carried the shadow of a horrifying death. All those deceased bodies writhed in her direction. Their arms raised high above their heads, resembling weapons. A weapon, Francesca realized, meant to kill her instantly.

The hatred was too much to bear. She wanted to close her eyes tight. To run away and hide. To be locked in the protective arms of Travis. But this was a nightmare. There was nowhere to go. All the while, the voices came closer, closer, closer...

Their screams shocked her terribly. With shaking fingers, Francesca lowered her face to the ground. She simply couldn't stand to look at these horrific figures a second longer. The energy she felt from the ground was pulsing, like a heartbeat. It was disastrous in nature. All of a sudden, Francesca's eyes began to burn. They glowed a red, a color that twinkled like rubies. And then...

BAM!

The trees shook in their roots. The windows of the cabin blasted open. Every single blade of green grass was singed, wisps of smoke rising from the Earth. Lifting her face upwards, she killed thousands of the dead with nothing but a single stare.

In a shrill voice, she cried out, "Leave me alone! I am *not* a killer."

Francesca fell back on the ground. Heavy tears filled her eyes. Repeatedly saying to herself, "What am I? What have I done?" She hammered the ground with both of her fists. "Taking the lives of those who deserve it is not killing," Francesca yelled, trying to convince herself. "I am not a killer!"

The horror of the act was too much. Francesca's eyes snapped open.

She woke up immediately in her bed. Her body was shivering, and she had tears in her eyes. Same as always. And surprisingly, Travis was by her side. He blinked awake and searched her face.

"Francesca?" he murmured sleepily.

Ignoring him, Francesca rushed toward the mirror. In her reflection, her eyes were still blood red, but there was now the absence of strength. Examining herself in the mirror, she was immersed in deep thought. Trying to figure this out. Travis threw aside his blanket. Seeing her panicked and red eyes was a clear sign that something had happened. Facing her, Travis knew that there was something very, very wrong. Her face showed a depiction of her innocence.

"Another nightmare?" Travis asked with his low and gentle voice.

She nodded her head and gestured that it was the one she had been experiencing for the past two weeks. Breathing heavily, she sat in the chair just beside the bed.

Francesca dropped her head, and her hair fell long around her face. She was trying to collect her thoughts. Again. It had happened again!

Travis sighed deeply. "Be back in a minute," he whispered.

He slipped out of the room and came back with a tall and fresh glass of water. Francesca smiled her thanks. With every sip of water, she was able to make herself calm. After a while, she placed the glass down on the side table. This was the time to reveal herself. Tell Travis about her terrible past, all the way to the unending journey of these horrifying nightmares. Francesca inhaled. It was now or never!

Then, it all came tumbling out.

She spilled every detail about herself. Her crimson red eyes. Her past. The deception and raw, unhinged power. Like a waterfall, she had gone over the edge. Now, there was no turning back. Travis listened intensely; his face hard as stone. For him, everything that she was saying confirmed his suspicions. He remained quiet, his fists balled tight, trying not to panic but also interested in this new, strange side of the girl he loved. While for others, this might just be a story, a made-up story for attention, to Travis, this was a real foresight. From literature to reality, there was a complete journey, and on this path, Francesca was the sole pedestrian.

There was silence in the room except for the trembling voice of Francesca. According to her, everything that happened to her was because of the strange powers that owned her body.

"It's beyond my control," she finally admitted. "I barely understand it myself."

"Can you... can you tell me what it feels like?" Travis stuttered.

Francesca shrugged. She could try?

"These celestial powers are one of mighty magic that incapacitate the human body only when there is unjustified treatment of innocent lives," she explained. "At least, that's what I think is happening."

"So, why did the powers just choose you?" Travis asked with a huge sense of inquisitiveness. His mouth hung open in awe.

"I don't know, exactly... but maybe the sole purpose of these powers is to protect the mortals," Francesca answered with a low-pitched voice.

"Mortals!" Travis exclaimed. When Francesca nodded, he continued, "And a celestial power?"

It seemed like he was conceptualizing all of this brand-new information and trying desperately to understand. But it was hard. Everything he thought he knew about reality was being turned upside-down.

"Maybe I was born among celestial beings who have devastating powers," Francesca answered calmly. "Maybe it's my duty to protect the innocent," she said quietly. "And make the bad ones pay for their wicked deeds," Francesca answered further. "The celestial powers will make every single person pay for their vile actions. That, I am positive."

Now, the nightmares were all making sense. The celestial powers themselves were revealing her true identity to her. The nightmare that had been disturbing her from the day she was first bullied.

Exhausted and out of words, Francesca rose from the bed. The sheets stuck to her thighs; she was still drenched in sweat from her nightmare. Fearing another episode, she asked Travis if he would spend the rest of the night with her, hold her, and keep from relapsing into another fit of terror. He agreed without hesitation. With a click, Travis slid the deadbolt across the door to lock them in the room together. Only Travis was there for her.

But unbeknownst to the couple, there was someone else who had been eavesdropping on their conversation. Samantha Walden herself.

Instantly displacing herself from the doorframe, she lifted her ear off the wood. Then she rushed toward her own cubby of a room. She had to collect her thoughts. And what wild thoughts they were!

The suspicions held by Agnes were true. All those murders, the bodies of orphans hanging from the tree, placed symmetrically in concentric circles, they were all Francesca's doing. Her celestial, or rather demonic, powers had reigned evil upon their orphanage, killing them off one by one.

"Unbelievable!" Samantha exclaimed to herself.

The following morning, she called Agnes to the cabin to discuss what she had heard. Something simply had to be done. The two enemies, once separated by hate, suddenly found themselves sitting at the same desk. Together, they both agreed that as gentle and meek as Francesca was, an investigation into her origin had to be carried out. And there was no one better to form the plan than Agnes and Samantha themselves.

Working in unison, they decided to collect the shreds of

evidence about the true identity of Francesca. With the assistance of Marianne, whose sole motive was to take down Francesca, Samantha revealed every piece of information that she had overheard at the orphanage. Turns out, her snooping paid off.

With a crooked grin, Agnes puffed her chest. "I knew it all along," she bragged.

But Samantha was more careful. Serious potential harm could come from such accusations against an orphan under her care. If their mutual suspicions were indeed true, then soon, there would be destruction ahead.

Before the welcoming of such a devastating event, Samantha decried that they first needed to understand the motives of Francesca. After all, what if the supernatural powers were simply temporary, like a curse? Or perhaps a spell?

Immediately, a team of experts were hired to investigate the curious Francesca. After a week of observation, there were significant findings made in this case. The team discovered that there was a boy who had regained consciousness following the fiery explosion on the Beauchamp farm, Pierre, the younger brother of Lucas Beauchamp. After the team traveled to France for an interview, he agreed to tell the investigators about the incident that happened on the farm.

The tragic deaths at the royal farm were a hot topic for the people of Europe. The identity of the boy was not revealed by the authorities — better to keep him anonymous, they figured. There were serious threats that were ahead; therefore, both Samantha and Agnes traveled with them, leaving the orphanage in the care of the other staff members. They needed to find the answers.

"It must be done," Samantha Walden said, trying to

convince herself just as much as the others. "Francesca poses a risk to us all. We must find this boy. Talk to him. Only then can we know the truth about her."

This happened on the outskirts of Paris, France. The city torn apart and dilapidated just like the rest of the country, trash littered the ground and stenches so potent that the team struggled to breathe. Following the cobblestone roads, they finally reached the farm. The well-known place had gained popularity after being abandoned.

On the outside, it seemed to be the most luxurious farm to ever exist, exhibiting regal and status, but there was something else at play. A thing that depicted a terrible foresight, an act that had taken place there. A mysterious one. Following the pathway from the front door, the team paused to view the spot where Francesca was first welcomed into the home. The greenery was not the same as it had been before. There were hardly any live plants. Patches of dying, yellow grass speckled the ground. Walking on the barren land, each member of the team remarked on how positively dreary the place had become.

"Lord have mercy..." gasped Samantha.

They stopped in their tracks when they found the dead bodies. Well, if they could even call them that. Pieces of human flesh was probably a more apt description. Walking from the farm to the dungeon took roughly five minutes. And yet, it felt like an eternity to those present.

"It's empty," said Agnes. "Our sources must be wrong. There's no one living here."

Rightly so, it seemed that no one was inhabiting the overgrown place. But out past the collapsed wood, there was something that was hidden from their sight. A boy *was* living over there. He had been there from the day the farm was first abandoned. The boy had never interacted with another human being, not in a long time. In fact, no one knew that he was still alive! He was injured, but he somehow managed to cure himself.

As the team approached the feral boy, he crawled back into his alcove and made small defensive noises, like an animal. It quickly became obvious to the team that the boy would not be revealing anything.

"Can he even speak?" wondered one of the researchers.

This would evidently be the biggest challenge. Gaining the trust of the boy was not easy. But Samantha knew — they had to try! Only by getting him to talk and spill everything he knew would they ever solve the mystery of Francesca. Luckily, there were two members on the team who were well-educated in the art of both psychology and language. They began to investigate the boy. Ultimately, after a combined effort of no less than six hours, the boy agreed to talk about the incident.

"Good," said Samantha slyly. "You are doing the right thing, child. Tell us everything. Help us."

The team assured the boy that his life would be spared, and his confidentiality would be kept. Then it began. An incredible story so wondrous, it was almost unbelievable! The boy narrated the whole incident. He closed his eyes, the words rising and falling as he told of how the innocent girl named Francesca was tortured and belittled until she had no choice but to act out, her strength more powerful than even she could've imagined.

He spoke of the cold nights when she was tormented, and the dazzling rays of the sun that were just tickling her soul. Every single thing that happened at the farm was for a purpose. A purpose to make those who lived here pay for their actions.

"Interesting," Agnes said. "The same sentences were uttered by Francesca herself."

Samantha nodded. "Yes. This sounds an awful lot like our Francesca, does it not?"

Samantha's mind was spinning. But how could that possibly be? The identity of the mysterious killer... none other than a child left in their care? Impossible. And yet, it appeared to be true.

They left the boy at the farm. The team decided to stay with him, to make sure he stayed safe, while Samantha and Agnes returned to the states. The testimony of the boy was written on a piece of paper, for recordkeeping purposes. Samantha packed up her bag, said goodbye to the Pierre, and turned away from the disastrous scene. Hoping for the best, but simultaneously, fearing the worst...

On her way back to the orphanage after resolving the mystery of Francesca, Headmaster Walden was stunned. She had to pause many times just to catch her breath. There was a ringing in her ears, like a hammer hitting a nail. She still couldn't believe what she had just witnessed! It seemed like, every day, there was a revelation of something new about the girl. It seemed that this was not a human being at all, but Pandora's box. One that she was in charge of.

Each secret was scarier and darker than the previous one.

"How can Francesca be the embodiment of evil?" she mused.

The child was so quiet. So docile. As she entered the orphanage after returning home from the farm, Samantha was greeted by the orphans. She made sure to keep her distance from Francesca, lest the girl really was supernatural and sensed that something was amiss.

From that day on, every night, the headmaster went to

Francesca's room, finding her sound asleep. And each time, she saw Travis curled around her. On one occasion, when the moon was full and shining beams down into the hallway, Samantha caught sight of Travis hovering alone in the hallway.

"Travis," she called out. "What are you doing up so late?"

But she needed no answer. Travis' eyes told her everything. He was standing outside the bedroom, analyzing Francesca. The headmaster would tell him to go back to his room, but every night, she'd only find him outside once again.

And that's how they continued to cross paths, staring at each other in front of Francesca's room like they understood each other. Samantha's look was one of horror and fear, while Travis' was one of coldness and apathy. He simply glared at her sleeping body, eyes wide open, and a nervous pattering of his heartbeat against his chest.

What could they do?

THE NEXT DAY, THE ORPHANS WERE BUSY DOING THEIR regular exercises. Jumping jacks, skipping, running laps, and such. Francesca sat under an oak tree. Alone. She was going through deep sorrow. The nightmares were still following her. She wasn't sleeping well. Every nightmare was a new revelation of the celestial powers. Her soul itself was guiding and initiating the presence of the ultimate power that she held. Emotional imbalance began to emerge, and gradually, Francesca was no longer a gentle person. She started to lose her temper over the tiniest of things. This change was creating many hurdles for her and Travis.

"Geez, you're grumpy lately," he complained one morning. "What's going on with you, Francesca? You're not acting like yourself at all."

To that statement, she simply rolled her eyes.

"Leave me alone, okay?" she snapped. "If you aren't going to help or say anything nice, then just go away and shut the hell up. All I'm asking is to be left alone. I just want some peace and quiet."

Francesca kicked a pebble. It skidded into a tree.

"Jesus, why is it that everyone is constantly on my case and in my face?" Francesca continued angrily. "Silence. That's all I am asking for. Just a few minutes of silence where no one is whispering behind my back or insulting me to my face."

Travis' face crumpled. His feelings were wounded. He mumbled something and then took off, not wanting to make the situation worse. Sure, the orphans could be cruel. They did like to pester Francesca. Rightly so, that she would wish for silence. But still, her words cut like a knife. Travis slunk away to gather with another group of children huddled in the yard.

One day — like all the other ordinary days — the orphans were gathered in the garden for their daily lessons. This was the day when Francesca finally came out of her room. The bright sunlight welcomed her, the beams of warmth kissing her skin. Admittedly, the sunshine felt nice. For the first time in ages, she smiled.

Everyone was busy with their tasks. Francesca glanced around, looking for Travis. Examining the environment of the garden, she spotted him and made a move forward. Seeing her, he looked up. A timid grin crossed his face.

"Hey," he ventured tentatively. "How are you feeling today?"

Francesca held out her hand. Gently, Travis took it in his own. His eyes locked in on hers as he tried to read her face.

"Look, I'm sorry," she apologized. "I know I've been... weird... lately. Forgive me?"

"Of course!" laughed Travis. "I could never stay mad at you for more than a few hours. You know that."

They hugged. But then the headmaster called Travis, and he left immediately. As he did so, Marianne made her way toward Francesca.

"Oh, here we go," murmured Francesca.

Marianne was one of those orphans who seemed to get a perverse pleasure from ruining Francesca's day. She would constantly insult her, call her rude names, and gossip behind her back. With narrowed eyes, Marianne made her way through the crowd of orphans. She had words to say! Now, the time was here. It was the perfect opportunity.

Marianne walked up to her and started an unnecessary conversation about the relationship she had with Travis. She was cruel. Nasty. Instigating. As happy as Francesca was about resolving her argument with Travis, she just couldn't take Marianne's nagging anymore!

Francesca balled her hands into fists. Marianne's high-pitched voice was carried by the wind. As each word reached Francesca's eardrums, she could feel herself becoming more and more agitated. Suddenly, the memories of all her previous fights came flooding back. The noise clapped like thunder. In Francesca's mind, images of the other orphans — and how they liked to taunt and tease her — were fresh and raw. Like the time when one of the older orphans had purposely locked her bedroom door from the outside and wedged a piece of wood underneath, blocking her exit.

Or the night when they had all formed a circle. Francesca had been alone, reading a book by herself, when out of nowhere, five orphans materialized in the yard. They towered above her like giants. One of the orphans grabbed the book. He tore out a page, crumpled it like a tissue, and laughed as he threw the tattered paper at her. With tears in her eyes, Francesca pleaded for the boys to stop. But it did nothing to stop their assault.

Each bad memory pierced through Francesca's heart. She didn't want to hurt anyone. Not at all! However, they had to be silenced. This could not go on. Not at her expense, or anyone else's.

"Enough!" she screamed.

"Wait. What the hell are you doing, you crazy freak..."

Francesca couldn't hold her anger any longer. It erupted like a volcano. Her eyes flared bright red. In less than a millisecond, she had destroyed the entire orphanage. Boom! Just like that. Marianne died on the spot. The fiery tornado ripped across the space between them, dissolving her into a pool of melted flesh and blackened bone.

The others weren't so lucky. Their deaths took longer. Many people were decapitated. There was intense scream-ing, and all of a sudden, there was no one left. Silence. Just like she had wanted. The building was detonated in the exact same way that the Beauchamp farm had been. It seemed that no one was left alive. Instantly, flames rose from the ground, burning whatever, and whoever, was left.

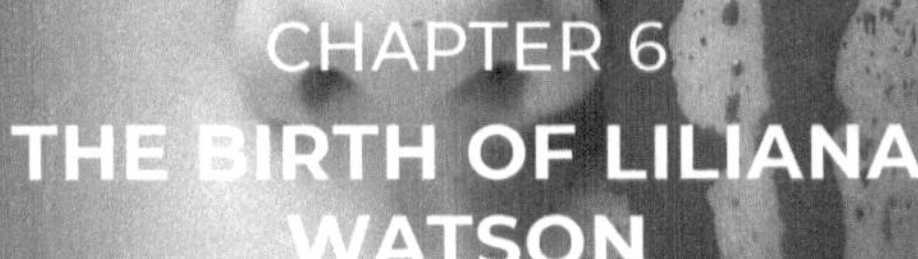

CHAPTER 6
THE BIRTH OF LILIANA WATSON

Seventy-One Years Later...

T he year was 1924 in the small town of Stockbridge, Massachusetts. Stockbridge was famously known as the quiet town of Massachusetts, where crime and chaos usually remained nonexistent, unlike its neighboring cities of Boston and Cambridge.

It was a place where families came to raise their children and where the elderly came to relax and retire. The children played on the streets safely at night, with the parents never having to worry about kidnappers or serial killers.

The only unfortunate event that ever happened in this peaceful town was the incident of a German Shepherd chasing after a frightened child for over three blocks, all because he wanted the cracker that was in the young boy's pocket. It was so unusual and terrifying for the residents that it became branded as the most disruptive incident to have happened in the past seventy-one years.

Other than that, Stockbridge remained a sleepy town that many people simply drove through for gas or refreshments on their way to Boston or Cambridge.

During the chilling winter morning of April 23, 1924, a woman stared out her bedroom window, observing the sprinkling of beautiful snow on the ground while holding a steaming hot cup of coffee. She gently placed her hand on her abdomen, feeling the kick of a baby that was due any minute. Her contractions had grown closer and closer together while her tolerance for pain had gone slimmer and slimmer.

Unbearable agony continued to shoot up her back, causing her to lie down on her bed. This was her seventh pregnancy, and though she knew what to expect, she never imagined the lengths of excruciating discomfort that came with it.

After several minutes, the pain increased, encircling her body as if a venomous snake was grappling her. Tears pooled under her eyes as her voice strained while calling out to her husband. Upon hearing her cries, he instantly ran into their bedroom, just to find his wife lying on top of bloody sheets.

"She's coming, William. She's coming. Call the midwife!" Esmeralda cried out as she continued to scream in agony.

William hurriedly made his way out the door and bustled out into the cold air of the April morning. It didn't take him long to arrive with the midwife beside him. Esmeralda continued to pant and struggle through the pain. Her screams of distress were so piercing that her cries could be heard through the walls of the old Victorian home.

"Congratulations, Mr. and Mrs. Watson. Meet your healthy baby girl. What shall you call her?" The old midwife placed the baby in Esmeralda's arms.

"She's beautiful." Esmeralda looked over at William as he sat down by her side. "Her face is so lovely and pure. We shall call her Liliana, or Lily, for short."

However, Liliana Watson was no ordinary child. There was something unique in her that no other children in the surrounding neighborhoods possessed.

She was born with a very rare genetic disorder that caused her pupils to become red as blood. Her eyes never closed, even when she was sound asleep. Her pupils would just continue to dart from side to side, left to right. In fact, this disorder was so rare that Lily was the first known case of this kind in decades. They called her condition, "Remphelia."

However, William and Esmeralda didn't notice this fine detail until several days after she was born. Commonality in this town reigned supreme as those born with genetic defects were immediately branded as outcasts and derelicts. Because of her condition and their fear of being rejected by the town they loved, her parents were forced to reject their daughter and cast her aside. They had to sacrifice their own daughter in order to save themselves and their reputations.

So, one dark, cold night, William and Esmeralda Watson bundled up their little girl, placed her inside a woven basket, and left her on the doorsteps of the infamous Baylor Orphanage.

Baylor Orphanage was known for the horrors that lurked behind its metal doors. It had been rumored that those who entered through the doors would never be seen again. Seventy-one years ago, the orphanage faced horrors of its own, horrors no one really understood.

It had burned into debris and ashes before being rebuilt again by the humanitarian society of Stockbridge. The volunteers found the bones of those who once resided there crushed beneath. Because of this unknown phenomenon, rumors had spread all over town that the orphanage was cursed, with children having nightmares whenever they walked past the building and parents experiencing chills down their spines.

Headmaster Walden finished her last rounds of the night when she heard a faint cry on the other side of the wooden doors.

"Those damn hooligans! If I find them one more time tarnishing the walls of this place, I swear I'll..." Headmaster Walden stopped in her words as she swung open the front door to find a woven basket sitting peacefully on her doorstep.

She picked it up, unsure of what she would find, until she saw the most adorable baby sleeping inside. The child was wrapped in a velvet blanket; a piece of paper with the name "Liliana Watson" was tucked into a corner beside her, along with a check for a thousand dollars.

Unbeknownst to the headmaster, she took Liliana in as just another unwanted child who was left abandoned. A lot of people moved into this town to start their own families, but many who lived there did not desire children of their own, leaving their unwanted newborns at the orphanage instead.

As Liliana became older, it grew more noticeable that she was a special and unique child, with a large set of eyes that perfectly enhanced her structured cheekbones. She was a child with unexplainable and divine beauty. However, it didn't take long before she started to stand out among the other orphan children.

At the age of five, several unexplainable events began to occur inside the orphanage. One night, while being tormented by the other children, little Lily began to experience tingling sensations throughout her body as she stared back at the children. Suddenly, the orphans began to float right before the eyes of everyone. As they levitated in the air, Lily felt her body becoming more and more powerful, a feeling she wanted to experience forever.

As Headmaster Walden rounded the rooms for her nightly checks, she noticed a commotion coming from the room Liliana shared with several other children. Upon entering, she was bewildered to see the children floating above their beds. Her knees felt weak as she held onto the sturdy post of a bed beside her for support and balance.

It was then that she saw Liliana sitting calmly on the edge of her own bed, her eyes glowing crimson red. It took all the courage the headmaster had to creep closer toward Lily, her long, skeletal fingers grappling the shoulders of the little girl.

"Lily, Lily, please stop. Whatever you're doing, please stop," she spoke with an authoritative voice, the surprise causing Lily to break her trance.

Unfortunately, upon removing her gaze from the other orphans, they each fell, one by one, colliding with the posts upon landing. The sounds of their spines cracking and skulls crushing were heard upon impact. Several children screamed in terror as they walked by and witnessed the murder, huddling in the hallway away from Lily.

However, it wasn't the death of the children that made Headmaster Walden decide to grab Lily by the wrist and drag her down into the basement of the penitentiary-style orphanage. It was her fear of Lily's untrained power, and the shame that it would cast on the institution. She had to ensure that any news of this incident would never leave the premise of the building; the safety of the world depended on it.

The headmaster didn't want to admit it, but she had heard of this horror of a nightmare before; the distant memory she tried so hard to push out of her mind still burned into her skull. She couldn't tear her mind from what she had seen in the bedroom, still lingering onto the fact that the young child was able to make several human bodies float effortlessly.

Soon, she stopped, opened the glass door of an isolated and solitary room, and pushed the child inside before clicking the lock tightly shut from the outside. The room looked like nothing more than a prison cell, completely barren of all substance other than metal chains and a white marble floor, completely surrounded by glass walls. Liliana Watson was all alone.

Suspecting that Liliana's ability was caused by Remphelia, a condition similar to what the orphanage had reported in another child nearly a century ago, Walden immediately contacted a lab at Elyson University that specialized in rare neurological diseases. They had been aware of this condition for decades now, spending years designing the pill that could finally suppress it. The pill was made with Naphazoline and designed to turn the crimson eyes of Liliana into midnight black, leaving her absolutely powerless.

However, the exact cause of Remphelia and its mechanism were not yet fully researched as it was too rare to study. The pill they created only acted as a suppressant rather than a cure. Trial and error it may have been, but once scientists found a remedy that worked, they decided to mass produce it. Lily was given these pills every morning since that terrifying incident, her psychokinesis never witnessed again. As for the children who saw what happened, Headmaster Walden made sure none of them ever repeated that night to anyone else, convincing them that it was all a horrible nightmare.

So, for the next fifteen years, Liliana Watson remained trapped inside her isolated cell, never able to walk through those chained doors. She was fed through a small slit that was barely wide enough to fit a thin plate. Since Lily was a young child when the incident occurred, she had no recollection of what happened that night, as if the memory was completely pushed out of her mind.

Still, she never questioned why she had to live and sleep in the basement of the orphanage while the other children roamed free; she just thought that was the way it was. The darkest moment of her life started to unveil as she continued to experience the feelings of guilt and shame with no ways of repenting, the agony piercing deep inside her mind with each passing day.

Dᴀʏ ᴀꜰᴛᴇʀ ᴅᴀʏ, ᴛʜᴇ ᴏᴛʜᴇʀ ᴄʜɪʟᴅʀᴇɴ ᴀɴᴅ adolescents would come by her room, sneaking out of the headmaster's observing eyes. They taunted and teased her for being locked up inside that lonely room while the rest of them were able to socialize and go outside to play on the grounds. They continued to bully her for being different.

Soon, the rumors began to spread outside the walls of the orphanage. Waves of reporters snuck their way inside just to take pictures of the poor girl, tarnishing the reputation of the orphanage even more. They wanted proof for themselves, the dark and opaque tears that flowed from her pale face, as they wouldn't believe it otherwise. It didn't take long before Liliana became branded as "Creepy Orphan Lily."

More and more tragedy continued to happen to Lily that made her life miserable. She began to feel insecure for being different from the other kids. The frustration from being trapped in confinement was eating her up from the inside out, the longing for socialization creeping inside her. She wanted to feel the grass tickle against her feet, the air breeze brush against her skin. But most of all, she wanted to laugh with the other children. Lily missed the feeling of human touch and human connection.

The thoughts of being swaddled and held by Headmaster Walden when she was younger lingered inside her head even though many of those moments were as simple as moving Lily from one crib to another as more influxes of abandoned babies came pouring into the orphanage like a swarm of bees. Despite being minimal, those were the moments she cherished most and longed to experience once again.

For the past fifteen years, the only human touch she had been able to receive was the touch she felt from herself. Even then, those always felt cold and distant. Having been trapped inside that dungeon for so long, with no one to socialize or communicate with, her ability to speak eventually vanished. Her vocals had not been used for so long that they completely shut down, Liliana never hearing the sound of her own voice again.

With no voice and no efficient means of interacting with the rest of the orphanage beyond her glass cell, she had to find alternative ways of communicating. She was forced to cut deep into her skin to access the blood coursing inside her to use as ink on the walls. Often times, she would bleed out more than she had intended, the medics rushing in to resuscitate her while dosing her with more pills.

But even as all the other orphans grimaced in pain while witnessing her lying on the ground, Lily remained emotionless, her emotions so detached that she never expressed any pain, anguish, or sadness.

Damaging her body soon became her only hobby, so much that several guards were brought in to chain her hands together to prevent Lily from further hurting herself.

During those times, with nothing else to do, she would stare out her small window with her forehead pressed against it, imagining her life out on the grounds with the others. They seemed so happy enjoying life, a feeling that she couldn't remember experiencing. She longed to play outside rather than stare at nothingness, spending her days counting the number of stitches and scars on her pale skin, accepting the fact that her life would remain in solitary confinement forever.

CHAPTER 7
AN ILLNESS SPREADS

"**B**reaking news! We just received notice from the CDC that a deadly illness is spreading like rapid fire across the continental United States. When contracted, those infected will develop mental paralysis, impairing their ability to function consciously and logically. We are strongly urging all citizens to stay as far away from each other as possible. Even a mere breath can transmit this debilitating illness from one specimen to another.

Major cities like Philadelphia and San Francisco have already seen soldiers and civilians fall victim; all that remains in their places are vegetative states of once human beings, unable to think for themselves.

As an extra precaution, we are also closing down all borders between cities and counties, and barricading all premises. Everyone will remain where they currently are. No exceptions. Anyone who attempts to bypass these barriers will be shot immediately.

There will be no transportation or shipments of any kind across these borders. Stay put, and stay tune, until further notice," a journalist from ACC Times announced alarmingly on national television during a chaotic Friday afternoon on April 23, 1939.

"Sir, this illness is very serious, and it's spreading fast," 25-year-old, fresh out of Elyson Medical School, Yin Suzuki, explained to the committee that she reported to. "If we don't find a cure for it soon, it will destroy our society, and we won't be able to do anything about it. We will have to work toward a cure, put our best scientists on the team, or we're basically dead. This illness-induced laziness is turning everyone in town into noctambulant creatures, taking over their wills to live. We have to stop it now before it spreads!" she continued.

The head of the committee, Dr. Mikazaki, leaned back, his eyes not betraying the slightest of emotion. He refused to be bothered by the seriousness that Yin was demonstrating to him, despite the evidence and figures she was sharing.

"She's new to the field of pathology and doesn't have much experience. What does she know?" Dr. Mikazaki whispered quietly to himself.

In fact, no one in the committee seemed to care about

the seriousness of the illness as Yin noticed that no one was listening to her. Before she joined the committee, she suspected that none of them really cared about what happened to the world. They were so used to staying in the sanctuary of their own labs, too stubborn to explore the world beyond. That thought itself frustrated her even more.

How can they even call themselves 'scientists' if they refuse to use their brains for the greater good of society? They're acting like they're already infected! Wait, what if they are? What if I'm all alone in this? I need to fix this. I need to find a cure for this illness! Yin thought as she clenched her fists.

She needed to get somebody, anybody, to acknowledge how bad this situation was, that it could potentially destroy the world. If they didn't do something soon, they would all turn. It was only a matter of time. Complete zombies with no purpose or life to live. They needed a cure for the illness, or they would all be done for.

She stared at the people inside the room. Just the idea of them not caring about what would happen to the world burned rage inside her. She needed to find someone who would listen.

"We understand that, Dr. Suzuki," Dr. Mikazaki said, finally speaking louder. "And we also understand the sheer seriousness of what you are saying. Our question to you is, what proof can you give us that you will find a cure in the time that has been provided to you? What is the assurance that you can give us for successful research and an end to this illness of inevitable fate? Because, how we see it, precious resources are going to be wasted on trying to find a vaccine for an illness that cannot be cured. It's just that we cannot waste those resources, you know, since we're in a crisis."

"Sir, with all due respect, I cannot promise anything," Yin answered bluntly, surprising many as she was usually so calm and confident. "However, I only know that there is a way this illness can be cured; we have succeeded in finding potential weaknesses of the virus and have developed a hypothesis for how to kill it. With just a couple months and the opportunity to work on extracting the antibody from the xerocole responsible for this spread, I will be able to show you a positive response before the worst of it hits us.

Other than that, well, everything is up to you and the committee to decide. Send me and a small group of researchers to the Arabian, or watch the world crumble at your hands. I'm simply informing you what I have found over the past several days. The choice is yours," she confidently said as she stared in the dead eyes of her mentor.

And with that, Yin and a couple of her colleagues were shipped off to the Arabian Desert. It didn't take long for Yin to realize that this illness was a strange one, unlike any Yin had seen before. It was far more devious and contagious than the other viruses that had preceded it.

Not only did this virus weaken the immune system of its victims, but it also altered their mental states of intelligence, causing them to become lackluster and unmotivated for change, far more complex than anyone could have predicted. It didn't take long before the world had to truthfully accept that this was a real disease, a truly horrific and dangerous disease.

However, how can one accept something without fully understanding it? This, unfortunately, was something Yin failed to realize during her time in the Arabian until it had become too late. It took her eight painful months in Jordan to try and get a handle on how the virus, referred to as "Coxin," was operating. It was an extremely difficult task for her research team because they struggled to realize that the virus was slowly seeping into their brains, changing the way they perceived it, and removing their motivation.

Even so, because Yin never figured out the true nature of Coxin, she didn't realize until it was too late. Her colleagues didn't simply stop caring and communicating with each other; they were infected. Coxin started off like any other virus, infecting an individual and forcing the cell that it had infused with to multiply in numbers until it overtook the entire human body. But Coxin was much different, much deadlier.

The Coxin virus mainly targeted the human brain, entering through the cerebral core and penetrating the brain until it stopped functioning. Unfortunately, Yin and her virology team did not specialize in neurological functions and could not figure out exactly how bad it was before blowing all their resources into a potential cure that was far from what they needed. Finding a cure for the virus, let alone a virus that infected the brain, was insane. Yin didn't know where to even begin looking. Writing her report to the World Health Organization about her progress proved to be a real struggle in itself, struggling to form coherent sentences that described the situation, let alone a full solution.

Case Report: The Coxin Virus

Reporter: Dr. Yin Suzuki

Description: Coxin is a heavily infectious and transmissible virus that can infect mass populations at once if even one infected subject is present in the area. The virus is airborne in nature, often transmitted through a single breath, making it difficult to contain. We have yet to see any signs of this contagion slowing down or even ceasing when subjected to different conditions or temperatures.

The main components include heavily potent protein chains that cannot be broken down by any enzymes known to mankind, making it impossible to isolate. We now also have reason to believe that Coxin can become waterborne, spreading through the sewers and infecting the world's drinking water.

The Effect: As of now, Coxin seems to be affecting the cerebral core of the brain, although it still remains unknown the exact mechanism the virus has. We have tested the virus on other species of life and found that only human beings are able to become infected, therefore, making it impossible to test potential cures on animals. Nonetheless, animals are able to act as carriers, transmitting the virus from one person to another.

The Research: Research on the virus has been thoroughly mandated via all privacy laws and are kept completely confidential. We have no signs of malpractice, and the research is only helping us properly find a cure. As of this moment, it is impossible to determine if this virus even has a cure and what steps are needed to properly stop it.

The Cure: There is no way to determine whether this is curable or not. As mentioned above, the protein chains that make up the base of this virus are impenetrable. Every single enzyme combination has been tested and failed, and at this point, we are open to any suggestions that anyone has. The interior components of Coxin also show a high amount of electron activity, further solidifying evidence that this is a neurological virus.

As of this moment, we still do not have any data as to

how this is affecting people. There is a possible thought about how it can affect the logical reasoning and common sense of a human being, but there is no proof to conclude this case.

Therefore, at this stage of research, it is impossible to deduce if a cure is possible to synthesize. However, success had been found in my original research. There is a chance that proactive thinking and use of the brain can stop this virus from attaching. How and why still require more research, so does finding a cure based on this observation.

CHAPTER 8

A DICTATOR IS BORN

Meanwhile, towns across the country entered a midst of chaos. With limited resources and supplies due to border shutdowns, people were battling each other as they panicked. Looting had become common as people stormed supermarkets and convenience stores, disregarding those they injured as long as they obtained the coveted items first, coveted items they weren't even sure they needed.

There were also the unfortunate civilians who began climbing over the border walls with insanity, all of whom either fell victim to their own slip-ups or from the bullets of guards standing on the other side.

The town of Stockbridge was turning into a destructive disaster, but the events that loomed behind the gates of the orphanage were about to prove more damaging.

"What do you mean you aren't able to get me those pills? I don't care if the borders are closed. I don't care if transportation of shipments isn't allowed. I need those pills! Do what you must! Kill the guards if you have to. I need those pills! You don't understand!" The shrill voice of Headmaster Walden echoed from down the halls of Baylor Orphanage as she slammed the telephone receiver down, the side table on which it stood crumbling below its weight.

"I need those damn pills!" she mumbled to herself.

Like many of the other times when the headmaster lost her temper, the orphans who saw the sudden change became frightened. Her temper was becoming volatile, and it confused most of them, especially the orphans who fully understood what was happening. Little did they know, the headmaster herself was becoming terrified of what would happen if she didn't receive the pills right away.

"She's mad again," Bethany, one of the elder orphans, said.

"I heard it's about Lily again. I was passing the headmaster's office when I heard that her pills couldn't be delivered," Katerina replied.

"Why do they need to give Lily pills? Oh, I know. She must be crazy. She's nuts. It's probably the reason why she's always locked up in that cell, right?" Eduardo asked. "Why don't we ask her ourselves?" he added as he pointed in the direction of the basement.

"You know what? That's a good idea. Come on." Bethany gathered the children, and they went straight to where Lily was.

Seeing how the headmaster changed from one personality to another infuriated even the orphans. They already hated Lily for being different, and whenever the headmaster was angry, that usually meant more chores for them.

Meanwhile, in the basement of the building, an oblivious Liliana was lying on top of her thin mattress in the empty cell. Her mind was filled with possible actions she could take to escape this forsaken place. Her hands were still bound, with nothing to entertain herself with. Soon, Bethany, Katerina, and Eduardo reached her cell, ready to torment her fragile heart.

"Hey, Lily! There are rumors all over town that you're known as the 'creepy orphan!' You're creepy! Why are you so creepy?"

A loud laughter echoed inside her cell. Lily sat up straight, trying to burrow her head in between her legs. She tried to cover her ears so she could drown out their voices, but her restrained hands refused to budge.

"Yeah, Lily! You're like one of those creepy girls in those bloody horror movies. You give me nightmares!"

The orphans started to bang the door to her cell, their shrieks sending shivers down her spine.

"Lily! You're weird and ugly! That's why you're stuck in there alone. I hope you stay in there forever and die!" Eduardo cried out.

"You have to take pills because you're all messed up in the head! You're both creepy *and* crazy!" Katerina added.

"Creepy Lily! Creepy Lily!" the three continued to cheer ominously, taunting Lily.

As Lily's tolerance began to weaken, a small crack was

beginning to form from the external pressure. Lily barely had enough energy remaining from the significant loss of blood she experienced, but she still managed to muster the strength to stand up and stare at the others. She wanted them to stop, to leave her alone, but without her voice, she wasn't able to communicate that. A single drop of tear dripped from Lily's right eye, and a light tint of red began to appear.

OVER THE NEXT SEVERAL DAYS, THE TOWN REMAINED sheltered from the rest of the country, from the rest of the world, with no access to additional necessities or resources due to this unknown and unforeseen virus. Those infected were distinguishably noticeable, their facial expressions blanking and their focus deteriorating.

The townspeople shielded themselves inside their own homes, choosing starvation over death from the deadly air. Even the newscasters and journalists stopped reporting, as any hope for a potential cure had died since Yin Suzuki and her team went radio silent. Stockbridge, Massachusetts had become a ghost town.

Inside the orphanage, Lily began to feel changes in her body. There was an unexplainable force of energy occurring inside her brain, yet she could not fathom what was happening inside her. After fifteen long years of having been drugged daily, her body suddenly began to feel different without the constant systemic interactions with the chemicals. She noticed her faint reflection in the glass of the window, the color of her eyes changing into a crimson red. Her frail body began to fill with strength and power as her hair whisked against the strange chilling wind blowing through the vent above her.

Suddenly, an aura of light began to surround her. The fiery matter lighting up the darkness of the building. Liliana had come to life. Because she had been suppressed for so long, Liliana never became aware of her special ability as the rage of energy continued to flow inside her body. Therefore, she was never given the chance to control them and not let them fall under the dictatorship of her emotions. The angrier she got, the more powerful she became.

A few of the children walking down the hallway noticed a glowing light toward the basement where Lily's room was located. Curious, they walked toward it to see what was going on. Their eyes widened when they saw the flaming orphan. Terrified by the vision, they began to pound their fists against the glass.

Bethany raised her binoculars and witnessed the crimson eyes of Liliana becoming more and more intense. Lily glared back at her, melting the binoculars in her hands, Bethany following shortly after. Frightened, the remaining orphans started to run, hoping to escape the wrath of Lily before she could get a hold of them.

However, despite how quickly their little feet moved, their speed remained no match for Liliana. Seconds after they began running, they levitated into the air, one by one, the same levitation that Liliana had done fifteen years ago. Her rage pumped harder as the children screamed for help.

"No, Lily! Please stop! I'm sorry. I'm sorry!" Eduardo pleaded as his body continued to float.

"Lily! Please put me down! I promise to never call you names again!" Katerina pleaded with fear.

But before their pleas could register in Liliana's mind, they flew against the brick wall of the basement, the crushing of their bones echoing down the hall. Their lifeless bodies fell to the ground; their lives instantly terminated. With her newfound power, Lily turned her focus to the glass screen in front of her, staring, until the entire wall shattered.

Blood now trickled from her sockets as she stepped out of the isolated cell for the first time in fifteen years, her bare feet scraping and tearing against the shattered glass shards on the tiled ground. Everyone in the orphanage had done her wrong, and she wasn't about to let any of them get away with it.

One by one, she destroyed those residing at the orphanage, twisting the necks of those playing on the grounds and forcing the maids to run their own heads beneath their vacuums. The blood of the innocent splattered against the white dress of Liliana as she silenced the servants who tried to seize help, zippering their mouths shut and preventing them from being able to speak.

The rage of the energy on her body added to the hatred she had been holding deep inside. The servants, maids, and other orphans were all just collateral for who she really wanted revenge against, Headmaster Walden. She had been dosing and physically abusing Lily for years, treating her like a prisoner when all she ever wanted were connection and love.

Instead, she was raised by someone who instilled hate and vengeance inside her, repressing who she really was and lying to her instead of sculpting her into someone who was able to control her feelings.

THE SILENCED SERVANTS SOUNDED THE ALARM, THE alarm blaring through the old building. Unaware of what was happening, Headmaster Walden grabbed a gun from the safe in her office and bolted down the winding staircase, just to find the bloody bodies of orphan children decapitated in front of her and smoke coming from the library.

But she wasn't scared. She had been trained for this very moment, just like all the headmasters before her time had been trained. She expected this inevitable moment to occur, but with the sudden attack of the mysterious illness spreading around town, she didn't have enough time to prepare herself against the demise of this orphanage.

"Lily! I know that's you! You're being a very bad child, and you need to stop this right now!" Headmaster Walden yelled into the library as she carefully stepped over the children, her gun cocked and held tightly with both hands. "I'm coming in! And when I get there, this better be over!"

Walking closer toward the library, children continued to levitate across the orphanage, some in flames while others were partially intact, most of them with snapped necks. She stepped over the corpses that surrounded her feet, careful to not track blood on her heels, as she entered the library and saw Liliana levitating in the air, books surrounding her and children being flung left and right.

Headmaster Walden could see Lily's eyes burning bright, turning more and more red the more frustrated she became. The strange wind inside the orphanage blew stronger as the headmaster forced herself further into the room.

"Lily, stop! Now! I order you to stop!"

However, her command only made Lily angrier. She threw the children against the walls of the library, their blood forming her response.

You betrayed me, Headmaster Walden. You were supposed to take care of me, and instead, you left me to rot inside a cell, where I was forced to live in solitary with no human interaction. You are the reason I became like this. This is all your fault!

"Lily, please, listen to me. You have to stop this," Headmaster Walden stuttered in her words as she didn't want to say anything that would trigger Lily even more. "This wasn't my fault. I promise. I was only trying to help you! You had a power that was out of control, and I needed to suppress it for your sake and everyone else's. I was only trying to keep you safe!"

Liar.

Lily spelled out once again, using the blood of a maid to write against the dusty window. Refusing to listen to more of Walden's excuses, she focused her eyes into those of the headmaster until Walden's eyes exploded, leaving her blinded to rot on the ground of the library as Liliana floated out of the orphanage, setting the remaining rooms on fire and burning the building of hell to the ground.

Fury did not even begin to explain the wrath that Liliana still possessed inside of her. Murdering those who taunted and contained her was nowhere near enough for her revenge. She had spent fifteen years of her life trapped inside a cell with no interaction with other humans other than the occasional insults from the orphans and the demanding voice of the headmaster forcing her to swallow her pills, leaving her completely mute and utterly alone. Growing up, she had only ever wanted positive communication with others, a chance to socialize and play.

Lily looked back at the burning orphanage that served as her shelter over the past twenty years. Only the pillars and one wing remained standing; everything else had crumbled into debris. Feeling a small boulder lifted off her chest, Lily stepped foot outside the metal gates for the first time. All she wanted was a home, someone to take her in and care for her.

However, little did she realize, the once peaceful town of Stockbridge was now filled with those infected by the illness; those who normally would've taken her in as their own now shutting her out instead. Everyone in town refused to open their doors. They all feared contracting the deadly virus and saw Liliana as another infected.

"Go away!" one woman screamed.

"You're infected! Get off my porch!" a man shouted through his door when he saw Lily walking up his steps.

Suddenly, the feeling of rejection hit Liliana once again, her rage forcing her to silence all those who rejected her. If she couldn't experience companionship, neither could they. She then vowed that the rest of the world would also suffer the same pain and agony she had felt. She swore to banish everyone's ability to socialize and communicate. Forever.

Speaking now ceased to exist; those who disobeyed her had their lips sealed shut and a dagger pierced through their vocal cords. Humans of the world would now solely communicate through messages and messages only. She didn't care if they had to handwrite their conversations in their own tears and blood, like she had to do.

The world would never speak again.

CHAPTER 9
A NEW WORLD

The year was 2010, seventy-one years since Liliana took over the world. She had claimed her place as the new ruler, projecting what she experienced as a child. Under her ruling, voices had not grazed the ears of human beings in decades, communicating solely through letters and written messages. Those who tried to oppose her were instantly banished and never heard from again.

Some had tried to oppose her new laws. Some had even

tried their luck in murdering her. But none of them succeeded, all ending up dead in a blink of an eye. Several country leaders tried defying her, banding together in hopes that strength in numbers would rule. All that landed them were several broken necks in front of millions of supporters.

The more people who tried and failed, the more the world became fearful of her, more so than they were of the virus. All the authorities and world leaders were under her control, enforcing her rules that were punishable by death if disobeyed. She had the world at the palm of her hand. She watched as all the people slowly lost oral communication, just like what she had experienced in her childhood. Alliances began to disband as those who tried to attack all ended up being seized.

Still, the world continued to change despite being under the dictatorship of Liliana. During those times, citizens of the world had to forego any long-distance communication. Telephones had become obsolete as oral conversations were banned. The mysterious virus had infected almost the entire country, causing postal services to go completely out of business. The world became isolated. People became distant and alone. Socialization ceased to exist.

It wasn't until the year 1992 when Sir Frances Beckerman of Hull Brix, California invented text messaging, where people could send electronic messages through mobile phones. For forty-two years, Beckerman had been locked inside a bomb shelter, the closest human being nearly a hundred miles away. He had locked himself up, dedicating his life to reuniting with his lover, thus shutting himself off from the rest of the world.

Frances Beckerman was a former soldier back in 1950. He was one of the most respected soldiers in Hull Brix, with more knowledge than any single human could handle. He was bred into a wealthy upper-class family, where he could have whatever he wanted, even the beautiful maidens of the land.

All except for one, Juliet Sawyer, a servant girl from the lower-class society who instantly stole Frances' heart when they first met at Hillside Park. It was love at first sight, Juliet with her white blouse and brown peasant skirt, and Frances with his navy-blue petticoat and black bolo tie. The connection they made on that day was beyond wonderful.

They spent most of their time walking the beaches of California, sharing their first kiss under the glimmering stars while sitting on the white sand with the cold water immersing their feet. They consummated their love in Malibu, sneaking around and defying all orders.

Their happiness didn't last long as their families soon discovered what was going on between them. During the 1950s, members from the lower class were forbidden to interact with members from the upper class. A cross between the boundaries of status was seen as humiliation to those of the upper class.

Frances' parents found out about their illicit love affair when the couple shared a kiss while professing their love to each other in the woods near the Beckerman's estate. They immediately used their connections and turned them into the authorities.

They gathered all the possible evidence they could find about the lower-class peasant breaking the law, severing the ties between the two lovers completely. It wasn't long before Liliana heard about this forbidden love. As a result, she created a law that would forever separate the upper class from the lower class across the country, never allowing the two classes to interact ever again.

Devastated by the loss of his love, Frances retreated to a bomb shelter that he built with his grandfather when he was just a little boy, a secret hideaway only the two of them knew the location of. Over the next forty-two years, Frances locked himself inside that bomb shelter, refusing to come out until he found a way to reach Juliet. He swore to himself that he would spend the rest of his life trying if he needed to; he would see Juliet once again. He believed that love conquered all. He knew that his love for Juliet would guide him to a plan.

"Don't worry, Juliet. I'll do everything I can to reunite us. I will make sure that we meet again," he stubbornly repeated to himself.

Forty-two years later, he finally invented a mobile phone that he soon called the "Apt." The phone had the ability to transmit messages from one phone to another, despite the distance between two people. No longer would the separation of the classes tear them apart. If he couldn't get his messages to Juliet physically, he was going to do it virtually. He just needed to find a way to get the receiver over to Juliet.

Now, hopeful for the success of his invention, he knew it was the perfect way to finally reach Juliet; a measly wall could not come between them. He would leave this shelter and find her once again. He would make her feel the love they shared.

During the chilly morning of January 22, 1992, Frances finally crawled back out into civilization, eager to reignite the flame between him and Juliet.

Unbeknownst to him, Juliet had joined an alliance with several others to fight for the rights of the lower-class society. When Liliana heard of this news, she knew she was being betrayed, immediately liquifying the eyes of all members of the alliance, including Juliet. This caused people to become more terrified of their dictator, more inclined to obey her wishes.

After weeks of searching for the love of his life, Frances Beckerman soon stumbled upon a notebook that listed all the names of the fallen victims from the alliance. His heart dropped from his chest when he found Juliet's face plastered against the wall of a light post. Her neck had been strangled; her eyes were torn out by Liliana as a warning to anyone else who wished to go against her.

Frances felt weak to his knees, knowing he would never see her again. Tears flowed from his eyes as he realized all his sacrifices over the past several years were all a waste.

Hungry for revenge, the strong-willed Frances tried to hunt Liliana down so he could kill her. His motivation was so strong that he failed to realize how much more powerful Liliana was than him.

"How dare you step foot in my sanctuary without being summoned?" Liliana's voice reverberated inside his head the moment he was presented before her.

Frances was frightened. He didn't want to turn his head for the fear of facing the monster that had taken over the world. Slowly, he finally turned, just to see a young and beautiful woman covered in scars, her eyes shining crimson red.

Ever since Liliana stopped taking her suppressants, her power made her stop aging, giving her the power of eternal youth. As she stared into Frances' eyes, he could feel his pupils dissolving, soon rendering him completely blind.

Luckily, several months later, his nephew, Malcolm Betterman, stumbled upon his shelter and discovered his notes for the Apt. He created a company that soon manufactured the creation as a worldwide form of communication in the Machiavellian-ruled nation.

THE WORLD TRULY WAS CHANGING, TEXT MESSAGING evolving into artificial intelligence, chatrooms, and social media. The world once full of promise and substance had now turned into one hollow and shallow; those living in it had all been infected and unable to break out of their zombie-like states.

However, the world didn't used to be like this, cold, emotionless, and disjointed. The world used to be a joyous place before the reign of Liliana, where connections, integrity, and conversations all thrived, people developing a sense of community and compassion.

Families sat together at dinner tables and talked about their days. Strangers sitting next to each other on buses and trains engaged in small talk about their mornings and evenings. Baristas and clerks knew about the personal lives of their regular customers. Romantic and platonic partners went out on dates and enjoyed each other's company, uninterrupted and free from distractions.

Children played together on the playground in parks, laughing and chasing each other without a care in the world. Even bullying used to be the good old-fashioned punch in the face or stealing of lunches, not what it had become now. Adults often traveled back home to stand by their parents as they lied to rest, and businesses enjoyed each other's company during team-building exercises.

No, the world was no longer what it used to be.

Now, since the vanishing of vocal communication,

social life had dissipated into something no one recognized any longer, a society where the beings living amongst others, somnambulistic. With the creation of the Apt, making communication and the transmission of messages no longer a struggle or a chore, people had stopped trying to end the reign of Liliana, for they had accepted the new way of life, seeing texting as a convenient alternative to speaking.

The creation of the Apt had ruined authentic human interactions. True, it allowed for long-distance connections and quick access to information; however, it also tore people apart, forming social connections with a piece of technology rather than with other human beings.

Families no longer sat together at dinner tables, eating in isolation and alone while taking images of their food to share with the world. Strangers on buses and trains robotically typed away on their phones, not a single word or sound to be heard except for the hustling and bustling of wheels on dirt roads and tracks.

Baristas and clerks no longer had jobs, as people had turned to virtual shopping with the simple click of a button. Relationships were falling apart as people cared more about their connections with the messaging community than their connections with other people, the rate of divorce skyrocketing as people no longer found a need for their partners.

Children were no longer seen at parks, the playground sets rusting and falling apart from the lack of maintenance and use, while bullying had gone completely virtual, with cyberbullying dominating the cause of suicides worldwide. Companies turned all team-building exercises into online chats, with no personable moments or face-to-face interactions.

Worst of all, parents and grandparents were left to die on their deathbeds alone, their children and grandchildren finding themselves too distracted or too busy to grant the dying wishes of their elders.

In all honesty, technology had always been predicted to cause more harm than good to the human population. True, it represented convenience and a betterment of life, creating an ease in the lives of those already hectic. But it was also very fickle, a complex and intensive development that people found themselves struggling to live without.

However, the modern society humans now lived in did not appear overnight. Technology that existed in the modern world needed to be developed, researched, and carefully crafted, far more than other aspects in the world, to prevent it from developing into the bad reputation that it was predicted to have, one that laughed in the face of humanity and turned it apathetic.

But all in all, technology had changed the world, for better or worse. Some called it a "gift," while others call it a "curse." Some called it a "menace," with others going as far as calling it a "true gift from God reigning down upon the world." There was no hiding the truth; it did make things easier, a lot easier, with technology changing everything in the world, from the way people lived to the way people interacted with each other. There was no turning back. The world would never be the same as it once was.

It didn't take long for technology to go horribly wrong. It didn't take long for the citizens of the Earth to possess it as a basic necessity, an essential need that they simply could not live without. Without technology, the world would descend into complete nothingness, with everything else worth living for, forgotten. However, among what used to be most important, silence now ruled the Earth.

People simply weren't allowed to speak anymore, not to themselves or to those around them. No longer were people allowed to open their mouths to converse with those beside them, to engage in small talk about how their days were, to learn more about their personal lives as opposed to learning about them through blogs and captions.

Virtual interactions had become life. Virtual interactions had become the only way in which people could now live and breathe. The world was becoming a dark and depressing place under their new dictator, but people could no longer see that, for they had fallen victim to Coxin.

Apt was a system of connection, allowing everyone to message everyone else even if they didn't know them personally. The device was connected through a digital system that made everyone reachable. For those who already had phones, they were automatically linked. For those who didn't, they were forced to.

Even if they wanted to speak again, it's not like they could ever bypass the consequences that the ruler had set. No one wanted to admit it, but they had all witnessed the disappearances of at least one person they knew who tried to rebel against Liliana Watson, their voices immediately silenced, and they were never seen again.

With text messaging, any attempt at restoring vocal communication had become impossible. With text messaging, personal interactions had become simply non-existent. But this didn't hit as a big surprise to people; everyone knew it was coming. No one wanted to admit it, but they all knew that as soon as they heard about this new invention, basic human contact would cease to exist.

The matter of fact was, without their phones, there was no reason to continue living.

From the looks of this somnambulistic town, no one would ever guess that the population continued to thrive, relying heavily on technological support. Silence had ensued the world now, the world becoming dark, miserable, and dreary, so quiet that it only made things more unbelievable than they already were. The silence was deafening, making this noctambulant town more horrendous than what it could have been otherwise.

Clearly, the years before them had changed. The world which used to speak, the world which used to be able to distinguish itself from other alien planets, was completely destroyed by this technological boom. All that remains was a dreary nation of pure, cold silence. It was a world filled with havoc and indifference, a world under the control of a superior being. It had become a world that people used to only see in horror films and nightmares, a world isolated from the aspect that made them human.

And that was the world Remy Kimora was coming home to.

CHAPTER 10

A CHILD OF DESTINY

Thirty-two years ago, pregnant Belle Kimora fled her hometown of Boulder, Colorado to escape to the isolated island of Troft, a place of solitary seclusion off the coast of Antarctica. She had never seen Liliana, but she heard about the deadliness that the young woman was capable of.

Under Liliana's rule, Belle, along with the rest of her family, had been isolated from each other, their lives draining from loneliness and lack of socialization. She knew she couldn't continue living that way, and no way was she going to raise her daughter in such a toxic environment.

So, one day, she decided to plot her escape from the world where social interaction had been banned. Troft was the only place in the entire world that wasn't under Lily's control. The island was so isolated that Lily didn't dare step foot onto it. Belle knew that if she could just make it there in one piece, she would be able to interact with the few inhabitants and animals residing there.

"Are you sure about this, Belle? It's dangerous out there," Darian, her husband, tried to warn her as she placed the finishing touches onto her raft.

"We've discussed this already, Darian. I told you, you don't need to come if you don't want to. I can do this myself. Besides, it's for the best. I don't want my child growing up here. I'd rather take my chances out there than face my cruel fate here," Belle answered.

"But you don't know anybody there! What if Liliana catches you? You and our daughter will both be killed!"

"I've already decided, Darian. End of discussion. You're either with me, or you're against me. I'm tired of being suppressed." Belle walked back into their house, leaving Darian with a tough decision.

It was a dark night of 1964 when Belle set her journey through the tunnel to escape the forsaken town of Stockbridge. She managed to bypass the guarded borders, crawling her way to the state of New York that took almost two months. When she reached the end, she set her raft onto the ocean and disembarked.

She peacefully arrived at her destination nearly three months later. During her journey, she planned out how she was going to start her new life in Troft. There were several research stations left abandoned for her to stay. Goods and basic necessities were still available in the area that would last her for years. There were greenhouses that were still functional and hunting supplies that she could use.

Belle was even lucky enough to have befriended the wolves in her area, which had been her companions since. Before Belle arrived, she carefully studied how she would give birth to her child alone. She was prepared.

Two months before her expected date, she discovered that one of the female wolves was also pregnant.

"We might have our babies on the same date, Nala," Belle said to the wolf while she was lying on the front step of Belle's home.

Nala looked at her and laid her head on her lap.

It was another ordinary day, and Belle was sitting in the front of her window when she felt a searing pain shoot down her back. Suddenly, her water broke. It was time. With staggered steps, it took all her strength to prepare herself, giving birth to a beautiful little girl nine hours later.

"Remy. I think I'll call you, Remy," Belle smiled.

Belle and Remy spent the next six years together, Belle teaching her daughter how to build her own shelter and hunt animals for nourishment. They didn't need anyone or anything else.

Meanwhile, back in Stockbridge, Darian, Belle's former husband, had settled down with a new wife after Belle left him for Troft.

But Belle wasn't the only one trying to escape; there had been reports of many others trying to flee to other countries and islands in hopes of escaping the dictatorship. Several were able to run and hide successfully; many others were caught trying to cross borders and were killed.

As a result, a law was enforced that ordered all civilians to turn in anyone who tried to escape. Afraid for his and his new family's lives, Darian quickly turned Belle in as one of the fugitives who escaped six years ago to Troft.

"I'm sorry, Belle," he whispered.

"Mom! It's my birthday today!" Remy yelled back in Troft as she jumped out of bed and toward her mother.

"Yes, sweetie! Happy Birthday! I'm going to make your favorite meal for dinner. So, I need you to behave." Belle smiled as she looked at her daughter who was jumping for joy.

"Yay! You're the best, Mom! Can I go outside first? I want to see Nala and the others. Pretty please!" Remy hugged and begged her mother.

"Oh, alright. But make sure you don't go far from here. Do you understand? It's a dangerous world out there," Belle firmly demanded.

"Yes, ma'am!" Remy gave her a salute and went on her way.

About an hour later, Belle heard a loud bang on her door, followed by demands and screams. She thought she had heard everything there was to hear here, but this sound was different, different but familiar. It reminded her of the sounds she heard back in Colorado when Liliana...

"Oh, no!" Belle whispered to herself. "How did they find me?"

After six years, Belle thought she was free from the grasps of Liliana for good. She thought she had made it, that she had finally escaped, safe and sound in Troft. Interrupting her thoughts, the front door ripped off its hinge, with armed soldiers storming through her home. It didn't take long before they discovered her hiding beneath the dining table and immediately dragged her to their ship.

"No! Let me go! Let me go! You can't take me! I refuse to go back!" Belle proceeded to scream as the soldiers continued to drag her behind them.

UNFORTUNATELY, HER CRIES WERE TOO LOW FOR REMY to hear. As Remy socialized with the pups of Nala, she failed to notice that her mother was being taken away.

"Happy Birthday to all of us! Luna, Ariella, and Josiel. May we all celebrate this special day with love and friendship." Remy raised her glass of water as she rested her elbow on Luna.

The three pups loved playing with Remy. They didn't have much human interaction, and Remy brought much joy to their family. The pounced on her, slobbering over her face. Remy fell back in laughter, happily enjoying what she believed was the best day of her life.

As Remy and the wolves cuddled in front of the warm fire, they heard the anguish cry of Nala. Something terrible had happened. The other wolves guarded around the young ones to protect them as they witnessed a strange ship departing the coast.

Thinking it was just another group of researchers who came and went, Remy proceeded home several hours later for dinner. However, she was surprised to find the front door missing and several pieces of their furniture destroyed. The hare her mother had prepared was embedded in the deep snow, and Remy trembled as she searched the home for her mother, stepping on the glass shards scattered across the floor.

"Mom? Mom, where are you? I'm home! I'm ready for dinner!" Remy called out as she continued searching. "Mom?"

There was no one to be found. Afraid of being alone and a victim just like her mother, Remy slowly made her way back to the wolves' den. She didn't know what had happened to her mother, but she wasn't about to find out, either. Her mother would never abandon her so suddenly. Something bad must have happened to her.

She was welcomed by Nala and the others, and soon found comfort beside them, walking back to her home every day in case her mother suddenly re-appeared. Every day she would walk over; every day she found nothing but disappointment.

On her eighteenth birthday, while picking up the remnants of her home that hadn't been destroyed by animals, Remy came across a note her mother had apparently left for her, taped to her bed. Remy failed to see this sooner as she hadn't slept in her bed since the incident. She picked it up, unfolded it, and read.

Remy, if you're reading this, you probably discovered by now that I am gone. I have been captured and brought back to a world I tried so hard to escape from in the first place, a world I couldn't bear to raise you in.

I'm sorry, Remy. I wanted to keep you safe, to keep us safe, but I have failed. But please, know that I love you with all my heart and will always love you for as long as I live.

Even in my absence, I have faith that Nala and her tribe will keep you safe.

Live. Survive. Don't get caught. When you're older, come find me in Boulder, Colorado, and we can be a family again. I'll be waiting.

Love, Belle

"Mom," Remy whispered as tears poured down her face. "Mom, I miss you."

She felt guilty that she had held a grudge against her mother all these years, part of her believing that her mother had left her. As she fell to her knees, Josiel approached and snuggled up against her.

"Josiel, I am going to find my mother, no matter what it takes."

CHAPTER 11
A WARRIOR'S ENDURANCE

Living in Troft was rough, despite how long she had been there. Remy imagined that this was how cavemen used to live. Things would get especially bad whenever a storm struck. She could never predict the voracity and disaster that came with each storm, despite how many she had lived through. The timing was also always off, giving her little to no time to shut down the electric generator she was incessantly running, a generator that required almost five gallons of kerosene to charge.

Life was always terrifying when a storm came by because Remy knew that, in order to get her next supply of kerosene, she would have to walk three towns over, brutal enough one time, much less several. Storms in Troft always prevented her from going outside because she knew they were a life-or-death situation.

The biting cold, the horrifying nature that was already slashing her skin without the storm, would turn homicidal, tempered force wings striking her with enough vigor that could send her flying off her feet.

She once found herself outside during one of these violent storms, causing her to fly across the sky and into the side of her wooden shack, crumbling it as the stability hadn't been checked in nearly a decade. She feared the worst for what murders may have occurred behind the walls, but living without it was out of question.

No one here lived in igloos; that was always a myth. If they were to try, they would freeze within seconds. It wasn't the lack of light that scared her during these power outages; it was the lack of heat. She was already wearing more than humanly possible. She couldn't imagine how she would ever make it through a storm with no heat.

"Shit," Remy cursed to herself as she closed her eyes.

There was no point in trying to read, anyway. The small lamp beside her was flickering so much that it began to hurt her eyes. So much for not being bored and finding something to do.

She could feel a gust of wind strike near her, causing her home to vibrate against the icy ground. If there were mountains near her, they definitely would have triggered an avalanche. She hated the idea of her camp being so close to sea, the fear of the glacier she resided on cracking any minute and causing her to float away. However, it was during times like these that she was glad she did, a thought that always crossed her mind whenever a storm passed by.

She knew Troft would try to break her, and several times, she did break. Her most memorable moment was when she almost lost her arm battling a Troft lynx, the deadliest of its kind, while strolling the icy edges for some fish and krill. But as long as she wasn't dead, she refused to give up. She would burn in her misery and shiver in her loneliness before she gave into Mother Nature.

If she could prevail the time the strong winds blew down her home, forcing her to rebuild another as the fiery blizzard pierced her eyes, she could endure any storm that crossed her path. Even when her situation looked like a lost cause, she still needed to hold onto some kind of hope that would allow her to keep surviving. The hell was she going to perish the same way she came into this world, cold and alone.

And that was how she slept at night, covered in sweat from her nightmares, alone, scared, and cold, curled up beneath a thin blanket that barely sheltered her from the worst storm she had ever seen. Kimora could only pray that, one day, she would be able to forget about these worst years of her life, forget the endless horrors that she had endured here.

Her skin was cracking from the cold and dryness of the air, blood trickling out as she tried to wrap her scarf around her wounds. Just when she thought the storm couldn't possibly last any longer, she found herself curled up for nearly twelve hours, shivering and bleeding. She had gotten this far in Troft. What's a few more days?

She only had another two days, at most, before her food

supply depleted. She would need to go out again to replenish her goods.

THE NEXT MORNING PROVED TREACHEROUS, A nightmare that resided in reality. To wake up and have to walk through snow, waist deep, was something she never wanted to have to do again, something she never thought she would have to do in the first place.

The harsh wind blew against Remy's emaciated cheeks as she pushed forward back to her lonely wooden shack. The nearest fishing hole was miles away, and without the ability to drive through thick inches of snow, Remy often had to trudge on her own two feet back to her home. Living in the cold midst of Troft had truly tested her strength.

The place proved to be nothing but a chilling and barren wasteland, thoroughly and utterly ruined. Despite spending her whole life here, the things she had seen, the emptiness and hollow aura of Troft, were something she wouldn't want to find herself in ever again.

There was just nothing here. No contact with human life forms, no communication with the outside world, no interactions whatsoever. But she wasn't completely ignorant to the world beyond her. Over the years, she was able to study the books left behind in several stations by researchers who had either left or perished in the cold.

Soon, it became difficult for her to find food as the bitter cold killed off the remaining life forms. The cold proved extremely brutal, much, much worse than any of the other sufferings she had experienced before. She foolishly thought that after thirty-two years of biting and enduring this brutal cold, she would eventually grow and become accustomed to it. But she was wrong, wrong about the cold that sent her running under her lynx-skin covers every chance she got.

But it wasn't the cold that killed many of the residents here; it was the wildlife, the natural citizens of the terrain.

"Come on!" she cried out, looking behind her.

The lynx continued to chase her while she ran near the cold waters to check on her crab trap. It growled ferociously, a massive beast of a thing. It had followed the scent of the hares she had caught a couple miles back.

Remy didn't even know hares were local to Troft until she struck the jackpot one early morning, starving and desperate enough to eat frozen tree bark. She knew there were hares up north, but down south? That seemed like a stretch. But, hey, not like she was complaining. She'd eat anything she could get her hands on.

"Is that the best you can do? Get at me!"

The lynx roared, its voracious breath nearly blowing her off her feet. Its limbs remained powerful, vibrating the ground they stood on while hers felt ready to crumble. Remy grinned, looking ahead at the track she had taken today. Usually, she wouldn't dare let a Troft lynx chase her like this, seeing her as a snack rather than a full meal. Today was very different, and hence, why she was luring him in.

Thirty-two years stuck in this infernal hell that was Troft turned her into a survivor, a fight to the finish. A complete survivor who had only lived and breathed for one thing. Existence.

A growl removed her from her thoughts, and she jumped to the ground, tumbling over as the wild animal went flying above her and right into the trap that she had set up, a set of broken rovers and drilling equipment specifically set up to impale the brute if it lunged toward her. She was glad she had been charged up and ready for this, overdosing on buckets of caffeine she found far away at a station.

Remy was completely stoked and ready for this chaos of a chase. Otherwise, she was done for, turning into a chew toy for this lynx she foolishly lured in. Adrenaline pumping, fear coursing through her veins, she somehow managed to defeat the seven hundred pounds of beast.

"Oh, yeah. I knew I could do it! I fucking knew it!" Remy grinned with her fist pumping in the air as she looked down at the groaning, broken lump of a body that was the wild beast.

With massive drill-bits impaling its body, it didn't take long before the creature closed its eyes to rest, for the last time. Living alone in the wild, Remy trekked daily for food and water, any means possible for her to survive.

Unfortunately, not all days had been as successful as that day, returning home with nothing but tears in her eyes. It was not often that she found nourishment; hell, she was lucky if she was able to eat once a day.

Lynx were her biggest threat in Troft, but they were also a gift, a gift of substance and nourishment enough to last her for weeks. Not only were they themselves food, but they often left behind carcasses of their prey with enough meat still on them to satisfy Remy's hunger for the day. She came across the carcass of an albatross once. Before then, she didn't even know she could eat an albatross.

Sickness and frailty kicked in every day, and she no longer had the energy to move around as much. She knew she was taking a huge risk by eating the albatross without knowing what sort of poisonous insects had been crawling inside it, but she was desperate, resorting to eating whatever she could find.

Finding food in the cold of Troft was a blessing, and she wasn't going to let any piece of meat go to waste if she could help it. Nothing slipped from her skeletal fingers. Not a chance in hell.

Dragging the carcass of the albatross back to camp truly was a workout. She had to meticulously plan out her steps and cover her tracks to prevent predator wolves from finding her base. The albatross was *her* food, and she'd be damned if she let someone, or something, steal it from her.

She'd fight with her bare fists before she'd let that happen. It got especially tricky when she realized that the blood of the bird was smearing against the white snow, but she managed to push the surrounding snow over it to cover the scent as she continued to haul the bird back to camp.

She winced as she heard a crackle, staring off into the distance where the storm was brewing. Thunderstorms were rare in Troft, but also extremely dangerous if one were to ever arise. Luckily, the stormy blizzard naturally covered the remainder of the blood infused in the snow. She'd be a fool to linger outside during these times.

Bolting the door behind her as she entered her camp, Remy sighed heavily, leaning against the wooden door and shaking her head. Trudging in the snow with massive boots was difficult as is. Sometimes, she wished that she had the wolves to help her lug her food back home. But that was also out of question as the wolves would starve to death after day one, eating each other to survive until there were none left.

She had never extracted meat from a bird before; she didn't know how to make the most out of this creature other than eating the thing whole, bones and feathers included. The lynx didn't leave much for her, but she was able to extract enough for three meals from that decaying bird. Lynx were known to be picky eaters as they always left something from their prey, mostly the heads.

However, she needed to remember to carefully preserve the meat without it rotting or turning into ice; otherwise, the meat would spoil, and she would become dangerously sick. She didn't want to make the same mistake she did her first time hunting down meat. She had been so happy snaring her first hare that she preserved it in her sleeping bag for special emergency, just to find out that it had completely decomposed after just one day, turning into meat even the wolves didn't want to eat.

After stuffing herself with what she rationed out from the bird, she went out into the woods to continue gathering all the logs she could find. She was going to need more than eight if she ever wanted to make it across the Atlantic Ocean. Though she had never been on the ocean herself, she had witnessed more than enough currents to know that if she didn't prepare, she would never make it across alive.

Most of the time, she had to starve herself to save the minimal supplies she could find during the months of famine that the island experienced every so often, not even able to find the carcasses of animals that alpha predators left behind.

Still, if that wasn't enough, she found herself actually facing the alpha predators, running away and barely making it through the biting cold, the almost impassable landscape, and a maneater chasing her down. She couldn't muster the strength to steal the hunts of the wolves as they were also having a hard time finding their prey.

Remy was too scared to lose any of them as Nala, Luna, Ariella, and Josiel had died years ago, Nala dying from old age while her pups were killed by some hunters trying to survive. Their deaths had devastated her as they had become her family, raising her as their own. She now had a new generation of wolves to call "family."

She remembered the day she stepped back into the wolves' cave as she tried to find comfort beside them. Ryu, the largest male wolf, laid his head on her lap while she stroked his thick fur.

"You know, Ryu, I keep wondering what it feels like to wake up with the sun shining on my face. Feel the warmth of its rays on my skin, the sweetness of the warm air. I long to hear the swaying of tree branches against the wind, like my mother always told me about. I'm so tired of this solitary life. I hate seeing snow all day. I want to see more. Smell the beautiful scent of roses I've read so much about. Dip my toes in water that won't give me frostbites," she sighed as sadness consumed her while Ryu whimpered in her sorrow.

Still, she couldn't bring herself to leave Troft just yet. She was so worried about what her life would be like if she chose to live in Boulder. She had no idea what her future would be once she stepped foot onto green grass. She wasn't even sure if her mother was still alive or if she still remembered her. The thoughts had made her anxious for years. Every time she set foot to start her journey, her stomach started to churn; her visions blurred and made her dizzy.

She had been in isolation for so long, relying on herself to get through each day, that she had forgotten how many times she had fallen and failed in the process. A lot of times, she had injured herself trying to get to more and more unreachable places, both in her surroundings and in her mind. She had forgotten about the number of times she had neglected her health by not venturing out for food because she feared being eaten by the alpha predators she so often tried to kill.

She had forgotten the number of storms and blizzards she had to endure but stood against, with a wide grin on her face. Remy had thoughts of giving up on trying to live through natural disasters as they were inevitable, that one of them would eventually kill her. She had forgotten about the first few years where she suffered unconditionally, praying her death came before the next creature.

Troft was brutal, utterly brutal.

Shuddering lightly, her hands shaking, she looked into the horrifying atmosphere of the white barren land as she slowly pulled on the dead body of the wild lynx. She made sure it was dead by slamming a poorly constructed machete into its head repeatedly, several, several times, before turning her back to the rotting carcass. She had once been mauled in the calf by a lynx. Remy thought she was done for, and with that lethal mistake, she barely escaped the horror alive. Never again would she make that mistake.

How she had lived without hunting for food all these years, surviving on berries and tree bark, she would never, never know, but she had. She should have sucked it up and began killing for nourishment sooner.

However, now was not the time to think about how Troft had tried to break her, tear her apart, and eat her alive for breakfast. No, now wasn't the time to think about how she had stood up against the cold, biting, utterly horrifying, freezing cold.

It wasn't the time to think of the negativity and loneliness she had gotten used to over the past thirty-two years that she had endured, but rather, the joy and content of finally hunting down a big lynx herself, piercing it before it had the chance to kill her.

Suddenly, a blasting air of pure cold and sudden chillness caused her to shiver, despite being indoors. It was so damn cold that if she ever left her shelter without proper insulation, she would be dead instantly. There wasn't even enough time for her to feel cold as she would immediately become an icicle. That's how cold it was. A human popsicle.

After having messily killed that lynx, she craved a much-needed shower. She didn't used to have trouble snaring animals, but this one, in particular, refused to go down, flailing in all directions until Remy was completely covered in blood, murderous blood. She almost didn't persist with killing the lynx as she watched it screech in pain, but she also didn't want to leave the innocent animal in pain, putting it out of its misery with one final crack of the neck.

The thought of removing her warm layers sent shivers down her spine as she walked into the bathroom, but she needed that shower, that shower with barely any warm water coming out of it, making the filthy blood much more appealing. Water was often difficult to come by in the barren terrain, and her shoddily-made filter system was of no use. Sure, it was a good idea to turn snow into lukewarm water, but that plan quickly foiled as the winds grew stronger.

Water wasn't even her biggest problem; food was. Finding food in Troft wasn't as simple as waltzing out into the forest and eating an apple from a tree. The unfertile land made those trying to survive hunt down their food; there weren't any animals or plants wandering around at their beck and call, waiting to be eaten. But the cold also made it so difficult to hunt that the lethargy was what drove most of Remy's starvation.

So, she did what anyone would've done in that situation. Searching through her camp for her chiselled, rusty axe, Remy placed her left hand against her cracked bed. With her eyes closed and a deep breath, she swiftly lowered the axe and dismembered three of her toes to keep her alive for at least another day.

Blood rushed out from where her toes once were, pain throbbing as she positioned her foot over fire to sterilize it. Throwing her bony toes into a pot of boiling water, she prayed to the gods that this nightmare would soon end, before she ate the rest of her own body.

Nearly an hour later, the starving and near-frozen Remy trekked across the slopes in her thermal boots, always staying within visible distance of her shack in case she ever got lost in the frequent blizzards. Growing up raised by vicious animals, her priority had always been survival, pure survival. She desperately needed some animal fat in her system, or else her weight would astronomically whittle away.

CHAPTER 12
THE JOURNEY HOME

At the age of thirty-two, after realizing that there was life outside of this cold, isolated, and brutal island, traveling to a world unbeknownst to her may prove much more difficult than the life she was born with.

But enough was enough on an island where she was torn apart from her mother, the only other human she had ever known. Being raised by wolves for so long, she knew she couldn't continue living among them. All she wanted to do now was go to the person who gave her life and see what she had been missing out on all these years while living in isolation.

What a surprise it was going to be.

After decades of trying to engage in conversation with wild animals, she was desperate for some human communication with the outside world. But she knew the outside world would be more than she expected. Complete anarchy was possible. But she didn't care. She needed a life that was more than just this.

THAT DAY FINALLY CAME. WHILE STARING AT THE endless abyss, she was ecstatic. Finally, after so many years, she was going to reunite with her mother. She had been in Troft for so long that she thought this was all there was to the world, a life where she had to wrap her feet in fish skin to prevent frostbites.

Anything had to be better than this. Still, she wasn't ready for a world that awaited her outside of this secluded island, the home she had grown familiar with.

Day after day, she waited until she was able to gather enough materials to construct herself a small boat to take up the shore. Now that she was finally ready, her anxiety of the unknown began to frighten her.

Will she recognize me? Will I be able to live amongst civilized humans without trying to maul them with an arrow? Will I be able to cope with their lifestyle? Things must be way different there. How will I survive?

Many questions began to course through Remy's mind as she began packing up what little she had.

She didn't belong here. She knew that now. It was time to go. This was her home, but this wasn't her true home. Gathering her strength, she walked toward her boat.

Remy Kimora remembered how she endured thirty-two years of hell while she climbed in her shoddily-constructed wooden boat, awaiting a life that was hopefully better than this. She thought of the wolves she learned to love, letting her tears fall from her eyes.

Before she departed, she set fire to her home as one final gesture that she would be gone for good. Pushing her boat off shore with an oar that gave her splinters, she headed north, up the Atlantic Ocean, saying her farewells to the land of no return.

As she passed Argentina and up toward the Caribbean Islands, Remy smiled at the thought of reuniting with her mother, having her hold her in her arms like she used to when she was a baby. She didn't know what would await her ninety-four days from now, but she was excited to find out.

Day after day during a freezing winter, Remy continued to row, seeing no sign of human life other than the several dead bodies she found floating near her. She wasn't sure where they came from, but she imagined it was from the small island in the South Atlantic Ocean everyone referred to as "the island of death."

At times during her brutal journey, wind scraping against her pale skin and rocks almost destroying her only form of protection from the icy cold water beneath her, she considered eating the bodies that she came across.

No, that would be too cannibalistic, wouldn't it?

Sailing alone in the middle of the ocean was rough. If the harsh conditions didn't destroy her, the mental challenge she had to face with herself definitely would. Whoever said living with yourself was easy never truly had to do it. Life alone and isolated threw her across cycles of emotions, from anger toward herself and the world to contemplating suicide.

Ninety-four long days later, she finally crossed the Gulf of Mexico and into Galveston Bay in the heart of Texas City. With barely two cents to her name and a lack of awareness of what currency even was, she realized her potential struggle to make it across several states into Colorado. Living in isolation truly made her different.

The port was surprisingly warm, and for the first time, she could see people, people who weren't trying to kill or eat her. Attempting to get some help from strangers, she rushed over to a man lowering his sail. She lightly touched his shoulder, and as he turned around, she saw blood in his eyes and stitches over his mouth.

Shocked, Remy quickly backed away, tripping over her feet and falling as a sudden wave washed over the dock behind the man. She picked herself back up and ran away. Terrified by the world she just arrived in, she found a group of relatively normal-looking citizens. She quickly skipped over to them and asked if they could help her get to Boulder, Colorado.

However, when they turned around, all she could see were blank stares in their eyes, blank stares that looked up at her, back down at their phones, and back up toward her again. They remained so quiet that she could hear their breaths, gusts of air pushing in and out of their lungs.

"Excuse me. My name is Remy Kimora. I'm trying to

find my mother in Boulder, Colorado. Can someone help me?" she asked the silent crowd.

However, she received no answer. There were over ten people in the crowd, and not a single one spoke. Sure, they acknowledged her; she wasn't invisible. They just refused to speak. The people continued to remain silent, until one of the women in the group lifted her phone. On the screen, the word Hush appeared as the rest of the crowd placed their fingers over their lips and walked away.

Why aren't they speaking? Is there something wrong with me? Don't I speak their native tongue? she thought. *Speaking is the most important aspect of human life; it's how humans survived for so long, by communicating with each other for support and by communicating with their predators for survival.*

Without speaking, it's impossible to properly convey feelings and desires, something that can never be fully understood when read from a screen. Without speaking, what's the difference between humans and inanimate objects? Sure, they can move, but their level of intelligence drops to the point where they might as well be dead. Her thoughts continued to argue with her.

Life became stranger when she was met with silence again at the William P. Lobby Airport in Houston. She had hoped to use pity and guilt to snag a free flight from one of the pilots.

However, when she arrived, hours later on very sore feet, the people there also refused to speak. Complete silence. There were no announcements of departing flights or gates. There was no one shouting out orders of food that were ready like what she had seen from the tapes that were stocked in the station back in Troft.

Everything seemed to operate based on a machine, with

people receiving texts for every announcement a human used to do. It was a strange sight to behold, but at least, the once-busy airport seemed much less chaotic.

Everything around her was so much different than the bustling nation she had imagined. For better or worse, she wasn't so sure yet. She observed as people received their boarding passes on their phones, as their phones vibrated when their food orders were ready, as they texted those sitting beside them, and as they faced machines at gate counters instead of attendants.

The only sounds she could hear were the constant clicking and tapping on the phones. Not even a whisper. Not even a murmur.

Remy lived in isolation for nearly twenty-seven years without human contact, and coming to a metropolitan city, it felt like she never left the unfruitful island. She still felt alone, despite being surrounded by people. Even when she tried to speak, ordering her coffee with her voice, she was turned away and given strange looks like she was an alien unable to abide by the rules of society.

Left and right, people refused to look up from their phones as if they had been sucked inside of them, sucked inside a piece of technology that was supposed to assist them, not absorb them. The people in line at the coffee shop refused to look up. They simply typed in their orders. The barista then prepared them and set them down on the counter, all without a single word spoken.

Some looked over at Remy like she truly was from out of town. They sensed that she was different, that she didn't belong. It also didn't help that she was wearing a shirt stitched from animal hide.

She needed to find someone to talk to, someone to help her find out where her mother was. Her hope fading, she plopped down on a vacant chair and stared off into the crowd.

How can this world even function? It doesn't make any sense. What's wrong with these people? Do all these people just hate me for some reason? I need answers, now!

Getting up from her seat, she watched as several passengers began to board their plane. Each and every one of them stared down at their phones, paying no attention to their surroundings. She watched the gate close automatically with a loud beeping sound, and she sighed as she watched the plane take off.

Turning back around, she noticed something on an empty seat.

Could this be one of those devices?

Remy picked it up, looked around to make sure no one saw her, and she shoved it into her pocket before running into the restroom. She flipped it open and saw a screen with numbers ranging from zero to nine.

This must be it! Maybe I can call my mom.

Digging into her pocket, she pulled out the note her mother had left her. It included a number to call if she ever made it out of Troft alive.

Hoping to God the number worked, she dialed it on the phone, the one and only number she had in her possession.

The phone rang. It rang several more times. But no one answered. Remy felt devastated and frustrated.

"That's weird. Why won't she answer her phone? Is this the wrong number? Did she change her number? This better not be a fake!" she whispered to herself.

Remy proceeded to call her mother eight more times, only to be met with silence. Panic began to send shivers down her spine.

Why isn't she picking up? Did she forget about me

already? Did she give me the wrong number? No, she wouldn't do that to me. She couldn't. She would never abandon her only daughter like that. This isn't happening!

As thoughts of doubt and confusion rushed through her mind, she received a text message from the number her mother gave her.

Who's this? Please do not call me. Never again. You can send me a text message if you want to talk. I only communicate through text messages. — Mom

The text message that popped up sent Remy's mind on a loop.

"What?" Remy whispered louder. She was genuinely confused. "Why the hell not?"

Remy tapped on the phone, spending several minutes trying to figure out how to use it before finally sending a reply to her mother.

Mom, this is Remy. Why text? Why can't I call? Mom, answer me. Why don't you want to talk? It's me, Mom, your daughter. Pick up the phone. I finally made it out of Troft, and all I want is to see you. Please answer, okay? — Remy

Remy anxiously texted back, proceeding to call her mother once more. As the phone rang, another text came through.

I said, no calling. — Mom

Typing a response back to her mother's agitation, Remy leaned against a pillar at the airport and wondered what happened to the world, what happened to her mother.

What is going on here? Remy thought, desperately looking around for someone who would speak.

However, whenever she tried to approach someone with words, she was met with silence, a grim glare, and a point of a finger toward a sign that said Quiet. Even more concerned, she quickly bolted to the exit and out of the airport, looking for her mother who texted that she would be at the parking lot in sixteen hours to pick her up.

As she rushed out, she was met with the same incidences she had witnessed inside the airport: silence. This could not be normal.

"I want to know what the hell is happening. This is nothing like the books I've read about America. Where is the industrialized society I always dreamt about?" she said out loud.

Suddenly, a strange woman approached her and showed her a message on her phone.

You need to be quiet right now, or you're going to be in big trouble.

Remy became more confused. She was finally able to interact with people, able to see someone who looked like her and without fur, but she felt more isolated here than she did back in Troft when it was just her and the barren land.

But maybe she was destined to be alone forever. Remy had lived a lonely life most of her life. It's not like there were many opportunities to make friends and have romantic relationships while living in a barren wasteland. Her best friend was a wolf that eventually died because of old age, and the closest she had ever gotten with a living being was the hare she constructed into gloves.

But she didn't care, did she? It's not like she ever lived a life where she had something to compare hers with. Besides, it was all about survival, right? Survival was much more important than connection.

After spending the night inside the airport, Remy walked toward the parking lot the next morning, longing to reunite with her mother. She was hoping that maybe her phone was just malfunctioning, and she wasn't able to call.

Her eyes teared upon seeing her mother from all the joy she was feeling. Even though Remy was mad that her mother had done nothing to contact her all these years, she ran up to give her a hug.

To her surprise, she didn't receive a hug back. Her mother just looked at her without any sign of affection, refusing to talk or hold her hand. It was as if she didn't feel what Remy was feeling at that moment.

Remy attempted several more times to get her mother to speak, but all her mother would do was point to her phone, not a single peep out of her mouth. Twenty-six, twenty-six long years without her mother, and she couldn't even get a single word out of her. She had more conversations with a tree than her mother was giving her right now.

This isn't right, Remy thought.

She had suffered enough alone in the wilderness; no way was society going to take those she loved away from her. No one bothered to explain what was happening. Her head was still full of questions.

"Mom! What the hell is going on? Speak to me! Say something. Please, I'm begging you."

Despite how much Remy shouted, it didn't take long for her to realize that she could only hear herself. Other than the wind blowing against the trees, her surroundings were silent. Cars didn't honk like what she saw on the tapes she had watched, especially in crowded airports. Everyone was on their phones, but not a single sound out of any of them.

At first, she thought something was just wrong with her

mother. There was, but the issue extended far beyond just her. Something seemed to be wrong with everyone. This strange phenomenon was something she couldn't have predicted.

Was this a result of an illness, or did everyone in town just become walking computers? She didn't even know where to begin to explain what she was looking at. Shouting over to some of the pedestrians passing by, Remy soon realized no one was going to answer back.

"Did everyone suddenly become mute? Am I going to get shot for speaking? Is Big Brother reigning upon us? Mom?" Remy leaned back, her eyes tearing even more.

Instead of the heartfelt and warm eyes she had hoped to be greeted with, she was met with a stone-cold face with eyes that continued to fixate down on a phone.

"Mom! What are you doing? I'm here! It's me! Your daughter! Remy! Remember? I have so much to tell you. About Nala, Nala and her pups."

Remy proceeded to repeat several more times as her mother still refused to acknowledge her.

Seconds later, her mother turned to her car, the cold air fogging up the windows, and robotically wrote, No talking, and I mean it. Your life depends on it.

Shocked and terrified, Remy stumbled back, tripping over her sack of clothing. She fell to the asphalt ground beneath her, scraping both her knees as she tripped over herself. Her mind completely froze. She could not believe what her mother had just written, so eerily creepy, so psychotic.

For Heaven's sake, they were literally standing in front of each other. Why couldn't she just fucking speak? God didn't give her vocal cords so she could tie them with a shoelace.

"Mom, we're standing right in front of each other!" Remy rolled her eyes, glaring at the strange woman she questioned was her mom.

Still no reply. The robotic woman in front of her still refused to speak; Remy was deprived of the motherly tone she had expected. Despite Remy getting noticeably agitated, demanding answers angrily out of the woman who gave her life, her mother continued to stare down at her phone, typing away like a college student, refusing to budge her head even as Remy tried to force it up.

But the blind look and hollow stare in her mother's eyes shook through her, fear coursing through her veins as blood rushed rapidly throughout her body. Her mother turned back to the car window.

I said, do not. Do not do that again, ever. Do you understand me? Never again.

"Oh my god, Mom! We're standing in front of each other! Why won't you even look at me?" Remy asked, her voice cracking. "Everyone is like this! What's going on, Mom? What happened? What's wrong with you?"

Her palms began to sweat as Remy became more worried and frustrated.

No response as her mother continued to type away.

"Mom! Speak to me!" Remy shouted, her teeth gritting and her face red. "Why can't you talk? Tell me what's wrong! Please, just tell me."

No reply. The only thing she could hear was her own grating voice, and nothing else. The world was silent. Too silent. Her mother turned toward the car one more time.

Get in the car. Get in the car right now. You are to text and nothing else.

CHAPTER 13
A STRANGE NEW WORLD

The next morning, Remy woke up feeling relaxed and strangely out of place in her bed in Boulder. She had been stranded in a wooden hut for so long that she couldn't adjust her body to sleep on something that wasn't a wooden board, leaving her feeling uncomfortable for being comfortable. She hoped that the happenings yesterday were just a dream, a delusion from the isolation she had faced.

However, when she went downstairs to greet her mother, she was met with the same ominous feeling she had experienced the day before. Her mother could only text her responses back, asking her if she wanted breakfast through a phone rather than asking her in person, despite them both standing in the same room.

Realizing this wasn't a dream, Remy grew more and more terrified that something had gone wrong with the world, that she had entered an alternative realm where everyone was controlled by some sort of invisible being.

She became even more horrified as she witnessed her mother turning on the television, the voices on the screen gone, replaced by actors simply typing their conversations.

Their messages were then received by the phones of those who had connected with the program, carrying on as if nothing had changed. Her mother didn't seem to notice the oddity of the situation either, reading from her phone the entire time the television stayed on.

How can they live like this? This is not normal! Who the hell watches television shows on their phones when the freaking TV is sitting right in front of them? How can people be two inches away from each other and still only communicate through a fucking phone?

Infuriated, she stormed out of her home, just to face the strange world that surrounded her. People were walking the streets, sitting, sleeping, all on their phones. Strangers, friends, partners, children, all on their phones. Not a single laugh, cry, or whisper to be heard. To the blind, this town might as well be a ghost town, not like it's any different from a world full of corpses anyway.

She continued walking, cautious not to bump into anyone as she feared they might combust or explode. She reached a tall glass building, with full intent on demanding answers on what's happening. Someone would explain to her how the world ended up like this.

"Hello," Remy smiled at the receptionist, hiding her disdain when the woman refused to look up at her. "I would like to speak to you about something. I have questions, and I know you have answers."

The woman didn't respond, not even looking up. She simply texted on her phone that was in front of her, and suddenly, Remy felt something vibrate inside the pocket of a coat she stole from her mother's closet.

What? she thought. *I don't have a phone.*

Suddenly, she remembered that she never returned the phone that she had taken from the airport. Now, not only was she stranded in a strange world, she would also be branded as a thief. Overwhelmed with guilt but also frustrated by the untold pattern, she sighed and looked down. As expected, a response from the woman stared her right in the face.

What are you doing? Stop speaking, and text. We don't speak, not anymore, not since... — Aubrey

Refusing to acknowledge her claim that speaking wasn't allowed, just like she refused to accept it when her mother had warned her, she shook her head and looked at the woman again, forcing a smile on her face.

"Look, miss. Can I call you that? I've been out of touch, for quite a long, long time. I've been alone for the past twenty-six years in Troft; I can show you the scars I got from being mauled by a vicious lynx if you want. I have no idea what's going on. All of this is making me crazy. Please, just explain to me what's happening, if you don't mind. Even my own mother refuses to tell me what's going on," Remy said, her tone barely holding her scorn. "So, I would like some explanation as to what is going on, especially from the fucking Boulder Inquirer! Please!"

Again, refusing to respond with her vocals, Aubrey sent another message. People inside the building were starting to look at Remy and observe her rebellious behavior. Some of them started to take videos of her while she hysterically shouted nonsense. They were afraid for what would happen to her if she continued, for what would happen to them if they didn't do anything to stop her.

I cannot speak. No one can speak. Please stop speaking. — Aubrey

Sighing explosively, Remy stormed out of the building, snarling and almost screaming. No one spoke, and it was frustrating her more. She didn't want to live in a world like this; she refused to live in a world like this. The place she was in was no different than where she came from.

Growing desperate, she walked over to the police station. As she went, she noticed a young couple snuggling beside each other on a park bench, again, only using words that could be found on their little devices, texting their conversations to each other.

Remy wanted to rip her hair out. She wanted to scream at the top of her lungs and cry, shout hateful words to everyone involved if the world was playing some sick joke on her.

"Somebody speak!" she yelled as she marched over to the couple and ripped their phones out from their hands. "Speak, idiots! Just fucking talk to each other! You're right next to each other *for fuck's sake.* Just talk to each other!"

The couple stared at her as if she was out of her mind. With a blink, they quickly stood up and ran away. Remy saw their reaction, and she became aware of what she was doing.

By this point, Remy could feel herself becoming insane, the sole psychopath wandering this new world and telling everyone to speak. She was the idiot now. Everyone else was normal in this world.

The world wasn't meant to be so silent. It wasn't what she saw on the tapes. The world used to be lively; everyone was engaged in fruitful conversations. The world used to be colorful. All her dreams of connection and running grass between her toes had flushed away.

Texting was a lazy man's way of communicating when they wanted something but were too lazy to open their mouths to get it. She felt surrounded by a communication style she never really understood, everyone around her forcing her to abide by it. Never in her life had Remy felt such confusion. She expected that at some point in her life, she would be alive to see a dystopian world, but this was much more than she expected.

This was a nightmare, a horror movie that personified straight from her biggest fear. She was supposed to come home from Troft to tears and long nights of staying awake with her mother, sharing her stories of everything that had happened in Troft as well as everything she had missed out on over the past decades. Never did she imagine coming home to an aloof mother who was obsessed with her phone.

Jesus Christ, she's in her 60s! Why is she still texting like her life depends on it?

It's as if people were now basing their lives on the next text message. People were crossing the streets while reading whether it was safe on their phones, as if the traffic lights were texting them. People were driving with their hands off the wheel, the cars somehow managing to navigate on their own.

People were behaving recklessly, yet the world was still

functioning. Was this the new age? Was Remy the only one who could not get on board with this? The only accidents that seemed to be happening were suicides from what these people were reading online, if they could even be called "suicides."

The world was so turned around that Remy no longer knew whether she belonged in it. She clearly couldn't cope with the change, and it didn't seem likely that she was going to get her way any time soon. Was she just supposed to accept it and move on? Is her being the only sane one left a sign that she needed to fix this?

Throbbing pain in her head waited to detonate as she rushed over to the police station and tried to speak with someone normal.

"Hi." Once again, she tried to talk to a policeman that was sitting behind the desk. "I'm Remy. I just moved here from Troft and have no idea what's going on or what I'm looking at. Can I ask you a few questions?"

The man didn't reply, and within seconds, she felt the phone in her pocket vibrate again. Remy groaned, looking at the phone and message she just received.

Lady, I don't care where you've been or where you came from. You need to stop speaking. If you don't, I'm afraid I may have to seize and detain you. Trust me, you don't want that to happen. Please leave. — Officer Andrew

Remy could have simply texted back in another attempt to get a response, but she wasn't about to give into this nightmare she was living in. She was determined to find someone who would speak to her, and actually speak, not pretend to and turn to their phones. Despite her hopeful efforts, she was ignored by person after person, all either ignoring her or fearing her.

Not only did they refuse to speak to her and answer her

questions, but they also ran away from her whenever she was about to open her mouth.

"Please just answer me!"

Officer Andrew became frustrated with Remy's behavior, and he immediately grabbed her by the arm and pushed her out of the station, dumping her on the steps. Remy cursed as she felt the sting from his hard grip.

Why? Why should I stop speaking? That isn't right. Why can't everyone else just speak instead? Why should I have to live under the rule of texting when everyone else should be living under the rule of speaking? Why should I have to waste my time texting my coffee order when speaking would be so much faster? Why did the world suddenly become so dark, so pathetic that I can hardly believe that this is the same world I had been so anxious to leave Troft to come to? This has to be some kind of Machiavellian dictatorship. What else could explain this?

Shaking her head, she decided to try the local hospital. Maybe they had seen a slew of damaged brains come by that could explain the situation. Walking up to the receptionist and hoping to hear the sound of a voice, she was met with another text message in its place.

Ma'am, you're not supposed to speak. I don't care who you are or how long you've been away from the world, but speaking is something that is not allowed here. You can get us all in trouble. Please, I'm asking you to leave. — Nurse Maurice

People in the hospital were moving away from Remy, like what had happened to her earlier this morning. Some patients nearby turned on their cameras and began filming her. She noticed this and gave them a glare.

"What is wrong with you?" she yelled as one of the security guards walked toward her.

Remy's instinct kicked in, and she bolted out the emergency door.

She was fed up. If people were going to be stubborn, then so was she. She refused to break and give into their warnings, despite how ominous they seemed. She was going to continue asking questions, pestering those around her, until she got an answer.

However, person after person, she continued to be ignored, even by the military guards sheltering the borders of the country.

No one wanted anything to do with her, a feeling that tore her apart much more than anything in Troft had done to her. It was almost as if her life would have been better if she stayed. At least the wolves spoke to her. This world made her feel like she was being victimized like a nerdy child in middle school.

Suddenly, her phone vibrated.

I've been observing you for quite awhile now. Stop what you're doing. If you continue speaking, you will die. Don't ask questions; don't talk to anyone. I'm warning you. — Damon

Confused and terrified, Remy peered around her.

Who the hell is Damon, and why is he texting me?

Her eyes automatically scanned the street corners, but no one was around except for garbage cans and street lights.

Is he a stalker? Is this what the cop was saying earlier? Is this my potential fate?

She stared at the phone's screen. Nothing made any sense to her anymore; the mysterious message definitely sent her over the edge.

"This is ridiculous," Remy sighed as she shoved her phone into her pocket and walked away.

BEHIND HER, LURKING IN THE ALLEY, DAMON WATCHED from afar.

You have to save the world from Liliana. You just have to. — Damon

However, before he could bring himself to press send, he immediately deleted it and walked the other way.

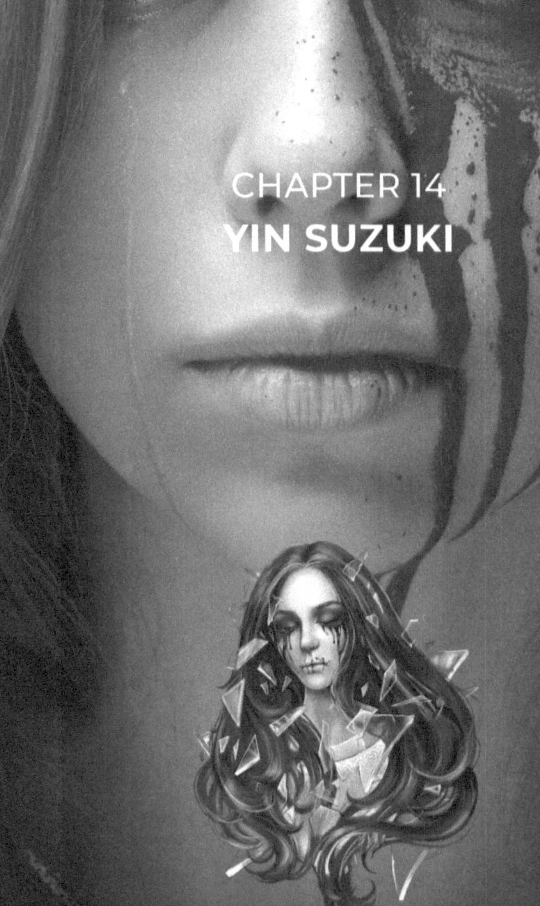

CHAPTER 14
YIN SUZUKI

Remy knew a lot had changed; a lot had gone wrong in the world. She expected this country to be different than the isolated island she had been living in, but this? This science fiction post-apocalyptic world she had just stumbled into? There was no way she survived hell in Troft just to come home to this.

She had to try and fix this, find out exactly what went wrong with this world and change it. This modern world wasn't meant to be silent. It was meant to be filled with tears and laughter, not emotionless creatures who now expressed their emotions through emojis.

What happened to all the children laughing on the playground, running around and having fun after school? What happened to all the hipsters chatting away on their phones while sitting in front of coffee shops? What happened to all the elders yelling at teenagers to get a job and stop vandalizing the streets? Thoughts continued to roam through Remy's mind as she sat on a bench, staring at the empty street.

Sure, those days seemed chaotic, but they were much better than this world, devoid of everything, turning everyone into mindless puppets of one divine machine, controlling their every movement. It was all a magician's spell that they were unable to break out of.

Life was supposed to be about the sharing of stories and adventures through voice. People shouldn't have to read about the personal lives of those close to them like an open book; these were called "personal conversations" for a reason.

Yes, there was evil in this world, sociopaths who liked to turn every positive situation negative and manipulative, but no one should have to give into this dictator that had taken over their lives and expressions.

Remy used to believe that in life, all the positives always found a way to balance out the negatives, creating a perfect equilibrium where humans were able to tolerate life without killing themselves.

However, right now, she wasn't so sure anymore. The negativities had been multiplying with no end in sight, bringing humanity to a lost cause that she wondered if it would ever climb back up again.

With life as it stood now, it seemed impossible for the world to balance itself out again, at least, not as long as people continued to refrain from vocalizing.

It wasn't like freedom of speech had been abolished. People just refused to take advantage of the First Amendment, using the Internet as their outlet for rights instead, and hiding behind screens as they insulted and bullied others, trolling them because they know people aren't able to interact with them physically.

This world was so populated, yet everyone seemed so distant and far apart, almost like they were each living in their own worlds.

Remy was beginning to feel like a hopeless case. She didn't want to go home because her mother didn't feel like her mother, and she didn't want to go back to Troft despite how terrible living in Colorado was. The mother she knew back in Troft was different from the one she met. She felt like they were different people. Her mother used to be so full of warmth and love; the woman she knew now was cold and distant.

Over the next several days, Remy found herself losing faith in humanity. Her energy and motivation to get people to speak was beginning to drain. She started speaking less and less and using her phone more and more to get through life.

One day, she found herself at a coffee café, ordering a latte through her phone. She picked a spot in the corner where she didn't have to look at the monstrosity people had become and began to write about the horrors in her journal.

It's been almost three weeks since I came to this country. So far, I have only been able to hear my own voice. What a tragedy. Maybe I should've never come. Maybe I should've drowned in the Caribbean when I had the chance.

Suddenly, her phone vibrated.

Don't turn around. Pretend like nothing happened. The message read.

"What is happening?" Remy whispered to herself, afraid to turn around in case someone had a gun to her head.

Trembling and shaking, she proceeded to type a response when another message popped up.

My name is Yin Suzuki, and I've been following you. — Yin

At least it's not Damon, Remy sighed in relief as the phone continued to vibrate on the table.

I know you don't belong here. I know you've been somewhere far, far away up until now. You're different. I can sense it. You don't know me, but I know a lot about you, and I know that you can help me, help all of us. We all used to be someone else, someone different than the people we are now. You thought you were leaving Hell to come to paradise, but what you don't know, is that you just walked right into the land of someone very dangerous.

Remy's eyes widened in shock. How could a stranger know so much about her, especially since she had been away for so long?

Did she see me in Troft? Did she know Mom? And what kind of name is Yin?

What are you talking about? How do you know me? I swear, if you're a stalker, I'm going to kill you. — Remy

But the message continued.

I know you want to know what's going on. To truly understand, we need to go back several decades. Our country, our world, used to be like the nation you imagined, full of life, laughter, communication, and connection. However, back in 1939, it changed forever under the control of Liliana Watson, the great dictator and queen. The story of Liliana was a strange one, a young child locked up and confined for years because she was different. — Yin

I don't understand. This is nonsense. There's no way one girl can be the cause of all this. This doesn't make any sense! Did Damon put you up to this? Are you trying to threaten me? — Remy

The creation of technology only made it worse. Markets crashed, and mass anarchy took over. People refused to accept what was happening, but the more they tried to rebel, the more Liliana fought back, destroying the nonbelievers. Soon, everyone began to rely on phones to communicate. When that happened, everyone lost their will to fight. — Yin

Well, why didn't you try to fight? You seem to know a lot about her already. There has to be a way to defeat her. I know there is. — Remy

We tried. For years, the citizens tried to fight against Liliana, never giving up even as they fell to their deaths. However, since the phone, Apt, was invented, people began to lose their motivation, living comfortably behind their own screens and refusing to risk their lives for the greater good of humanity. They grew tired and fearful of trying to be heroes, always losing. Instead, now we all choose to live in silence. — Yin

Remy stared at the screen, unsure of what to say. When she first saw this world, she thought the citizens had all just gone insane. Never did she think it was because of one person.

Who is Liliana anyway?

I know what you're thinking. Why haven't you heard about it? If Liliana has overtaken the world, why haven't you been affected by her? Back in 1963, there was an uprise in the nation when Liliana discovered that one of her pawns had escape. I'm going to tell you about why you grew up in Troft. — Yin

Tears streamed down her face as the messages were frightening her. This mysterious person seemed to know everything about her, more than she knew about herself. Did her mother put her up to this? Was this a joke?

Back then, no one knew why, but they knew she was trying to escape the dictatorship of the queen. It turned out that your mother became pregnant with her one and only child, and because she was afraid of exposing you to this massacre of a world, this society where people either killed themselves or got killed, she left. She hopped on a boat and rowed to Troft all by herself, for she knew that was the only way Liliana couldn't find you. Troft is the only place in the world where Liliana knew connections could never be formed. — Yin

How do you know all this? Who are you? How do I know you're not just making this all up? I don't even know you. Show yourself, and stop hiding behind a screen. — Remy

The phone vibrated once again, and Remy felt weak in her knees upon reading the new message.

Who am I? Like I said, my name is Yin Suzuki. I was a scientist, a doctor, before the reign of Liliana. Back then, we thought a simple virus was the worst of our problems. Little did we know, the virus was actually a gateway to unleashing the deadly power of Liliana. Back in 1939, a small group of us flew out into the vast desert of Jordan to hunt down the xerocole in attempts to contain the virus. However, it didn't take long before we found ourselves captured by a terrorist group who referred to themselves as "Witness." — Yin

Remy gasped as the message continued. What if this was all true? It seemed too detailed to be made up. Maybe there really *was* something happening beyond what she thought.

They invaded our base camp and captured us, forcing us to live in a dungeon with no access to water or air. We tried to survive for as long as we could on dirt and patches of the clothing we had remaining on our bodies, but we knew time was running out. Lucky for us, it didn't take long before the power of Liliana came into effect. When the leader of Witness tried to threaten us with their final plan, his mouth was instantly sealed with a zipper, leaving him mute, before he finally disappeared before our very eyes. — Yin

Remy felt a tear flow down her cheek when her phone vibrated again. Expecting another message from Yin, she picked it up, just to see a notification that her coffee order was ready. She stood up from her chair and tried to scan the room to try and spot someone who could potentially be Yin, but had no luck. Grabbing her coffee, she sat back down, just in time for her phone to vibrate again. This time, it was Yin.

It was very strange, and unfortunately, we didn't realize what was happening until everyone had vanished except for me. I guess all those years of being a timid child really saved my life. I tried rushing back to the states as soon as I could to warn my family and all the others, but it was too late.

Everyone had already fallen victim. Speech had ceased to exist. — Yin

Remy read the message over and over, finding it difficult to swallow as she digested the words. Nobody could speak. They *had* to rely on texting. Her mother had risked her life to save hers.

Remy didn't want to be the only one left. This wasn't what she expected at all. She thought things would be different. She thought that she would find her mother, and they would be able to speak to each other. There were so many things that Remy wanted answers for, but that didn't seem like a possibility.

Her hands shook as she slid the phone back into her pocket. She looked around, scanning the room one more time. But it was impossible to find Yin. Everyone was on their phones. But it wasn't Yin Suzuki that Remy was afraid of; it was Damon, the ominous presence that was trying to kill her. She needed to find him before he found her.

Though she hadn't been in the country long, Remy was already learning not to expect much from the world. She stared at her shoes for a moment, taking deep breaths to calm her racing heart.

She needed a plan. Something. What was she even supposed to do with this new information? Were these people expecting her to save the world or something? She could barely save herself, almost freezing her ass off during her time in Troft.

The phone in her pocket buzzed. Remy pulled it out, and her eyes skimmed over the screen.

What are you doing? You are wasting both my time and yours by standing there. You must leave now. Find out where and how this all started. Learn about Liliana. Do what all of us failed to do. You are our only hope now. You are the only one who can save us. Save us. Save us. — Yin

Remy's eyes darted from her screen to her surroundings. Cold sweats were trickling down her forehead. Her hands continued to shake, and her vision blurred. She felt the salty sting of tears on her cheeks as she looked around again.

If she thought she was alone before, now, she was completely isolated. Not a single person looked up from their phones while her world tipped on its axis. She wanted to go home — and by home, she meant Troft — at least there, she could talk to the animals.

She didn't belong in this world. She thought finding her mother would provide her answers to so many questions that lingered in her mind, but she felt more confused than ever.

"I never thought I would be wishing to go back to Troft," Remy whispered to herself, and with a deep sigh, she started to walk away.

CHAPTER 15

HOME

Life in Troft had been much simpler than life in the states. Remy knew how to stay alive there. She knew who she was there. In this strange world, everything she thought she knew was completely proven wrong.

She was the only person who could speak. The only person who appeared willing to try. However, all it got her was anger from her mother. Sure, she hadn't spoken that much in Troft before, but that was because she wasn't surrounded by people. She had an excuse. Here, it seemed like voice meant grounds for death.

If Liliana was this mysterious ruler, there had to be information somewhere about her. Probably in a museum or library.

Remy shook her head. Solving the problems of the world wasn't her job. She only chose to move to America to reunite with her mother. If she couldn't have that, then what was the point of even staying? She wasn't about to risk her own life trying to hunt down a world leader.

I'm just one girl. I didn't sign up for this, she thought.

People walked by, staring at her, as she headed toward her mother's home. It was a home, but it wasn't her home, so devoid of emotion and sound. Since she arrived, she didn't see her mother smile once.

I can't be the one responsible for saving the world. Remy thought as she walked straight into her room, watching the shell of her mother waste away on the couch. *Maybe I should just go back to Troft. I don't belong here. I'm sorry, Mom. I can't save you. All I wanted to do was get to know you. I have failed humanity.*

She sighed and shook her head. All around her were phones as Remy stared out her window. No one dared to look up as they walked. They walked into walls and didn't seem to care. Instead, they just adjusted their footing and kept moving. They didn't care that they couldn't express how they felt. There were no whispered conversations held by young lovers. There was nothing that made this world worth living in.

Soon after dawn, she packed up her belongings and was ready to go. She walked by her mother's room, kissed her on the forehead one last time, and walked out the door toward the location where she stored her boat. She felt a wave of disappointment as she climbed in, a feeling of lost hope toward the world. She had expected the world outside of Troft to be different. But this was just too much.

ALMOST A WEEK HAD PASSED SINCE REMY DECIDED TO return to her solitary life in Troft. Lucky for her, the fire left her most of her home, enough for her to repair it with a couple twigs and branches.

It's better like this anyway. They don't need me. They don't even know me. Their lives wouldn't be any different whether I was there or not. Remy thought to herself as she roasted the head of a hare over a burning flame.

She stared into the endless white land before proceeding to her home, her real home.

She felt safe back in her comfort zone, where she belonged. She tried to resume her normal life, hunting foxes and catching fish with her bare hands, but the thought of leaving her mother and everyone else back in the states to die didn't seem to sit well with her.

She knew for a fact that there was nothing she was capable of doing, but she was probably the only person left on the entire planet who hadn't been possessed and controlled. As much as she didn't want to admit it, she was humanity's last hope.

I can't. If I go back there and try to challenge the queen herself, I'd be dead for sure. No, I can't. I won't. Remy shook her head.

Over the next few weeks, Remy tried to forget about Colorado, America, and Liliana. She had been fine her entire life while Liliana was under reign. All she needed to do was stay out of her way, and her life would be spared.

But truth be told, living in solitude was beginning to become utterly depressing, especially after experiencing the human contact that she had up north. Despite not hearing the voice of a single person during her time up there, being around human faces and knowing that they were still interacting with her were much better than trying to start a conversation with an otter.

She tried to occupy herself by writing about her experience in the great North America, hoping that she could write her manifesto for travelers to find one day in the future, long after she had died alone in the cold. She may not be able to save the world while she was alive, but maybe her story would inspire someone else to. She just wished she wasn't such a coward, fearful of some woman she had never even met.

Remy tried to sleep night after night, but each time she tried, her wandering thoughts haunted her, leaving her restless and full of guilt. She tossed and turned, hoping the right position would give her the comfort she was looking for, but nothing ever worked.

This world isn't meant to be silent; this world isn't meant to be silent at all. This world is meant to be filled with voices and laughter, filled with emotions and grins. Thoughts coursed through her mind, leaving her feelings of guilt. *But instead, it had turned into a world devoid of anything else except for mindless phone-addicted clones.*

There is nothing left to do. Life is all about laughter, about joy. Life is all about dreams and about positivity. Yes, there are monsters in the world. Yes, there is evil in the world, but that doesn't change the fact that the positives always negate the negatives.

As they say, for every up, there is a down, but in life, every up negates the downs. But do I want to be stuck here and do nothing when I know I can? I should at least do something. Remy felt overwhelmed from what Yin had told her. She wanted to help, but it wasn't her responsibility.

What should I do?

Finally, nearly six weeks after she left Boulder, she knew she had to go back. She had to save those people. She was their only hope. She was going to die anyway. She had a choice, either die alone in solitude and loneliness, or die an attempted hero. She thought about it several times before finally coming to a conclusion.

So, she collected her minimal belongings, said farewell to Ryu, and hopped on her boat once again, rowing across the South Atlantic Ocean.

Don't do it, Remy. Save yourself. Remy's conscience screamed as she pushed on.

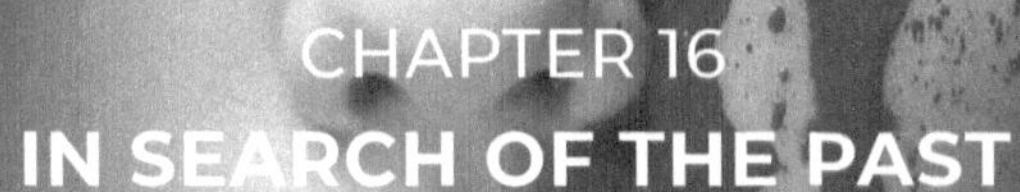

I need a plan. I need a plan fast.

The Boulder Library was as big as it was old. If she was going to crack this case once and for all, she might as well start with the one place with the most resources.

Floorboards creaked beneath Remy's feet as she walked into the building. There was a tiny old woman sitting behind a desk. Her glasses were too large for her face, and her deep wrinkles made her look as old as time itself.

Remy wrinkled her nose as she looked at the woman's floral dress and stern scowl. She hoped that she would be left alone in her search. She didn't feel like dealing with another text message conversation. If there *was* an evil ruler lurking, then surely, there must be spies everywhere. In all of the media she had consumed while stuck in the barren wasteland, the concept of good versus evil had stuck with her.

If she was honest, the concept of right and wrong, good and evil, yes and no, had intrigued her. She wondered what it would be like to live in a world that was governed by right and wrong instead of survival by instinct. In isolation, Remy had known no rules other than to survive at all costs. That definitely wasn't the case here as people didn't even know how to live for themselves. The world truly had become limited.

There were things that she wished she could unsee, like the ancient librarian. Remy smiled to herself as she walked to a table in the back and turned on a lamp. She set the phone on the table beside her and looked around. From floor to ceiling, there were thousands and thousands of books, old and new spines alike graced the shelves. Remy didn't have a clue where to start.

She sighed and walked around. *Liliana,* she thought. *There has to be a section dedicated to the woman who has a hold on the world. There was no way that one didn't exist. I just need to find it.*

Remy wandered up and down the aisles, looking for anything that would tell her what had happened here.

After running a hand through her hair, she looked higher on the shelves. Still, her search turned up nothing. *Were people afraid of documenting her life?*

It was getting late. The sun streaming through the

windows was growing dimmer with each hour that Remy spent wandering and looking for books. Finally, she returned to her table empty-handed. *I guess I'll have to try again tomorrow. There has to be answers here, somewhere. It was just a matter of discovering them.*

As she gathered her things, she felt someone staring at her. She looked up at the librarian, but the wizened old woman wasn't looking in her direction. Not even a little bit. Instead, the woman had buried her face in an erotic novel.

Remy giggled until a shiver crawled up her spine. She twisted this way and that, but she couldn't see anyone, failing to notice the dark and mysterious face of Damon staring at her from behind a large book.

Still, Remy was unable to shake the feeling of someone watching her as she left the library. Her hunting instinct was on alert. After searching several aisles of shelves, she gave up and walked outside. The world was quiet as she headed home, passing many faces illuminated by the blue glow of their phone screens.

When Remy walked through the front door to her mother's house, it was as if she hadn't even noticed that Remy had left and gone back to Troft. As usual, her mother's face was glued to her screen. Remy sighed and walked into the kitchen to make herself a sandwich.

There was no use in trying to get her mother to talk. It won't happen until she broke whatever hold Liliana had on the world. Once again, Remy felt overwhelmed. She knew the weight of the world would fall on her shoulders, but never did she expect it to be so difficult just to find some answers. She brought her sandwich upstairs and took a bite before plopping down onto her bed.

"At least this beats sleeping on twigs and leaves," Remy whispered to herself when her phone vibrated.

What you seek is not on the top floor. There is an older section of the library buried in the catacombs beneath it. You must go there and discover the answers you seek. There is an old door in the back of the restricted section. You must go in there. The librarian will try and stop you. Do not be fooled. She is stronger than she looks. — Yin

That mysterious message again. It gives me chills every time it pops up. Remy tossed the phone aside and fell back against her pillow once more. *I'll deal with it in the morning.*

However, as she closed her eyes to get some much-needed relaxation, the message continued to pound against her mind. She wondered whether she can trust Yin, or if she was actually a spy for Liliana, setting her up for a trap. She fell asleep trying to weigh the pros and cons of trusting Yin's messages.

THE NEXT MORNING, REMY FOUND HERSELF LOOKING up at the library again, the sun shining bright in her eyes as she stared at the murder of crows roosting along the cracked shingles. She watched for awhile longer before wishing away her nerves and walking inside the ancient building. It was time to get some answers one way or another.

She walked through the library without bothering to glance over at the librarian. Greeting each other and smiling were not how they did things in this world. She walked through the aisles, ignoring all the books around her, her mind focused on finding the catacombs mentioned in Yin's message.

And there it was. An old metal door shining as the entrance to the lower level of the building.

As Remy continued to stare, Damon was not far behind.

"Get away from that door! How stupid are you? Do you realize what you're doing? Who told you about the catacombs anyway?" Damon whispered to himself.

This was the first time Damon had spoken since the incident. His mind flashed back to ten years ago, when his best friend, Kyle, tried to stop Lily. They were supposed to work as a team, but Damon backed out last minute and watched his friend's body get crushed and incinerated by Lily's guards. His eyes were torn out, and his neck was snapped in half.

Ever since, Damon had regretted that moment, regretted letting his fear kill his best friend. As he watched, he felt the chill in his blood, the hollowness in his soul, and the unending ache in his heart. As a result, he swore to himself that he would never speak again. However, he didn't fall under the spell of Apt, allowing the device to take away his ability to speak like it did to others. He could still speak. He just chose not to.

Damon continued to watch as Remy ran a hand across the ornate door decorated with tarnished gold. He wanted nothing more than to run up to her and warn her, but he couldn't risk exposing himself. It's not like he could text her either; she was already suspicious enough of him.

Soon, Remy's phone vibrated again in her pocket as she admired the beautiful door. The message was from a strange number, one that she hadn't been in contact with before. She pulled it out, catching a quick glimpse at the librarian staring straight at her from between stacks of books. She had her phone in one hand and pointed at Remy with the other.

What do you think you're doing? Get away from that door immediately! — Gladice

This must be what Yin was talking about. With a grin, Remy decided to ignore the message and shove the phone back in her pocket. *What can she do anyway? Not like she can hurt me.* And she was right.

With the exception of Liliana Watson, Remy was strong enough to take down anyone who tried to cross her. She spent her entire life training in an uncivilized tundra, battling wild animals ten times the size of her. If she could take down a Troft lynx, she would have no problem taking down an elderly woman if she had to.

"And what if I don't?" Remy shouted back.

She knew she wasn't supposed to speak, that speaking would create greater consequences than she wanted, but she was tired of being suppressed. She didn't care who heard her anymore. She was tired of hiding. Maybe if she continued to run her mouth, Liliana would finally reveal herself.

Remy watched as Gladice's eyes widened in fear. But Remy didn't care. She was so used to people staring at her like she was a ghost that she simply gave up trying to fit in.

Without waiting for another text from Gladice, Remy pulled open the metal door and stepped inside. She pulled the heavy door shut behind her, hearing a loud thud as it came to a halt.

She looked ahead, but she saw nothing but complete darkness. *It would've been nice for Yin to give me a warning. I would've brought a flashlight.*

She pulled out her phone and started to swipe through the apps. *There has to be something here.*

Finally, she found a flashlight on her phone and turned it on. The light that emerged was dim, but enough to highlight that nobody had been down here for decades. There were cobwebs and dust decorating the walls, and no footprints were to be found. She then heard a scuttle behind her, but when she turned around, she saw nothing.

A rat maybe?

With a sigh, she made her way deeper and deeper inside, trying to duck as she approached the cobwebs so she wouldn't spend the next several days picking them out of her hair.

What am I doing? I don't see any books here. Not even one! This must be a trap. How could I be so stupid? Liliana would definitely kill me, for sure. But what if this isn't a trap? What if it's the real thing? What am I even supposed to do when I find Liliana? There's no way I'm powerful enough to defeat her. I'm biting more than I can chew.

"Right or left?" she whispered to herself as she came to a fork in the tunnel. From what she could see, neither direction was appealing.

Taking a turn toward the right, she began to hear whispers and voices echoing from the walls.

"This is really creepy, but at least someone's talking to me," Remy tried to joke to keep her nerves calm.

She kept on walking, listening to the sound of the rats scurrying out of her way. She could smell the stench of death and decay in the catacombs. It was not normal.

Someone had to have died down here recently, and the rats are finishing off their remains.

After a few more feet, she saw where the smell was coming from. The light from her phone was dim, but it was enough to highlight the rotting flesh falling from a woman's fractured skull.

Bile rose in Remy's throat as she looked around. Written on the wall in dried blood were the words, Get out before it's too late.

"Holy shit!" Remy screamed and fell backwards.

She had seen dead bodies before, animals and humans alike, but never did she think she'd find herself so close to one that she couldn't eat. Plus, the rotting corpse was something else entirely. There was a lopsided smile on her face, like she knew a secret nobody else did and paid the consequences.

"Damn it! I knew this was a trap! I'm so stupid. I need to get out of here. Fast!" Remy began to panic as she ran.

She didn't know where she was going. She just knew she had to get away from the body as fast as she could. Her legs began to ache as she ran, the uneven surface of the old stone floor jilting her from side to side. After a few minutes of bouncing like a newborn cub, she came to a stop.

In front of her was a room much larger than the library itself. Spread around the corners of the room were hundreds of tombs. Carved into the stones were the faces of past leaders who had died, all of whom lied beneath where she was standing. Another shiver went up her spine as she walked toward the center of the room, where there was an altar with a stack of books.

These books were old. How old, she couldn't even begin to guess. The leather-bound books were turning yellow with age, though the ice-cold catacombs had kept them preserved surprisingly well. Oddly, she didn't see any rats in this room like she did in the halls, nor were there dust or cobwebs, as if someone had been cleaning it.

Feeling the chill again, Remy felt the urge to turn back. Something was wrong. She wanted to run home to her mother and pretend that nothing had happened. The brief thought of falling in line with everyone else who lied in the tombs passed through her mind. She could just never talk again. Never saying a word seemed easier than approaching the books on the table.

Get out.

Turn back.

Run.

You're going to die here.

I will kill you.

She heard the whispers again, echoing around her. They sounded as if they were carried by the wind. Her feet seemed to have a mind of their own, moving toward the altar without her being aware of it. Remy stared at the books as the whispers grew louder. She took another step toward them, swallowing the fear that had blood pumping through her veins faster than ever. Her heart raced in her chest with distress as she took another step. The whispers grew even louder.

She couldn't explain what she was feeling. It was a combination of being both petrified and anxious. Her stomach was churning, and she could feel a hint of nausea.

You will regret this.

Turn back now.

You will die.

They will all die.
Murderer.
Death. Decay. Ruin.
Louder. Faster. The words blended together until they formed one long word that Remy couldn't decipher as she reached the altar and picked up the first book.
Remphelia.

CHAPTER 17

THE DISCOVERY

It didn't take long before the entire room began to shake, debris from the walls falling down onto Remy. She reached out and grabbed the remaining books, tucking them all under her arm. Her teeth rattled in her head as she ran through the tunnel with only moments left before it collapsed. Blood rushed in her ears as she continued to run. The whole tunnel was crumbling down.

I have to get out of here.

Twisting and turning, she no longer cared if the cobwebs got into her hair. She'd deal with them if she made it out alive as the debris of the tunnel chased her toward the entrance.

Come on, legs. Don't give up on me now! Her legs screamed in protest before she finally reached the door.

Pushing hard against the metal door, it refused to budge. Remy screamed as she pushed harder, throwing all her weight against it. The rats surrounded her ankles now as they also tried to evade their death, biting her legs as they fought each other for freedom.

Finally, she managed to get the door open. She ran out of the catacombs and dashed through the library to the front desk. Gladice looked up at her, eyes wide as she noticed the books that Remy hugged against her body. Gladice grabbed her phone and waved it at Remy. Remy's chest heaved as she pulled her own phone out from her pocket.

I did not think you would make it. Many do not. The last person to try had died in those tunnels. Be aware that those volumes only contain half the answers that you seek. There was a headmaster. Though I do not know more than that. — Gladice

Remy looked at her with eyes full of rage.

You couldn't have said something before I risked my life. There was another way to get this information instead of risking my life for some old fucking books? — Remy

The answers you are looking for cannot be found with the headmaster alone. To destroy the queen, you must first understand what she is made of. You must know her both inside and out if you wish to destroy her. — Gladice

If I didn't know any better, I would say that you were part of the resistance. — Remy

I suppose you better learn then. You know nothing of

life, child. You are too young to understand the intricacies of this world. I have lived for nearly a hundred years. I have seen the worst of the world. I saw the change. Do not make the same mistakes I did. There is no beating Liliana. There is only the acceptance of fate. — Gladice

As Gladice typed away, Remy noticed that half her face was missing, her right eye torn from her socket.

She got you, didn't she? How can you believe that things will never get better? There has to be something that can be done. — Remy

Foolish child. You may look like a grown woman, but you do not know of the world and its horrors. Do what you must, but in the end, nothing is certain except death. — Gladice

Remy shook her head and put her phone back in her pocket. She shifted the books around in her arms and shook her head as she left the library. Gladice was wrong. She had to be. All that trouble of getting these books had to be worth something in the end. If it wasn't, then why was she going on this wild goose chase after some woman who cannot be defeated?

REMY SAT IN THE MIDDLE OF HER MOTHER'S KITCHEN with the ancient tomes spread out in front of her. She had piles of papers and dozens of pens spread around her as she pored over the texts. Although they were written in English, they were old, using words that hadn't been used in hundreds of years. She squinted hard as she tried to decipher the meaning. Still, nothing seemed to make sense. The tomes read more like fictional horror stories than informational guides.

Remy tucked a pencil behind her ear and crossed her legs. She grabbed a piece of paper containing the text that she had managed to read so far. Her eyes traveled along the page, looking for anything that would stand out to her.

Suddenly, she saw the same word that the voices had whispered in the tombs: Remphelia.

Remphelia is a rare condition that causes those affected to have red irises. It is also believed that it allows those who possess it to have psychokinetic powers in which they can control the minds of those around them, a dangerous psychological disorder, especially in a time when the world is facing strife.

However, it is this institution's understanding that every eighty-seven years, a child is born with the aforementioned condition.

Remy scribbled down as much as she could while trying to digest what she had read. She couldn't understand what the condition had to do with Liliana. She read some more, hoping she could get the answers she needed.

For centuries, children among children have been born with Remphelia, creating each apocalypse known to mankind.

The common source? Baylor Orphanage in the heart of Stockbridge, Massachusetts. Apparently, it had been rebuilt since its destruction in the late 1800s. No one really knew what had happened. Most say it was some fluke accident that killed everybody. But most people know it was something else. They say the orphanage is cursed. Constantly built and re-built.

Unfortunately for humanity, records for who these children were go unnoticed until it becomes too late. These children must be stopped. These children are the death of humanity.

These seemingly innocent babies will bring about the destruction of the world if left unchecked.

The year is 1922, and if our timeline is correct, another child will soon be born. 1924 is predicted to be the deadliest year of the century. It is our institution's responsibility to capture the child and find a way to contain her. It will be our only hope of surviving. This child cannot be trusted.

For years, we have carefully crafted the perfect team to hunt this child down. When the clock strikes the first of January 1924, we will begin searching for the child. I only hope that we will be successful in our mission. It is the eventual goal of this institution to find the root of Remphelia and expel it.

However, since the beginning of time, we have not been able to find the answer. We are all in danger if we remain unable to isolate the cause. It is a shame to do what we must to a child, but it is a necessary evil.

There is only so much that can be done before further intervention will need to be taken. I am fearful of what this predicament will come to.

Remy sighed before placing the paper down and running a hand through her hair. Every eighty-seven years, the world must face another horror. She was glad that her mother had hidden her away all those years. She couldn't imagine growing up in a world where she couldn't speak to anyone. Yet, here she was in that very same world.

If she could find a way to stop Liliana, then those in the next century may also be able to find a way to stop the next child born with Remphelia. She shuffled through the stacks of papers until she found one that seemed different from the others, this one more recent. She roamed her eyes once again through the tomes, gathering as much information as she could.

The birth of the child will end us all. The year is 1939. The child is here. We do not know when or how she will strike. We have learned of the headmaster, the leader of the orphanage where the child resides, who witnessed the power of this creature. A once fearsome woman who was able to keep this beast in check.

But despite all her efforts, one woman was not nearly enough to contain this child's power. It was only a matter of time before Liliana made her escape, slaughtering the orphanage and leaving only mere crumbs behind. Everyone gone. Dead. All except one miraculous save.

Headmaster Walden. She only had seconds left to live when the paramedics found her. Luckily, they were able to revive her. Maine, that's where we need to go. Close to the edge of state, contained in a hospital on the outskirts of town.

The headmaster failed in her duties. She cannot be trusted to care for the next child that is born.

We have a terrifying reign ahead of us now that Liliana has escaped. None have been able to find answers to her terror.

To do so, we must speak with the headmaster, but thus far, she has been in and out of delirium and unable to speak. Perhaps it is more of an unwillingness than...

The final sentence ended with only a blood smear. Remy looked around and sighed. She thought she would be able to start a normal life, but that was far out of reach. If she was the only one willing to talk, maybe the headmaster would be willing to speak to her as well. If she had known it would be this difficult, she would've just stayed where she was and died in peace.

She gathered her stack of papers and books, stuffing them into a backpack she found in one of her mother's closets. Maine was nearly an entire country away. She would have to buy a plane ticket to get there. Remy had no clue how she was going to do that. She didn't know how to drive, and it was definitely too far to walk. There was only so much she was able to do. Everyone ignoring her didn't make it any easier.

"And do it I must," Remy whispered to herself as she pulled the phone from her pocket.

After forty minutes of endless arguments with the device, a plane ticket was purchased, and a cab was set to pick her up the next morning. Remy set her backpack near the front door. After gathering another bag filled with clothes and some food, she headed into the kitchen. This could be her last night with her mother. She may as well make it as memorable as possible.

Remy placed the finishing touches on dinner when her mother walked through the door. Her mother set her purse down on the table and pulled out her phone. Remy pulled her own phone out and waited for the message to come through after seeing her mother's thumbs fly across the keyboard.

What are you doing? — Mom

I'm making dinner. — Remy

Why? — Mom

Remy sighed and put her phone on the counter, turning to plate the food. "This is my last night here. I'm going to look for Liliana in the morning. It has been too long since people have used their voices. This reign of terror needs to come to an end."

She will kill you. You don't know what you're going up against with this chase. There are better ways to fill your time than hunting her down. Things are working here. We can still communicate and lead normal lives. You are about to fight a battle that doesn't need to be had. — Mom

"Normal? You think this is normal? Then why did you run all the way to Troft just to hide from her? Why did you choose isolation for me for the last thirty-two fucking years if I was not meant to come home and deal with this? You kept me in isolation. You may have saved my life, but I will be damned if all I have to live for is texting. Everyone thinks I'm crazy, bombarding me with messages day and night.

I'm known in town as the one human who is still able to speak. If you ask me, I'm probably the only one out of all of us who still has some sense. I'm tired of being called the 'stranger,' the 'blasphemer.' I get it. I get why everyone hates me, despise me even. I'm different. I know that. But I refuse to let you all throw away the one thing that distinguishes us from all other animals. Words.

What is life without free will? What is life without self-expression? Without freedom? The bitch must be stopped. Now, eat your dinner and pretend that you love me because, in the morning, I'm leaving."

BELLE WAS SCARED OF WHAT WOULD HAPPEN TO HER daughter. She remembered what Liliana's minions did to her after they found out that she had been hiding in Troft. The torture she experienced was unbearable. But nothing hurt more than when she was forced to abandon her daughter, not knowing whether she would survive. Maybe it was her destiny to save the world.

She wanted to show Remy how much she missed and

longed for her daughter, but because she had spent so long without speaking, she had forgotten how to express her feelings. Her face was emotionless. She wanted to cry, but she didn't remember how.

Belle didn't respond, instead, put her phone back into her pocket and walked over to grab her plate of food from her daughter's hands. Remy watched as her mother sat down and dug in. No other messages were shared between the pair that night.

THE NEXT MORNING, REMY QUICKLY BRUSHED HER teeth and tied her hair back from her face. She pulled on a pink floral dress she had grabbed from her mother's closet. Living in Troft meant all her clothing were made from animal skin and bones. She already generated enough stares from the unfriendly crowds around her; she definitely didn't need more. She peered closer into the mirror and looked at the dark bags beneath her eyes. Was she ready? Not even a bit. Was she scared of dying? Absolutely.

It didn't matter. Nothing mattered in this world anymore. The only thing anyone cared about was typing away on their phones. There was no longer passion or communication. There were only cold screens. Remy never wanted to live in a world like this. She thought everything would be like in the books she had read, where everyone in the civilized society interacted.

She imagined children playing together on the playground. She wanted to find her own group of friends to socialize with on the cute tables in front of bistros. She imagined her mom conversing with other moms as they talked about their kids. When she left Troft, she thought she would be coming home to a family. Instead, she came home to emptiness.

Remy glanced at the time on her phone. The cab would be there soon. She stumbled down the stairs, wiping the sleep from her eyes. As she pulled on her shoes, she could hear the squeak of the stairs behind her.

Standing straight, Remy looked over her shoulder and saw her mother standing with a hand pressed against her lips. Remy offered her a sad smile. There were so many things she wished she could tell her, so many things left unsaid. She was certain that this would be the last time she would see her mother. Either she would die in Maine, or her mother would be dead by the time she came back. Remy settled on a small wave before opening the front door.

"I love you, Mom," Remy whispered as she stepped outside.

CHAPTER 18

TAKING DOWN THE QUEEN

The journey to Maine took much longer than Remy had expected. With no knowledge of the country, she had no idea how far away Colorado was. When she stepped off the plane, her surroundings were exactly the same as they were back in Boulder. Faces were pressed into phones with complete silence.

Remy hefted her bags higher on her shoulder and

looked around. She needed to find the hospital that the headmaster was kept in.

She pulled out her phone and walked over to the service desk, pausing for a moment.

Wait, if I ask someone for directions, won't they get suspicious? Will that expose me as trying to end Liliana's reign of terror?

After spending several minutes coming up with a convincing alibi that would help her reach her destination, she decided to type out a message to the attendant.

Hi, I'm looking for a...

However, before she could finish, one came through on her phone.

Hello, Remy. Welcome to Maine. I see your research has gotten you quite far. — Damon

Startled, Remy looked around her surroundings, but she saw nothing but mouths that were sewn shut, fresh stitches coating the lips of many people. Everyone was on their phones, typing away, so she couldn't pick out which one might be Damon.

What do you want? First, you threaten me with death, and now you're welcoming me? Who are you? — Remy

I can't tell you, not here, anyway. We might be monitored. See that black car across the lot at arrivals? It's me. Get in. — Damon

No, I can't. I have to get to the hospital, the one at the edge of state. — Remy

I know where it is. I'll take you there. Just get in. — Damon

As she read the message, she heard an engine. Remy looked up and saw a dark car with even darker windows idled alongside the curb. The windows were rolled all the way up, but Remy could see an outline of a man.

She wanted to weigh the potential consequences of getting in the car. Could she really trust this man? Was he trying to help her, or was he trying to kill her? After a moment, she decided that it didn't matter. She was as good as dead anyway if she didn't at least try. Remy jogged over to the car and tossed her bags in the back. She ran around to the passenger side and opened the door.

Inside, was a handsome man with black hair and dark purple eyes. He was about the same age as her, and his smile glistened as he stared at Remy.

Okay, what do you want? — Remy

Remy had been around silence for so long that she had grown used to sending messages. She had been ignored for far too long that it wasn't worth wasting breath just for silent responses.

To her surprise, rather than typing out his response, Damon placed a hand over Remy's screen and opened his mouth.

"I want to help you. I want to help you defeat Liliana," Damon said.

Eyes wide, Remy could only stare in silence. This was the first time in decades that she heard another human voice, and it... it... it was beautiful.

"Oh my god... you can talk?" Remy asked, surprised.

"Yes, I may be the only one besides you who is able to speak. But we have to speak quietly to avoid getting exposed. I tried to warn you, many times, to stop speaking, but you wouldn't listen. Now, I hope you do. I'm going to take you to the hospital where Headmaster Walden is, room forty-four. In order to get her to talk, you have to catch her when she's lucid. Otherwise, it's useless." Damon explained.

"Wait, so you're not going to kill me?" Remy asked with relief.

"No, that was just a warning to get you to stop this wild goose chase and risk getting killed. But now that you have come this far, I may as well help you finish."

"Why should I trust you?"

"Let's just say that I have invested interest in the world speaking again. This constant silence, I can't take it. People are so absorbed in their phones that they no longer know who they are. I used to be so close to my father; now, he barely recognizes me."

The sad expression on Damon's face proved to Remy that he was telling the truth. It didn't make sense for him to lie about something like that.

"And I'm guessing you want something in return?"

"No, I just want to hear laughter and joy in the world again. I can't stand watching everyone look so miserable. Don't think of this as saving the world for me. I can't take down Liliana. I've tried, but I only caused more pain. Believe me, Remy. Save the world from Liliana." Damon took Remy by the hand and kissed it. "You'll be a hero, a savior."

"I'll do it," Remy blushed as Damon drove away.

THE HOSPITAL LOOKED MUCH OLDER ON THE OUTSIDE than Remy had expected, the bricks that made up the exterior rotting and crumbling away. Windows had been shattered, and the nurses all looked suicidal. There was nothing welcoming at all.

"This is where I leave you, Remy. Be careful." Damon finally spoke again upon arriving at the hospital.

"Are you sure you don't want to come with me?"

"I can't. It'll be too dangerous for both you and me."

Remy watched as Damon drove away with her bags on the back seat. It wasn't like she would need them anyway, not where she was going.

And there she was, standing all alone once again. There was just something about this moment that told Remy she would never see Damon again.

Taking a deep breath, Remy turned around and walked toward the hospital. Staring up, she could see hollowed eyes staring back at her.

That must be the headmaster. Man, she's old.

Stuffing her hands into her pockets, she lowered her head and walked into the hospital. She signed herself in as visiting her grandmother and headed straight for room forty-four. The lights overhead flickered, and there was no elevator in sight.

Remy didn't bother to ask any of the doctors or nurses where the stairs to the fourth floor were. She couldn't risk exposing herself even more. She continued down the halls before finally reaching a room barricaded with heavy bars. Remy pushed the door open and saw a frail woman sitting on a wheelchair, still staring out the window. A pair of hollowed eyes turned toward her as Remy approached.

"Hello, are you Headmaster Walden? The headmaster in charge of Baylor Orphanage that burned down seventy-one years ago in Stockbridge, Massachusetts?" Remy asked nervously, unsure of what to expect.

The woman frowned but nodded. She raised one thin hand and gestured toward her mouth. It was sewn shut like many of the others. Remy could see open wounds all over the woman's arms, and even more scars laced around her neck. There was a strange smell in the room, a strange smell of death.

"My name is Remy Kimora. I came here from Colorado to speak with you about Liliana. I need to stop her before she destroys the world."

As Remy spoke, the headmaster raised her forehead, and she shook her head. When Remy noticed her trying to wheel herself out of the room, she ran over to the door and locked it shut.

"You couldn't control her, could you? You tried to prevent her power from unleashing, but you weren't able to. You knew she was coming. You knew she was the destined child of the century, the one who must be stopped, and you let her escape." Remy tried to hold back her anger, but seeing Walden channeled rage inside her because she knew Walden was responsible for all this. "How did she do it? How did she destroy the orphanage?"

Unable to speak, Headmaster Walden brought her hands up to grasp around her own neck. She shook her head from side to side before jerking it violently to the right.

"She snapped necks?"

Walden nodded. She moved her hands down to her legs and tapped her fingers against her thighs. She then pointed at Remy before pointing out the window. Remy walked over to the window to see what was out there. However, all she could was empty terrain, with nothing of significance.

She turned back to the headmaster, "I don't understand."

The headmaster shook her head before picking at one of the scabs on her arm. She opened the wound; crimson blood dripped down her arm. The woman then dipped a finger into it before writing on the bedsheets.

Powerful. More than any other.

Could not keep contained in the orphanage.

Afraid of isolation. Afraid to be lonely.

Go to Stockbridge.

Orphanage. Basement floor. West Wing.

Remy took out her phone and snapped a picture of the words. Stockbridge, Massachusetts. That's where she needed to be. She didn't know how she was going to get there, but get there she must.

After a long bus ride, Remy finally arrived in Stockbridge, Massachusetts. She was relieved to stretch her back, but no way was she ready to face Liliana. The entire time on the bus, she wondered what Liliana looked like. She must be really old by now, being born in 1924. She also scrolled through images of the orphanage on her phone, images that had been published in newspapers almost a century ago. Although it had been long destroyed, there was still one wing standing. The West Wing.

Disembarking the bus, she walked through town until she came across the spot she had circled on her map, where the orphanage once stood. In front of her, was half a wing and a pile of debris. Deep craters had been carved out of the Earth, and there were imprints of long scratches made by human hands.

The wind was cold, and crows screeched as Remy entered the remains. Floorboards creaked beneath her feet in places where they hadn't broken away. She climbed the stairs, careful to test each step before she descended. It didn't take her long to find Liliana's room, and when she did, she saw the word KILL carved deep into the floor.

She looked around. The room was more of a cell than a room. There were little light and bars across what used to be bulletproof plexiglass that had been shattered. Remy had lived in isolation before, but at least she was free to roam around. She couldn't imagine being isolated and contained like a songbird in a cage.

Taped to the wall of Liliana's room was a single picture. Liliana didn't seem like someone who kept memories of her past, but this was no ordinary picture. According to the photographs taken soon after the collapse in 1939, this picture had not been here before. Also, the other scattered pieces of paper she found upstairs were all damaged and yellow; this one was fresh and white. This piece of paper was new. She stared closer and saw a portrait of two people, a man and a woman.

Below the image were scratch marks that spelled out: You abandoned me. Now, you will die!

Her parents. They must be her parents. The ones who gave her up to the orphanage when she was only a baby. I remember it was written on the old tomes. Shit, I have to save them!

Remy ripped the paper off the wall. Liliana was just here. She could feel it.

She must have come back to Stockbridge to murder her parents. Not if I can help it.

"Come on, Liliana. Show yourself," Remy whispered as the building began to shake.

The ceiling beams around her started dropping. Paint peeled from the walls. Floorboards ignited in bright flames.

Remy raced to the door and up the stairs, listening to the building caving in on itself.

Liliana is in Stockbridge. If I make it out of the orphanage alive, I am going to find her. I have to.

REMY SEARCHED STOCKBRIDGE FOR THREE DAYS straight without finding a trace of Liliana. She had asked everyone in town, hoping someone would know the address of Liliana's birth parents. And luck she did find. Turned out, Liliana's parents were William and Esmeralda Watson, members of the elite council back in the 1920s.

Rumor had it that they conceived a little girl. However, they attributed the disappearance of Liliana to kidnapping in order to protect their image. It was also said that the couple failed to conceive a more normal child after giving several of theirs up. As a result, they lived by themselves the rest of their years.

Eventually, Remy overheard a rumor that tracked several sources to Yorkshire Medical Center, a couple miles east of Stockbridge. Upon arrival and after speaking to several medical professionals, she discovered that both William and Esmeralda died in a car accident twenty-two years ago.

Twenty-two years ago? I don't think Liliana knows about this. She must be headed over to where they used to live!

Leaving the hospital with the address of the abandoned home in hand, Remy noticed a woman acting very strange. She didn't seem possessed or brainwashed like the others in town, but her behavior seemed very suspicious.

As Remy continued watching, the woman tucked her phone into her back pocket, her eyes losing focus as she turned south. Remy watched as the woman walked down the middle of the road, without a care that cars were driving across.

"This has to be Liliana's work," Remy whispered to herself.

She ducked behind several lamp posts to avoid being seen as she continued following the woman through town. Other than her suspicion, no one else in town seemed to notice this woman's strange behavior. They all carried about their days as if nothing was happening.

Finally, the woman led Remy to the old home of William and Esmeralda Watson. As Remy continued to evade the woman, she noticed a well in the middle of the ruins. She had read about this during her research. Apparently, William and Esmeralda had several children during their years alive. Liliana was the youngest of seven born in that household.

However, all their children were different, odd, not just Liliana. All their children were born with some sort of defect that caused the parents to get rid of them one way or another. Liliana was the only child they saved, sending her to an orphanage instead of sending her down a well.

Rumor also had it that there was something peculiar in their genes that made the children all abnormal. All the deaths of their children were William's idea; he couldn't bear being associated with defective children, blaming Esmeralda for her tarnished womb. As a result, Esmeralda fell into a deep depression, convincing William to spare the life of their last child or else she would end her own life.

Remy saw that the windows of the home were broken,

and graffiti covered the walls. The stench of death wafted from inside the building to the outside. It caught on the strong wind that blew, carrying the rotting stench along with it. Remy watched as the woman opened the door to the home before going inside. Moments later, she heard a loud scream.

Remy dashed over some fallen tree branches and wrenched open the door. She ran inside, but her foot was quickly caught on something. With a yelp, she fell to the ground, and her head landed on the lap of a decaying woman.

With a scream, Remy scrambled to her feet. However, she realized, seconds too late, that she should have stayed quiet. When she finally managed to get back on her feet, she found herself face-to-face with Liliana herself.

Her hair was scraggly and hung down her face in clumps. It resembled the color of darkness and hate while her skin was pale and white. Remy winced in discomfort as she saw the large crimson eyes turn toward her. A sinister grin then stretched across Liliana's face, blood running in rivulets from the corners of her mouth.

"Fuck," Remy said as she took a step back. But Lily only stepped forward. "Stay back. I will kill you if I have to. I don't want to, but I will," Remy announced, her voice noticeably shaking.

Do it, the words hissed through Remy's mind. *Kill me. See what happens. You have not been the first to threaten me, and you will not be the last. You are a foolish human who can do no damage. You are nothing. You are weak. You are pathetic.*

"No," Remy said, trying her best to calm her racing heart. "I am a lot like you, actually. I was left alone to live my life. I was kept in isolation. I was scared, and I didn't think anybody loved me. I know you feel the same way. I can help you."

The smile grew on Lily's face, and blood poured out rapidly, flowing down to create a puddle at her feet. Remy stepped back and looked around.

If this goes south, I'll need a plan to kill this woman. The headmaster did say that Liliana was afraid of isolation. Maybe that was where the answer lied.

"Why did you kill all those people? You're only taking them away from their families like you were taken away from yours." Remy watched as Liliana flinched at the word "family" and took a step back.

Maybe I need to remind her that her mom did care for her, enough to keep her alive. That she had someone out there who truly wanted the best for her. Maybe then, her anger would subside, and I will have a chance of surviving. If all else fails, I'll shove her down the well and burn the building down. Isolation in its finest form, Remy thought.

"I understand why you're suffering. All you wanted in life were human interaction and trust. Trust me, so did I. My mother was taken away from me when I was very young, and I was forced to grow up with no other humans around. Your parents *did* love you; your mom did, anyway. You see, your parents had several children before you, your siblings.

However, they all were born different, strange, and your father despised them so much that he threw them all down a well to spare himself from humiliation. But not you. You were saved, by your mother. She convinced him to give you up to an orphanage to avoid watching you die, too. Your mother wanted you. She only did what she thought was best.

Look down in that well behind you. You see all those

skeletons? Those were your siblings. You would've been down there also if it wasn't for your mother," Remy finished, fingers crossed that Lily would buy her story.

LIAR! You are a perceptive human, but that will not stop me from silencing you. I lost the ability to speak after being contained for fifteen years. I have been miserable, living in a hell of everybody else's making.

Do you know what it was like to be kept in a cell because others thought you were too dangerous for the world? Do you? I have made them all pay, and I will continue to make them pay. They are who created this mess, and they will be the ones to pay the price. Remy flinched as she heard the loud voice of Liliana boom inside her mind, the sound loud enough to make her ears bleed as blood dripped down her face.

Liliana tilted her head and reached out a hand. A strand of Remy's hair lifted to meet it. Bony fingers wrapped around her hair and pulled. Remy screamed as she was flung through the air. Her body collided with the cement ground as she rolled. When Remy's head finally stopped spinning, she noticed that Liliana was standing close to the well, too close. It was too good to be true, but she didn't care.

It's either her life or mine.

"You're angry," Remy said as she spat blood and got to her feet. Her head was throbbing, like a million drums beating in her ears. "I was really angry, too. My mother left me alone in isolation, and when I found her again, she wasn't the same. It made me really mad, but there was nothing I could do to salvage it. You can do something about it, though. You can help me. Undo all these damages, and let people reunite with their families again. You don't have to destroy everyone else just because you feel hurt."

You will all feel the pain that I had to feel for decades. The world will burn in loneliness and solitude.

Liliana raced toward Remy after carving into the wall with the blood of the fallen; her bony fingers curled into giant talons. Remy dove to the side, but the sharp nails grazed her shoulder, cutting through her jacket and ripping her skin. Remy screamed as she stumbled to her feet and turned to face Lily.

"You will not silence any more people!" Remy screamed as she charged at Liliana.

However, an invisible force caught her mid-air and tossed her against a wall.

Remy's body slammed hard against the bricks and landed on several corpses. She whimpered at the pain radiating through her back, but she couldn't stop now. Her life depended on it. She needed to stop Liliana if it was the last thing she did. There was no other option.

Stumbling, she ran toward her again, pushing her closer to the edge of the well. She screamed in pain as Lily's claws dug into her face and arms; her nails were deadly, but Remy had to keep pushing. As blood poured down her arms, soaking through her clothes, Lily's smile grew, flashing two rows of jagged and yellow teeth.

"No!" Remy shouted as she ducked. The swinging claws missed her neck by mere inches. "You are not going to hurt anyone anymore. Let me help you. It doesn't have to end this way. We can both be saved! We don't need to be alone anymore!"

Remy dropped to the ground and rolled, dodging another swipe of the talons. She got to her feet and teetered on the edge of the well. Liliana refused to back down, so Remy was left with only one option. Lily was a wounded animal who acted through anger and revenge, destroying for her own remedy.

Remy needed to isolate her, kill her. Isolation was the one thing Lily was afraid of, keeping all those dead bodies around just to experience some sort of company. Remy wrinkled her nose, the unbearable smell penetrating her nostrils. She gagged at the stench and stumbled away from the well.

Liliana charged, and Remy saw what might be her only chance. She stood tall; her arms outstretched. As Liliana closed in, Remy's hands wrapped around Lily's neck as she watched her eyes roll back in her head. She shook as Remy gripped tighter. They looked into each other's eyes and both knew what was to come next. Channeling all the strength she had, Remy picked up the waif and tossed her into the well.

At that, Remy sighed and turned around to look into the well. There was no sign of Liliana.

It must be a long way down, Remy thought, moments before a twisted hand grabbed her by the face and pulled her in.

The last thing Remy saw before her body collided with the ground was Liliana's melting eyes. Red liquid poured down the hollows of her cheeks and dripped down her neck, following the same path that the blood of so many others took.

As she fell, Remy knew that the second her body hits the ground, she would be dead. Memories of her childhood, laughing with her mother, crossed her mind.

She loved me. Mom truly loved me, Remy thought as she closed her eyes, finding a sense of peace during her last moments.

Liliana could no longer terrorize the world.

A sickening crunch filled the air as Remy's body hit the ground. A moment later, red-hot pain flooded her body. Blood seeped from her wounds. She was broken, dying, and unable to move. There was nothing but pain.

Remy glanced over at Liliana as she heaved through her final breath and smiled at the body lying beside her.

I did it. She's finally dead. The queen is finally dead.

CHAPTER 19
REBUILDING A NEW WORLD

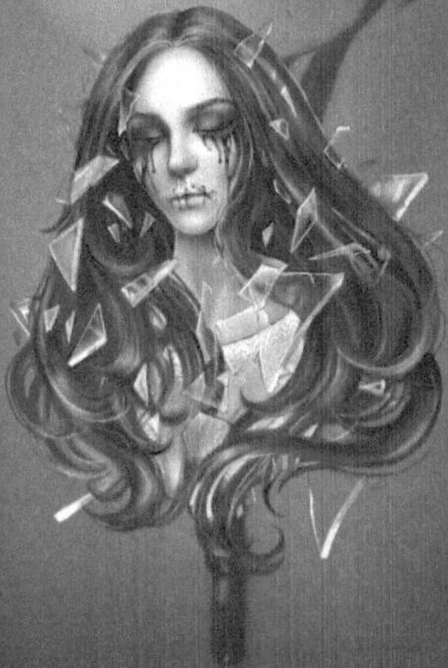

The body of a woman hung lightly from a tree as it drifted against the wind, with a strong rope holding her tight. Several crows rested on her shoulders, picking at the tender flesh. Hanging Day had become a new affair in town for all the bodies of the deceased. The crowd looked on as the body of the only woman brave enough to take down the queen danced with the breeze.

Liliana's death lifted the heavy weight from the world, as if a breath of fresh air expelled across the continents. The queen was gone. She could no longer restrict freedom of speech.

Soon, the stitches of those who had sinned started to come out. There were long lines in front of hospitals for days to remove the lengths of thread keeping people silent. It was only then that the real panic began to set in. The lack of remembrance. None of the humans could remember how to speak. They tried, but words refused to come out. Not even a sound. No one remembered how to say the simplest of words. They remained silent.

It didn't take long for people to turn back to their phones, like the battle had never happened. Once more, they became absorbed in their screens. It was all they had left, as if the reign of Liliana only existed to show them who they really were. Perhaps, one day, a new device would be created to replace the Apt.

Although Liliana was dead, more would soon follow, every eighty-seven years. Each would prove more powerful than the last. In truth, the humans hadn't learned their lesson. To them, everything was the same as it had been when Liliana was alive.

Their phones remained their only connection to each other. Oral communication was dead. The Apt was all they had left.

A man walked by the tree with his wife. She was in a wedding dress, and he was in a tux. Though they had only been married moments ago, in front of the hanging woman, they both buried their faces in their phones. The messages that contained their vows had already been deleted.

Even in death, there were still some followers of Liliana who chose to uphold her vision. Remy was accused of treason for killing their leader. Liliana's soldiers lifted both lifeless bodies from the well, giving Liliana a proper burial while Remy was hung to enforce their authority.

But the woman tied to the tree still bore a smile in death. She twisted and twirled as the wind grew more powerful. Passersby wondered when the rope would snap. Those who knew the truth saw it as a sign. Within a year, a new child was going to be born.

With the brave girl dead, who would save them next?

Damon looked on from afar. He continuously stared at the body as it twisted and turned in the wind. A memory flashed in his mind, of when he attended boarding school in Beddington, Maine.

The moment he heard that his mother, Elizabeth Walden, was in trouble, he remembered driving all the way back, just to hear that Baylor Orphanage had collapsed... with his mother in it.

It was a family tradition to care for Baylor Orphanage, generation after generation, to ensure that the new child of Remphelia did not create total destruction. All these years, Damon refused to learn from his mother, refused to accept that he was next in line. He would always hold that regret in his heart.

He walked up to the swinging body and grabbed a hand, sighing.

"I should've come with you. I knew there was a great chance you wouldn't make it out alive, and I let you go anyway. But I was so scared. I just froze. Please forgive me, Remy. Please forgive me. I have obligations that require me to stay alive. My mother was Headmaster Walden, and it's my duty to take over as the new headmaster for when the next Liliana is born.

I need to protect the world now. It's all possible because

of you, my friend. You did it. You saved the world. I'm so sorry. I should have done more. I could have done more," Damon whispered in front of Remy's lifeless body. "I will do my best to preach to the world your heroism and bravery. Without you, we would all be dead. I will make sure that you will not be forgotten." With that, he picked up the old tomes and walked away.

A FEW WEEKS LATER, DAMON OPENED UP A SCHOOL TO re-teach the citizens how to speak, starting from the basics. He wanted to help people rediscover the beauty of oral communication without having to rely on their phones. And slowly, but surely, people were making progress.

Damon was also fortunate enough to find several others who still had the ability to speak. They were all in the same boat as him, pretending to hide out in silence to avoid falling victim to the phones. Even Belle Kimora had volunteered to help him seek them out.

Although devasted by her daughter's death, Belle was proud of what she had accomplished. Her daughter was a hero. She just wished she was able to speak to her and love her when she had the chance. Remy grew up to be a beautiful and wonderful woman, and she dedicated the rest of her life into making sure everyone knew that.

Even in her elderly years, Yin Suzuki finally finished her research and created a cure for the Coxin virus, relieving the world from the crippling neurodegenerative illness before she failed to wake up one morning.

But it wasn't time to celebrate just yet, for people

started to lose their voices again as quickly as Damon had been trying to restore them. He didn't know why, why people suddenly chose to stop talking again. He knew the Apt still had a strong hold on the majority of people, but they seemed happy to be able to socialize again.

Then he saw her. Walking home from the library one day after gathering some books on speech, he saw her. Eyes were red as blood, and hair dark as tar. Liliana. Somehow, the fall down the well didn't manage to kill her. She was horribly damaged, but she was still kicking. That was more than Damon could say for Remy.

That bitch, Damon thought as he ran behind a tree to hide. If Liliana caught him, he would surely be dead. *Remy didn't die for nothing. I will avenge her death.*

While Remy was impulsive and acted on the spot, Damon was more strategic, carefully constructing all his actions before making a move. He spent the next seven days devising a plan to take down Liliana once and for all, a fail-proof plan guaranteed to work.

By this point, Liliana was much slower than she used to be, the loss of blood draining her essence. And with many of her supporters no longer following her, she was an easy target.

Ever since Hanging Day became a weekly event, more bodies congregated together each day to honor those brave enough to stand up against Liliana. It also became a temple for Liliana, a place she visited periodically to escape her crippling loneliness. She saw these deceased bodies as her companions, those who would never abandon her. And Damon knew that was the perfect place to lure and take her down.

Liliana was nothing without her crimson eyes, and

lucky for him, her fall down the well had already taken away half her ability.

ONE DARK EVENING, WHILE STAKING OUT NEAR THE Garden of the Fallen, Damon held his dagger close to his chest. He was ready. He was going to end Liliana once and for all. For several days, he had followed Lily, studying her pattern and discovering that she visited the garden every night at exactly 9:23pm. He hid behind a tombstone, several feet from Remy, when Lily approached.

To Damon's surprise, Liliana walked straight toward Remy's hanging body. She approached her and gently grazed her hand before reaching up with the other to stroke Remy's face. Damon could hear the loud breaths of Lily wafting onto Remy.

This is sickening, he thought. *How dare she?*

Damon continued to watch as Liliana ran a thumb across Remy's cold lips, about to lean in and embrace her, when Damon flew out from behind the stone and tackled her to the wet ground. He knew he couldn't look directly into her eyes as that was how Lily destroyed most of her victims. However, as he quickly glanced at her, he noticed tears pouring out like an innocent child.

If it wasn't for Damon's rage, his sympathy would've caused him to stop. However, he was so furious that he drove his dagger straight into her forehead, hearing a loud shriek follow. Her shrieks were loud enough to deafen anybody, and Damon knew he didn't have much time. He carved her eyeballs out from their sockets, stomping on them hard, before driving the dagger into her chest, leaving her immobile.

As Damon stepped back to admire his work, embers began to glow inside her body. Soon, flames emerged, and she voiced one final shriek before her body ignited into flames, engulfing her and turning her into ashes.

They were finally free.

CHAPTER 20

THE NEXT GENERATION

Death, by its very nature, brings the looming cloud of darkness and a certain disparity of affliction with every step it takes, engulfing the joys of human life and consuming them in sadness and misery instead. With its presence, chills of horror surround the living creatures of humanity, destroying the trust of society.

Death is an enemy, a demonic presence that drives

people away from their true selves, and a chaotic whirlwind that disturbs the normal functioning of everyday life, all the while, snatching the power of optimism from living creatures on Earth, those still left behind to deal with the consequences.

Even just one single death of a living creature can completely reshape thoughts into those of pessimism and vengeance, ideas and plans circulating their minds without even a morsel of light. The darkness and evil remain, their minds and bodies like psychotic tendencies, fueling their desires and motivation toward the dark side and abolishing anyone in its way until the deeds are done.

The controversial death of former dictator, Liliana Watson, triggered the spark in the lives of her haters and worshippers alike, a pathological monster with a deadly condition known as "Remphelia" who destroyed colonized America and nearly the entire world. She seized her position as queen, obliterating anyone who dared step in her way or go against her. She stole the lives of the innocent and banished their natural abilities due to childhood trauma that she could never face until it was far too late.

However, her ruling came to a fated end as she perished the same way she entered the world: sad, alone, and rejected, her life finally taken by someone no more than a mere mortal; the balance of the Earth was once again restored.

Under the control of the queen, an influx of technology took over control of the human mind and brainwashed people into believing that it was normal to abandon communication for good, losing the very skill that made humans different from other animals, all just because they feared the consequences that would happen if they did speak. Liliana's social abandonment and humiliation as a child made her develop a socially-destructive personality, silencing society so they would no longer have the opportunity to taunt her ever again.

Her plan seemed perfect, the key to a more civilized and respectful society, until it was fatally taken away by someone she hadn't accounted for.

After the death of Liliana, time began to pass, and technology began to lose its hold on people's lives. Faces frozen in place in front of phone screens, silence between confidants and strangers right beside each other, the constant vibration when text messages passed from one phone to another, the trend began to slowly diminish, and communication began to restore.

It had been nearly a century since people were able to vocally interact with each other, with babies after babies being born with nothing but detachment, isolation, and apathy toward one another. Family structures weakened and crumbled under deep layers of silence, all of them becoming clueless as to what speaking was even after it had been restored, turning human beings into true robotic specimens. It had taken years for emotions to return, for people to begin feeling the sensations inside them again, to regain human consciousness and morality.

However, the good news was, all these things eventually returned, and society was finally free from the grasps of Liliana Watson, a death that generated more relief and freedom than it did grief and sorrow, free to live life the way human beings were supposed to live it, free from fear. Freedom from the debilitating addiction to technology was also starting to return, voices wandering rambunctiously as vocal communication became a thing of the present again.

Families ate meals with each other at dinner tables. Children played with each other on playgrounds, laughing and screaming as they chased one another. Friends reunited with cups of latte while chatting outside of cafés. Even strangers resumed their daily conversations on buses and trains while heading off to work. The world was slowing becoming what it used to be, a life of closeness and collectivism.

Technology was slowly being destroyed, and people could not be happier. Memories of the past began to come back to those old enough to remember, and with oral communication, towns were resuming back to their democratic states.

With each passing day, memories of Lily faded more and more from people's minds as they realized she was gone forever. Many who used to worship her turned their attention to the new hero of the world, the one who took down Liliana, Damon Walden, believing they could also destroy evil, just like him. Their loyalty to Liliana was never genuine to begin with, so quick to turn their worship from one to another.

Remy Kimora was forever remembered as the unsung savior for Stockbridge. Though her life was short-lived, and the people never really knew who she was, her name continued to loom around town as one to never be forgotten.

However, this lifestyle was not unanimously accepted. There were still people who preferred the totalitarian lifestyle as it brought law and order to society. They called themselves, The Order. They hated the idea of people having separate opinions and freedom of speech. The country ran much smoother when there was only one leader in charge. Their loyalty remained so dedicated to Liliana and her purpose that they thrived on supremacy, dedicated to searching for a new powerful dictator.

Among them, was Colton Javernick, a young and stubborn man with a bright future, always searching for ultimate truth. Sadly, his parents failed to channel that intelligence into something beneficial and great, instead, substituting themselves with television shows.

Colton grew up neglected and isolated, his parents more focused on his older sister, Ella, instead. His opinions were always disputed, and his search for answers always came back with more questions. His deprivation for socialization eventually made him a loner, his intelligence wasted.

As a young child, he spent his time researching and discovering the world, like any curious child would. He continued to ask questions that everyone refused to answer. He spent a lot of his time alone, reading books in the library. That's how he discovered the life of Liliana Watson, a young girl who lived a life of isolation and solitude just like him, a young girl who was misunderstood.

Like all children who were neglected, Colton soon found himself addicted to drugs and ostracized by his family and friends. Rather than learning how to channel his brain for the greater good of society, he concocted ways to destroy it and all those ignorant who thought they had purpose in the world. By the time his parents realized how much he had changed, it became too late.

The more he learned about Liliana Watson, the more he loathed those who took her down, vowing to avenge her. He incinerated the corpse of Remy Kimora, the heroine who stood up to Liliana when no one else could, and made it his goal to destroy Damon for bringing this chaos into the world where everyone conflicted with each other.

Colton spent years in search of the old documents from the orphanage that mapped out who Liliana was since childhood, eventually discovering the early suppression of her powers by a special type of medication forced upon her when she was just a young child, kept in isolation, locked away from the world. She was taunted and teased her entire life, abandoned by her parents and unwelcomed by everyone who came across her, a life he was no stranger to.

If his research was correct, and the Remphelia tradition truly did exist, the next child would have already been born, a child far supreme, capable of drastically changing the world for better or for worse.

But society needed a new ruler, now. With each passing day, civilization was deteriorating as arguments instilled and compromises were nonexistent. He didn't have time to search for this new child; it could be anywhere. His hope for a new queen was beginning to fade, fast.

Within the abandoned walls of room forty-four, Headmaster Walden's life was fatally brought to a painful end by worshippers of Liliana. The world was beginning to divide, the believers and the progressives. The believers who searched the ends of the Earth for a new leader, and the progressives who valued freedom.

Colton watched from a distance as Damon slowly rebuilt the ruins of the orphanage, becoming the new Headmaster. He wanted nothing more than to strike him right then and there, but it was too risky as he now had a loyal group of followers guarding him. Any suspicious moves would be too risky. With the passage of time and the rediscovery of speech, people came to learn of and hold their different opinions. A new democratic society was born.

Everyone's useless and oblivious. They don't know what it's like to run a well-ordered society. They think they know what's best for themselves, their independence making them dumber than they look. This is not how people should live. We need to bring order back into this world. We need one leader, and one leader only, Colton thought to himself while smoking a cigarette on the hood of his car. *My time is now. Liliana Watson, I will avenge your death.*

CHAPTER 21

BIRTH OF THE NEW QUEEN

Far away along the Mediterranean Sea, laid a remote and secluded island, beautiful as the heavens themselves and so enchanting that it resembled something straight out of a fairy-tale book. The island of Zara was adorned with mesmerizing springs, pristine beaches, sparkling waterfalls, luscious mountains, and decorated with the most perfect weather to truly bring out the beauty of the land.

The island of Zara only had one village, a small village with a population short of just thirty residents, each and every one channeling their own charm of compassion and kindness. The native villagers all abided by the customs and traditions of the island, from baking fresh bread the beginning of every month and feeding them to the gods to playing beautiful and mesmerizing music every night of a full moon.

Many of the residents here were natives, descendants of those who managed to escape from the states unscathed during the rule of Liliana back in the states. The island of Zara was so secluded that it remained so off-the-grid that the guards of the Red Queen never managed to find them, leaving them to speak and die in peace. The curse of silence was never inflicted, and the people here were able to communicate and socialize without consequences, oblivious to life outside their island.

However, on this particular night, the evening of April 23, 2011, the villagers gathered around a small cabin, waiting for the arrival of a new resident. With the cold breeze brushing against their skin and blowing against their hair, the locals surrounded the home with bushels of flowers and gift baskets to welcome a new life.

Elvira Tempest lied in grimacing pain on top of her velvet sheets in her home. Her beloved husband, Leviathan Tempest, sat beside her, grasping tightly against her hands, reassuring her that everything would be okay. They had wanted a child for years, with no luck for almost a decade until, finally, a child was conceived.

Growing up, Elvira didn't have siblings, always feeling alone as her parents neglected her for their nights out at bars instead. When she met Leviathan, she felt like the gods had finally answered her prayers. Leviathan also lived a life of seclusion, finding themselves perfect for each other and tying the knot just a year later.

"Leviathan, honey, what if I don't make it? What if the baby doesn't make it?" Elvira winced in pain as she asked her husband.

"Don't worry, sweetheart. We CAN make it. We wanted this for so long, and trust me, nothing terrible will happen to this child. I won't let it. Just focus on your breaths, and imagine the happiness our daughter will bring to this family. I know you're strong, strong enough to push through. Just think, in only a few short minutes, we can finally hold our baby in our arms." His voice trembled as he spoke, but he knew he had to remain confident for his wife.

Leviathan watched anxiously from a near distance as the nurses and midwives gathered around Elvira. His ears pained as he heard her agonizing screams, wanting nothing more than to rush over to her side and comfort her. Three hours had passed since the sun had set, and Leviathan could hear the anxious voices of the villagers outside waiting for his daughter's arrival, as he looked at his watch, each click feeling like an eternity.

He was almost close to tearing out his entire head of hair when, suddenly, he heard the faint cries of a baby. He rushed over to his wife's side, and over the shoulders of the midwives, he saw a beautiful and flawless child yawning in front of him.

"I think we should call her, Mara. Mara Tempest. It has a good ring to it," Elvira whispered to Leviathan as she leaned over and kissed the baby on the forehead before leaning over to kiss her husband.

"She's perfect, just perfect," Leviathan smiled. He slowly picked up the child and walked her to the window.

"Everyone, welcome to the village, the newest member of the Tempest family."

As Leviathan spoke, the villagers all broke out into cheers and happiness, popping open bottles of champagne and dancing on the streets while the violinists eagerly played the "Birth of a Child." Leviathan was the first to greet everyone as they entered into the home, placing their gift baskets and treasures off into a separate room before heading over to the main den.

The night fell dark, and the crescent moon shone over them as guests showered the newborn with gifts before seating themselves down for a customary dinner.

Whenever a child was born in Zara, the entire island would gather together and sit around an ornately decorated table with candelabras while being served the best of feasts, from decadent wine imported all the way from Italy to the most succulent roast pig fed only the finest of food.

Moments later, Elvira slowly walked down the stairs, her long white gown trailing behind her, the child wrapped in a blanket in between her arms, and greeted the guests, one by one, before sitting down in her own seat. In such a small village, everyone knew everything about each other, from their most celebrated stories to their most intimate moments. Elvira loved conversing with the other villagers. Every conversation made her feel less alone.

"Attention, everyone. May I have your attention, please?" Leviathan stood in front of the guests midway through the feast, raising his chalice and clanging against it with a golden spoon. "Thank you all so much for coming this evening to welcome the arrival of the newest member of our family," he began as the guests all turned their attention to him. "Please give a warm welcome to, Mara, Mara Tempest. May your wishes and prayers bring a lifetime of happiness and protection to this little one. Mara, you are loved."

The crowd broke out into cheers and hearty congratulations as they all raised their own chalices and toasted each other. As they lined up to each give Mara a kiss on the forehead as a sign of good fortune, she became the star of the evening.

Life in the village soon returned to normal as the excitement eventually died down. Mara, as the youngest of the villagers, was the center of attention for the whole island, so adored as a matter of fact, that Elvira and Leviathan never had any issues finding someone to look after their daughter while they were out.

Time continued to fly by, and soon, Mara was celebrating her first birthday.

"Leviathan! Come give me a hand, please? The pot roast in the oven is almost done, and I still need to run out and pick up the cake," Elvira shouted from the kitchen as she heard the front door close, Leviathan walking into the kitchen to place down a bag full of napkins and paper cups.

One of their neighbors, Leila Winters, had offered to look after Mara while the parents got ready for the party, keeping her distracted and entertained to relieve Elvira and Leviathan from the stress.

"Honey, it's okay. Stop stressing so much," Leviathan spoke in a calm voice as he walked over to his wife and massaged her shoulders. "It's just a birthday party. No need to lose a leg over it."

"I know, I know. I just want everything to be perfect. It's her FIRST birthday. I want her to remember it forever."

Her husband chuckled. "Oh, Elvira, you can be so silly at times. She's only a year old. She's not going to remember a birthday party, much less whether it was fantastic or not, which, I'm sure it will be." He walked back over to the counter to grab his keys before giving his wife a kiss on the cheek. "Here, tell you what. Why don't you finish up here, and I'll pick up the cake from the bakery? Sound good?"

"Alright," Elvira answered with a hesitant smile. She usually took matters into her own hands, wary of trusting others as they'd usually just screw it up, but in this moment, she had to admit defeat. She had to trust that her husband was capable enough to do something right. "But make sure they use the pink frosting. Not purple, not blue. Pink."

"Pink, got it." Leviathan smiled as he headed toward the front door. "By the way, whatever you have on the stove there, smells absolutely delicious. Is that ratatouille?"

"Nope, it's..." Right when Elvira opened her mouth, they both heard a scream from upstairs.

"Help! I need help!" Leila screamed at the top of her lungs from Mara's room. "Something's wrong!"

Leviathan dropped his keys on the coffee table while Elvira turned off the stove and oven, and they both quickly bolted up the stairs. Leviathan glanced over and could tell that his wife's heart was beating fast because so was his. They were finally blessed with a child; they couldn't let anything happen to her.

"What happened? What's wrong? Is Mara okay?" Elvira asked, breathless, as she ran into the bedroom, almost fainting when she found Mara motionless in Leila's arms.

"Elvira? Mara!" Leviathan shouted as he closed in

behind her. "Leila, what the hell happened here? What's wrong with Mara? What did you do?"

"I... I don't know," Leila stuttered, tears pouring from her eyes. "One minute she was fine, playing happily with her bunny, and the next, she... she just passed out. I don't know what happened. I swear!"

Leviathan moved closer to them, placing the back of his hand against the baby's forehead before lowering his ear near her chest. "Well, the good thing is, her heartbeat sounds normal. Her temperature's just flaring up."

"Leila, can you please run down and grab some ice?" Elvira turned to Leila and asked politely. "We know it's not your fault. You love Mara. We know that. We're just very concerned for our daughter."

Leila turned her head around from the doorway and said, "I understand. I would've done the same with my own child."

Elvira then walked into the bathroom to sprinkle some cool water on a rag. She walked back into the room and handed it to Leviathan, who pressed the rag against Mara's forehead and held her close.

Several minutes later, her tiny fingers started to move, and her eyes began to twitch. Her parents loomed over her with hopeful eyes and smiles as they crossed their fingers.

"She's doing it. She's doing it!" Elvira grabbed Leviathan's hand and squeezed it tight.

However, when Mara's lids finally peeled open, the mysterious look they received was not what they had expected. Elvira placed a hand on her husband's shoulder as they both leaned over and peered closer at the little girl.

"Hold on, let me grab a flashlight. It's a little dark in here. I just want to make sure her pupils look okay,"

Leviathan quickly said as he handed their child over to Elvira before running into their own room to grab a flashlight.

"Shh, it's okay, my love," Elvira cooed, rocking Mara back and forth, back and forth. "Mommy's here. Mommy will always be here."

Within mere seconds later, Leviathan Tempest came rushing back into the room. Elvira stood up and laid Mara on her changing table while Leviathan shone a bright light in her eyes.

"Open your eyes, Mara. Everything is going to be okay," Elvira reassured, holding her daughter still.

However, they were both surprised by what they saw under the light. At first, her parents were worried that Mara's pupils had dilated, but what they saw was much, much worse.

"Honey! Her eyes! They're... they're bleeding! Quick, grab me that towel!" Elvira screamed over to Leviathan, who quickly threw a small white towel over to her.

She caught it and began dabbing against Mara's eyes, hoping the blood would absorb. However, as she tried, the blood remained intact. She even grabbed some water and tried to wipe off the red substance. But nothing worked. The blood remained.

"I don't think that's blood," Leviathan stuttered hesitantly and anxiously.

Elvira tried several more times before dropping the towel and stepping back. She stared back at her child in horror, almost choking on her own saliva as she struggled to breathe.

"What... what is she? What's wrong with her? Leviathan!" she shouted as she grabbed his shoulders and started to shake. "What's wrong with our daughter? Is she going to die?"

Speechless for several moments, Leviathan managed to muttered a few words. "I'm sure she's fine. Maybe it's just allergies. It is springtime, after all. Let's take her to the doctor first thing tomorrow morning. She'll be okay, just okay. I know she will."

"I mean, I've had bloodshot eyes when I was younger, usually due to allergies, but they never looked like that. I don't think that's allergies... I think that's..." Elvira started to speak.

"Elvira, Leviathan. I have the ice," Leila interrupted when she walked back into the bedroom with a small bucket of ice. However, she took one look at the child's red eyes and immediately dropped the bucket. "No, no, it can't be. It can't be!"

Leila backed away into the corner of the room, crouching on the ground, and began to rock back and forth. "No, it can't be. It's too soon! The queen is here. The queen is here. The queen is here. I thought we had more time."

"Leila?" Elvira asked, now more confused than scared. "What's going on? Who's the queen? What are you mumbling about?" She walked closer to Leila and crouched down beside her. "Why are you so afraid of Mara?"

"Oh, you two are overly paranoid. It's just allergies. I'm sure she'll be fine tomorrow," Leviathan brushed it off, closing his ear toward her chest. "Her breathing's fine. She's perfectly fine."

"No! You don't understand. I've heard about this. I didn't think it was time yet, but I've heard premonitions of a new queen coming to take over and destroy the world, a queen with red eyes."

Leviathan stopped monitoring Mara's breathing and quickly looked up. "What? No, you're crazy! A dictator with red eyes? You really think our little innocent Mara is even capable of hurting a fly, much less the entire world? I think you need to lay off whatever new medication Mr. Shultz is planting next door. I've heard nothing but bad things about them. I think it's making you lose your mind."

"Leviathan! Stop it!" Elvira snapped before turning her attention back to Leila. "Leila, what else do you know about this queen? What about the red eyes? Is it contagious?"

"I don't know if it's contagious, but whatever you do, do not let Mara out of your sight, ever! Who knows what sort of danger she's capable of?" she answered before taking a deep breath. "My grandmother warned my family about this right before she died. She said she lived her whole life under the silence of Liliana, the former queen, forcing my parents to take me on a boat and sail far, far away, somewhere where Liliana could not hurt us."

Elvira saw tears begin to trickle from Leila's eyes and could tell that this was a touchy subject for her. She softly touched her shoulder and gestured her downstairs. "Here, why don't we give Mara some rest, and we can all go down and talk over some hot tea?"

Leviathan and Elvira gave their daughter one last kiss on the forehead before shutting the door behind them and heading downstairs. The mother went over to the stove to boil some water while the father sat directly in front of Leila, glaring at her to see if she was telling the truth.

"She's... Mara's the chosen one," Leila sniffled, grabbing a tissue from the box in front of her and blowing her nose. "According to the myth, once every eighty-seven years, a new child is born, a child deadlier than any other, a child with the ability to single-handedly destroy the world. Those red eyes, they're called Remphelia, an extremely rare condition that gives whoever possesses it supernatural powers."

"Oh, come on! This is ridiculous! Elvira, are you hearing this nonsense? You expect me to believe that our innocent baby is actually a demon with magical powers who will destroy the world? That's absolutely absurd! I've read my fair share of fantasy books, but this is by far the most ludicrous story I've ever heard."

"Leviathan! Refrain yourself!" Elvira shot daggers as she glared at her husband.

"No, Elvira. I don't care how close of a friend Leila is to you. I don't need some lunatic coming into my home and telling me that my newborn daughter is dangerous." He turned to Leila and pointed at the front door. "I need you to leave my home, RIGHT NOW, and never come back. Do you hear me?"

"No, Leviathan, you have to listen to me, please! I'm telling you the truth. How else do you explain what happened to the United States, where people began disappearing mysteriously and silence overtook the nation?" Leila pleaded for the Tempests to hear her story and believe.

However, Leviathan's stubbornness refused to budge.

"That's nothing more than a myth, a fable, a fairy-tale. Everyone knows it was just a virus, just a virus, nothing more. I don't believe you, and I definitely don't believe the existence of some killer queen. Now, get out of my house," Leviathan ordered again.

"Leviathan, please, listen..."

"I said, GET OUT!"

Elvira shrunk back in confliction as she watched her

dear friend slowly walk out of their home. Leila had always been one of her closest friends, the most honest and trustworthy person she had ever met, but she didn't know who to believe anymore.

"What do we do now?" she finally whispered after minutes of silence.

"We do what any parent does when they're child is sick. We take her to see a doctor, like we should've done instead of listening to Leila's stupid stories."

THE NEXT MORNING, ELVIRA AND LEVIATHAN BUNDLED Mara in a warm blanket, and all three of them headed out to visit their local doctor. The island of Zara only had one doctor, an old man who was a local his entire life and studied medicine from books his grandkids shipped to him from England. Although quite stubborn at times, he always knew what was best for his patients, always keeping their best interests in mind.

With baby Mara crying in Elvira's arms, the Tempest family walked past several homes, the village neighbors all staring at them as they passed, to get to the office of Dr. Brahms. They knew, just by the looks they were getting, that Leila had spread the word around about Mara.

"Why don't you all just take a picture? It'll last longer," Leviathan snared as he shielded Mara from the sights of his neighbors.

"Honey, calm down," Elvira whispered at him.

They continued walking, Leviathan throwing insults at his once close friends while Elvira tried to shield herself from humiliation. Soon, they arrived at the office of Dr. Brahms. He welcomed the family in and closed the blinds.

Everyone in town wanted to know what's wrong with Mara, nervous whether she truly was dangerous. Brahms jumped back at first sight, shocked by what he saw in Mara's eyes. It was nothing like he had ever seen before. Sure, he had seen torn vessels in eyes, blood pouring over sclera, but never had he witnessed pure crimson blood red eyes.

"This... this... this child. In the forty years I've been in practice, never have I seen anything like this before," Dr. Brahms replied after carefully examining Mara's eyes.

His voice was calm as he delivered the news, but his entire body was shaking with distress.

"What is it, doctor? Is it a vessel burst? Can you fix it?" Leviathan asked.

"I'm afraid not, Mr. Tempest. Never before in my life have I seen something like this, so heinous, so peculiar. I believe what we have here is some kind of genetic mutation, something so extremely rare that I'm not even sure where to begin fixing it."

"Doctor," Elvira spoke up after cooing to the small child curled up in her arms. "Can it be cured?"

"I'm afraid not," Brahms whispered with his head bowed down.

"Well, what are we supposed to do? We can't just leave her like this! She's a freak! Half the town is already after us." As Leviathan lost his temper and screamed, he pointed out the window.

Crowds of people were lined up outside, banging on the glass window, trying to get a closer look at the cursed child. Elvira wrapped her shawl around Mara while Leviathan pounded his fists against the glass, screaming at his neighbors and friends to leave them alone. As both sides banged on the window harder and harder, the window pane slowly started to crack.

"Elvira! We need to get out of here. Now!" Leviathan shouted over to Elvira, who looked back at him in dread of losing her only child.

"There's a door at the back of my office that leads out into the alley. I'll try to ward them off as best as I can." Brahms pointed to a narrow wooden door tucked behind his desk and gave the Tempest family a nod.

Quickly packing up their belongings, Leviathan and Elvira thanked the doctor and bolted out the back door. They ran down the narrow alleyway between the clinic and the grocer, with the initial plan of making it back home before anyone could see them.

"They're over there! Get 'em!"

They heard someone shout in the near distance, followed by many little footsteps thumping along the brick sidewalk.

At this point, Leviathan and Elvira knew they needed a Plan B in order to escape the mob. Their small town was extremely superstitious, and they all thought Mara was possessed by the Devil. If they caught up to them, they feared for the worst what their neighbors would do to them. Friends or not, they would find a way to remove the demonic child.

Luckily, the Tempest family built a small underground bunker deep into the woods several years back, in preparation for a nuclear apocalypse. Their entire community turning against them was a close second.

"Elvira, we need to get a hold of Leila, see what else she knows about this curse. I'll take Mara. She'll be safe with me. Go! Bring her to the bunker!"

At Leviathan's orders, they both separated ways, Elvira

running back into town, into the mob, to try and find her dear friend, Leila.

NEARLY AN HOUR LATER, ELVIRA ARRIVED AT THE bunker in the woods with Leila, her face still pale and her eyes still shocked in horror. She peered down at the small child lying on top of a thin blanket as Leviathan prepared the fire.

"We can't stay here, you know that, right?" Elvira said to her husband, who stared intently at the fire and refused to turn around. She walked up to him and placed a hand on his shoulder.

"Leila, please, tell us there's a cure for this. I can't live like this. Mara can't live like this. She needs to be saved. Please, tell me there's a cure." Leviathan finally said with a sigh. He stood up, kissed Mara on the forehead, and sat down on an empty wooden chair, devastated.

"I... I'm not really sure. From what I've heard, there's supposedly some kind of medication for it, to suppress the redness in her eyes along with any danger she might possess, but you can only find it in the states. It's also been so long, that I don't even know if they make it anymore. I don't really know anything. I'm sorry," Leila explained. "If you need to skip town, I understand. Take Mara, and go find somewhere far away and secluded to settle down, away from here."

"Come with us, Leila," Elvira invited. "It's not safe for you here if they find out what you know. They'll do whatever they can to pry the information out of you."

"I can't. My entire family's here. I can't just abandon

them. And don't worry, I won't tell anyone anything, even if my life depends on it. Your secret is safe with me. I swear."

"Then I guess it's settled. Tomorrow morning, we ship out and head toward the states to find the cure. We'll search every inch of that country if we need to. Our baby girl *will* be saved," Leviathan declared. He walked over to Leila and gave her a hug. "Thank you, Leila, for everything."

"Anytime." Leila smiled.

THE NEXT MORNING, LEVIATHAN AND ELVIRA PACKED up the little belongings they had in the bunker and loaded them up in their wooden raft. They rarely spent any time in the bunker, so they only had the minimal supplies of a few key pieces of clothing, a few cans of cold beans, and two bags of rice.

Elvira sighed. "All those years spent decorating our home with the most beautiful and luxurious décor I could find, now all gone. What a waste, what a waste."

Leviathan steadied the raft and slowly climbed in it first before helping his wife, who was carrying Mara in her arms.

"Here, take the blanket," he said. "The sea's going to get pretty chilly."

With that, he reached over, untied the rope, and pushed off the rock, propelling themselves out into the ocean, as Leila waved goodbye on shore.

"Stay safe out there! I'll never forget you!" she yelled out.

The Tempest family settled on heading far east, to the remote island of Jezebel, tucked between the continents of Australia and North America. They didn't think it was possible, but no one lived on the tiny island. Most of the time, it was reserved for military base camps, but they had no choice. Their boat wasn't going to make it all the way to the states in one go; they needed to find somewhere to take up shelter and rebuild the deteriorating parts of the raft. It was going to be a long and treacherous journey, but the Tempest family was determined to find that medication.

"How do we even know this cure exists?" Leviathan asked in doubt. "What if Leila just tricked us and sent us to our deaths so they could get rid of us? How do we know we can even trust her?"

Days and days out at sea was beginning to take a mental toll on Leviathan. He had been so hopeful back home to travel to the states, find the medication they needed, and cure their daughter so they could go home. Now, the hunger, the exhaustion, and the fear of the unknown, were starting to make him doubt why he even began this treacherous journey in the first place.

"No, I trust Leila. She wouldn't do that to us. We've been close friends ever since we were kids," his wife assured him, placing a hand gently on his arm. "Look at the rainbow, honey," Elvira gestured to Leviathan as she pointed toward a rainbow on their left. "It's so magical. This is like our first vacation." She leaned her head against his arm, resting as she admired the beautiful landscape before her.

"Yeah, vacation. If only we weren't running for our lives."

Elvira wanted to scream at Leviathan for ruining her moment, but she couldn't. He was right. In that moment, a thousand thoughts dominated her mind.

What was going to happen to them? What was going to happen to Mara? Could they ever go back to their island of Zara? What if they landed in Jezebel with hundreds of guns pointed at their faces? How much farther would they need to go?

Tears began to well up in her eyes as his mind raced with thoughts of horror.

"I'm sorry, dear. I didn't mean to be so negative. The rainbow *is* beautiful. I'm scared, but I shouldn't have taken it out on you." Leviathan reached over to give his wife a hug as she shivered in his arms.

"What if something happens to Mara? What if more people know about her and try to find her? How will we escape them? How will we protect her?" she cried.

"I will do everything I possibly can to save our daughter." He looked over at Mara, who was sound asleep, wrapped in a wool blanket. "They'll have to go through me first if they want their hands on her."

THE TEMPEST FAMILY CONTINUED TO SPEND THE NEXT several weeks coursing through the Pacific Ocean, trying to keep their boat from tipping over whenever Elvira struggled with a fish and avoiding large currents that could rip through their raft with one blow.

One night, Leviathan and Elvira found themselves stranded in the middle of a raging storm. The clouds turned dark, and before they could even prepare themselves, the sky boomed and rain came pouring down on them, followed by heavy winds that nearly blew the boat over.

"Hold on to the side of the boat, and no matter what you do, don't let go!" Leviathan shouted as he used his oar to keep the raft from flipping them all into the icy cold water.

Elvira huddled herself over her daughter, using whatever body heat she could generate from herself to keep Mara warm.

"I don't know if I can! It's too strong!"

She could feel her hands slipping from the wet wood, and when she tried to readjust herself, Mara slipped out from her other arm, sliding toward the front of the raft.

"Mara! No! Leviathan, grab her!" Elvira shouted with the pain of a mother losing her child.

Luckily, Leviathan saw the child slide toward him just in time and reached out to grab her. However, as he did, he lost control of the oar and lost his hold. The raft tipped over, and both he and Mara fell straight into the angry ocean.

"Elvira! Save Mara! Save our daughter!" Leviathan shouted as he pushed their child closer back toward the boat before floating away himself.

As if on instinct, Elvira jumped in and grabbed Mara just in time. She quickly placed their daughter back onto the boat before trying to save Leviathan. But he was too far gone. She shook as she saw the last of his fingers sink into the water, the waves washing over him.

"Leviathan! No!" Elvira screamed, tears pouring down her eyes as she watched the love of her life drown before her very eyes.

Defeated, she turned around to make her way back to the boat, struggling to fight against the waves as they pushed back on her. However, through sheer strength, she managed to grab the edge, hoisting herself up and rolling over inside. She could hear Mara crying next to her as the storm continued to rage down on them. Elvira reached over and held her baby close, tears continuing to stream from her eyes, begging for the storm to end.

The next morning, Elvira slowly opened her eyes as the sun rays shone down over her face. She woke up and looked around. It was calm. The storm had died down, and the birds were chirping as the boat glided smoothly on the peaceful waves. Elvira sat up and looked around her, hoping the storm had all been a dream. She found Mara sleeping soundly beside her, but her husband was nowhere to be seen.

"Leviathan," she sniffed. "Please come back. I can't do this alone. I need you. I love you."

She wanted nothing more than to just break down. But she had to stay strong, for Mara. She had to keep heading east to Jezebel, like they had planned.

"Don't worry, honey," she turned to her daughter and spoke. "We're going to make it."

Ninety days after their journey began, Elvira finally reached the island of Jezebel.

"Hello?" she shouted as she stepped off, Mara tucked in her arms. "Is anyone here?"

No one responded back. The island definitely looked like it hasn't been lived in for decades. The trees were overgrown. Trash littered the ground from when the military came and went, and there wasn't a single cabin or hut on the entire island.

"This place is a dump," Elvira whispered to herself as she continued to explore the island, searching for anything that could help them live a sustainable lifestyle.

Nothing. Eventually, Elvira decided to settle down on the driest spot she could find on the damp island and used a blanket as their tarp for the night, settling under it and falling asleep under the stars. She would figure out how to build a cabin tomorrow.

"Mommy! Mommy! Look what I found!" Mara came running into their Jezebel cabin four years later, holding a handful of snails as her mother was stirring a pot of fish stew.

Mara's eyes were still glowing bright red, and several times, Elvira spotted her casually lifting the fish and snails straight out of the water with no movement but a simple stare. Despite the terror of who or what her daughter actually was, Elvira had learned to accept her daughter's condition

The two of them had lived on the island of Jezebel for the past four years, ever since their escape from Zara, undisturbed and undiscovered. During their first few weeks, Elvira lied awake every night, restless that the military was going to come and discover them, killing them on the spot for trespassing, or Leila was going to crack and expose where they were to her neighbors, and they'd come after her and kidnap Mara.

However, that fear began to fade when months started to pass by, and Elvira and Mara still found themselves alone, safe and alone.

"Mara, honey! That's great! Quick, plop them in the pot so they cook with the fish. We are eating well tonight!"

Stepping on the mini foot stool by the stove, Mara reached her hands up and dropped the snails in, taking in a deep breath of the delicious aroma that brushed across her nose. "That smells so good!" she exclaimed happily as she stepped back down.

"Go wash up, the soup is almost done. We'll have a delicious meal by the fire and then lie outside and watch the stars. Sound good?" Elvira suggested.

"Yes! My favorite!" However, as little Mara headed toward the metal bucket outside to clean herself up, a moving body caught her eye in the distance. "Mommy, did Daddy finally come home?"

"What?" Elvira asked.

"There's someone outside."

Elvira swiftly dropped the bowl she was holding, grabbed her binoculars. She saw several men walking around in heavy armor and carrying assault rifles.

"The military," she whispered.

"Mara, honey, stand behind mommy," Elvira gasped as she pushed her daughter behind her.

Holding her breath and trying to avoid making too much noise, she ducked down below the window and waited. She prayed and prayed that the soldiers were simply there for precautionary checks and would leave them be. She looked down at her daughter, who was shivering in fear on her lap, tears trickling from her eyes.

Their biggest fear had finally caught up to them, and the people of Zara had found them, here to take Mara away and brand her as Satan's daughter. But she had to stay strong. Panicking was the worst thing they could do in this situation. All they could do was wait.

Nearly four hours later, the sun began to set, and the day turned to night. Silence filled the air outside, with nothing but the quiet chirps of crickets.

"I think we're safe now. I think they're gone," Elvira whispered to Mara.

"Mommy? Are we going to be okay?" Mara asked.

"Yes, honey, we're going to be okay. Now, come on, let's go make some dinner. What are you think…"

Just then, Elvira was interrupted by the front door of the cabin slamming open, cold wind and snow blowing inside; the force so strong that Mara was knocked off her feet.

"Mara! No!" Elvira screamed and rushed over to her side, using her sweater to shield her face from the masked men standing by the doorway.

"Take her," one of the masked men ordered.

As the other two reached forward, Elvira pushed her daughter toward the back door.

"Run! Mara, run!"

"But, mommy…" Mara hesitated.

"I said, run!"

Mara ran out the back door as the men tackled Elvira to the ground and tied her hands to her feet.

"Find the girl," the leader ordered again.

The leader of the masked clan grabbed Elvira by the collar of her dress and pulled her toward their boat while the other two men chased after Mara, pushing aside the dead trees and untrimmed weeds as they ran in the bleak of darkness.

"Look! There she is," one of them shouted when he heard the sound of panting, and he reached out his arms to grab the child.

"No! Let me go! Let me go!" Mara screamed, her arms and legs flailing in the air.

"Oh, you're not going anywhere except with us, little girl." He turned to his partner. "Look at this helpless child. She couldn't save herself even if she tried."

As Mara found herself dangling in the air, the rage and

anger deep within her began to grow stronger and stronger with each taunt and insult she heard from the masked men, both of them laughing at her expense. She could feel her blood coursing through her veins, and her fingers tingling as red smoke began to travel out through her fingers.

"Shut up!" her voice boomed and echoed in the air, and Mara soon found herself exploding out of the man's grasp and sending them both in the air with nothing but the power of her hands.

She glared at the two grown men floating in the air, her eyes glowing bright red. Her fury and wrath grew stronger and stronger as her mind flashed back to the sight of them grabbing her mom and tying her up mercilessly. Mara tilted her head to the side, her eyes refusing to blink, and she stared at the man on her left until blood started to trickle out from his eyes, his pupils melting shortly after.

She then turned to the man on her right, and with one flick of her eyes, the man's entire head twisted around his neck and snapped, his limp body instantly colliding with the ground below them.

Four-year-old Mara released the other body and stood back in distress, her body trembling as she realized what she had just done. She didn't know where her power came from or how she was even able to access it. Terrified and confused, she ran off into the woods, refusing to stop until her little legs gave out on her, and she collapsed onto the frozen weeds.

The next morning, Mara found herself waking up to the bright sun and chirping birds. The dream she had felt so real until she found herself lying in the snow.

"Mom? Mom? Where are you?" she cried out, but her mother was nowhere to be found.

As the memories of last night found their way back into her mind again, Mara began to panic. She didn't know what to do. She was barely tall enough to look over the top of the kitchen table, and now, she had to try and survive all alone on an empty island. And she was hungry, tired and hungry. The massacre from the previous night took all the energy out of her, and she didn't know if she could continue on.

"Mom, where are you? Mom…" Mara whispered to herself as she continued trudging along the snow. She didn't know where she was headed, but walking seemed to be the only way to stay warm in the bleak of winter.

Suddenly, she heard a voice behind her, far in the distance. A woman's voice.

"Hey, Shawn! Look over there!" the woman called out. "I think I see someone. Maybe it's their cabin. We can see if they have any food."

When Mara turned, she blinked several times and saw two people running toward her direction. She rubbed her eyes, thinking it was just another dream, but when she opened her eyes back up, she only found them closer.

"It's a little girl," Shawn exclaimed. "Man, Ella, when you said you wanted to explore the island of Jezebel, I bet you never thought you'd find a little girl."

A look of concern washed over Ella's face. She took the coat off her own body and wrapped it around Mara. "You must be freezing! What are you doing out here all alone? Where's your mom?" she asked.

Mara turned toward her, her blood red eyes so shocking

that both Ella and Shawn fell back. "Help me," Mara whispered. "Please help me."

"Ella! Don't! What if she's contagious?" Shawn held Ella back with one hand. "What if she has it? Coxin. What if it's back?"

However, unafraid, Ella pushed his arm aside and proceeded toward Mara. "Don't be stupid. Coxin has been extinct for decades. There aren't any cases of it anymore." She leaned closer toward Mara, lowering herself down to eye level.

"Hi, there. Don't be scared," Ella said as she tucked a strand of hair behind Mara's ear. "My name's Ella, and this is my friend, Shawn. We can help you. Can you tell me where your mom is?"

Mara could only shake her head.

"Can you tell me your name?" Ella asked again.

Shaking her head again, this time, Mara reached her arms out from the jacket, her hands covered in blood as she showed them to Ella and began to cry.

"Oh my god."

"What the hell?"

Both Ella and Shawn became even more fearful of the little child. They didn't know what was going on, what she had done, or who she had killed. They looked at each other and knew that danger was nearby.

"We can't just leave her here," Ella insisted as she stepped back to where Shawn was standing.

"What if she's dangerous? I mean, you saw her hands. Even if she didn't kill anymore, she's got to be involved with someone who did. If we take her with us, whoever's looking for her will probably kill us, too. Do you really want to take that chance?"

Ella stayed silent for the longest five minutes of Shawn's

life, looking at Mara, and then back at Shawn. She was conflicted. She didn't want to risk Shawn's life for her own selfishness to help the little girl, but she also didn't want to leave her here to die.

"We're helping her," she confirmed, a look of disappointment washing over Shawn's face. "I need to make sure she's safe and find her parents before we leave."

Ella knew she was risking Shawn's life. Shawn was her long-term travel partner. Ever since they met on a tour of the rainforest in Brazil, they had been inseparable, always by each other's side, no matter what. He had always looked out for her, keeping her from running into dangerous situations that could get her killed, and she'd never let him down in returning the favor.

So, why was she so hesitant now? Why was she so fixated on helping this strange child even if doing so could lead to death?

"I'm sorry, Shawn," she whispered, taking the little girl's hand and walking deeper into the forest. She turned to Mara and said, "Let's go find your mom. I'm sure she's around here somewhere."

"Oh, great," Shawn muttered and followed them through the thick trees.

I never did get your name. Do you want to tell me what it is?" Ella asked after about two hours of walking through the thick forest, with Shawn trudging heavily behind them.

"Mara, my name's Mara," Mara replied.

"Hi, Mara, that's such a pretty name. Do you know where your mom is?"

That's when Mara stopped in her steps. Her body began to tremble again, and tears poured profusely from her eyes.

"Mara? Mara, are you okay?" Ella asked as she knelt down to console the child.

Suddenly, they heard the sound of cracking wood, followed by loud masculine voices. "There she is! Get her!"

"Shit! I told you they were gonna come after us!" Shawn panicked and started to run.

Ella quickly picked up Mara and followed him, both of them trying to dodge the flying bullets coming toward them. One by one, metal bullets were colliding with the trees and breaking off the branches to block their path.

"FUCK!" Shawn fell to the ground as one of them grazed his arm, a chunk of his skin tearing off, and blood profusely pouring down his right arm.

"Come on, Shawn! Get up, please! We have to go. We need to make it to the boat!" Ella pleaded as she helped Shawn to his feet and threw his arm over her shoulder.

"I swear to God, Ella. If we make it out of this alive, I'm never going with you to crazy, obscure locations ever again."

Limping, with Shawn's blood dripping a trail in the forest, the three of them managed to reach Shawn and Ella's boat, docked just several feet from Mara and Elvira's cabin. Ella placed Mara inside the boat, pushing Shawn in right after, before climbing herself. She hurriedly untied the rope that anchored it to shore and pushed hard against the ground with her oar.

"Come back here with that child!" one of the masked men shouted when he reached them and began to shoot.

"Duck!" Ella cried as the bullets came flying toward them, the boat floating slowly away simultaneously.

Soon, they were far enough into the ocean where the masked men could no longer see them.

"Whew, that was a close one!" Ella sighed.

She noticed an angry glare of daggers coming from Shawn but chose to ignore it.

It had taken her awhile to get there, but she eventually realized that the best apology she could give Shawn for almost getting him killed was time alone from her. Instead, she turned her attention to Mara.

"They... they killed my mom," Mara finally whispered.

"They? Who's they?"

Mara pointed to the men back at shore, who looked like mere ants from the distance. However, Ella could still see them jumping up and down, continuing to shoot toward the water.

"And that's why they were coming after us? So, they could get you, too?"

Mara nodded.

"What about your dad?" Ella asked. "Do you know where *he* is?"

"Gone," Mara whispered, shaking her head.

At that, Shawn broke his silence and turned to them. "I think we should bring her back with us to Stockbridge. We certainly can't take care of her, but maybe we can put her in an orphanage. We can't just leave her to survive in the wild on her own."

Ella smiled. Shawn always did have a soft spot for children, ever since he lost his parents in a car accident at a very young age, forcing him to live with his grandparents until he was eighteen. He could relate to Mara. He knew what she was going through, how it feels to grow up without parents. And he wasn't about to let that happen to anyone else.

"Yeah, I think that's a great idea, just great," Ella agreed beside him, leaning over to kiss him on the cheek as they rowed back to the states.

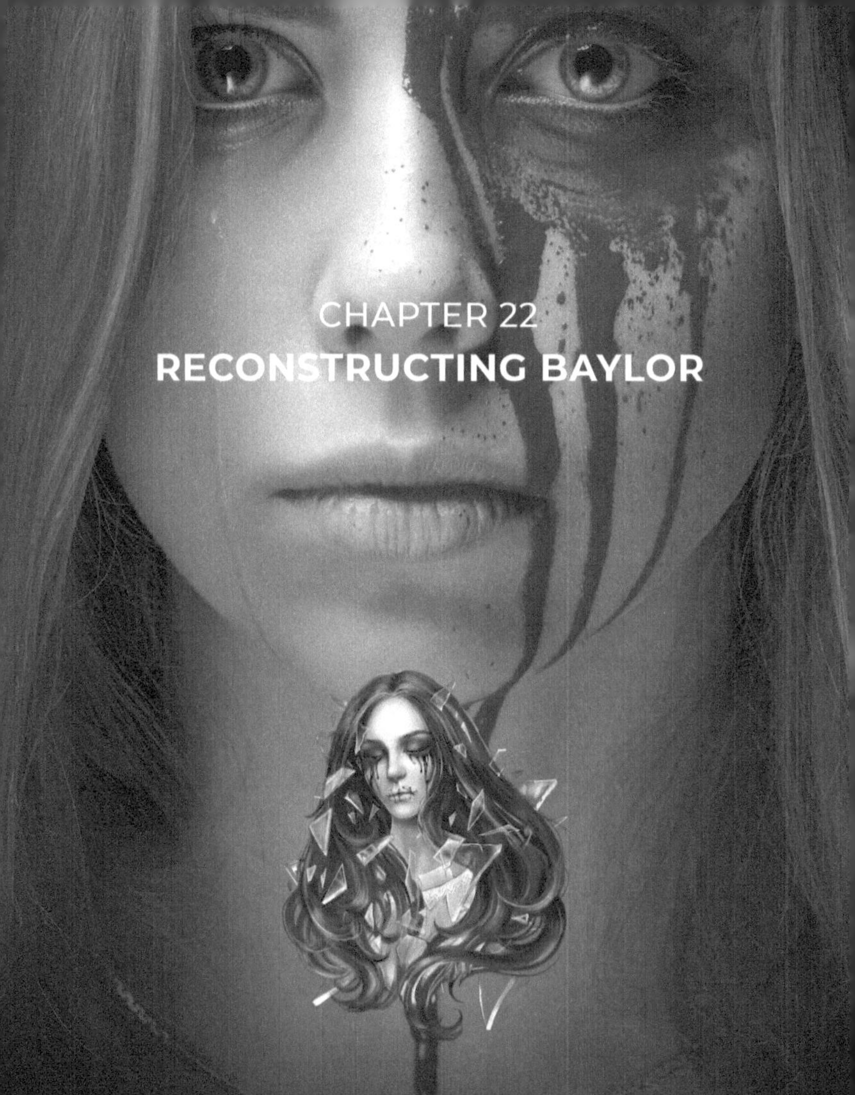

CHAPTER 22

RECONSTRUCTING BAYLOR

Two years have passed since the ruling of the Red Queen, Liliana Watson. Since her death, life was slowly getting back to normal in Stockbridge, memories fading away, some even believing the chapter had closed.

However, others knew about the history of Remphelia, the expectance of a new Red Queen once every eighty-seven years, and they prepared themselves for their next supernatural leader. Some hoping to worship her while others hoping to execute her. Baylor Orphanage became the new hot spot for both authorities and civilians alike.

Damon Walden had managed to rebuild and reconstruct the orphanage to a much better state than it was in before the collapse. The massive walls of the building had a well-decorated interior, adorned with luxurious chandeliers and spacious rooms. It also featured a ballroom for gatherings and events, several classrooms so the children could continue their education, and even a lounge for relaxation.

Damon also decided to expand Baylor into several buildings, each with its own beautiful garden. The ones that came prior were all too small for the vast number of orphans that graced the orphanage, with five to six children sleeping in one room.

Now, one building was reserved entirely as the sleeping space for the children, the second was allotted for education and rehabilitation, and the third became the space for management, meetings, and most importantly, the basement that housed both Liliana Watson and Francesca Billings, an empty white room from top to bottom, a thick glass wall, and enough security cameras to fill an entire city.

Everyone wanted to know more about Remphelia, whether it was an actual health condition or some sort of demonic curse. How someone could be born with such powerful, yet heinous, ability like clockwork? But although many tried to discover more, obtaining the source proved to be an impossible task, with the bodies of those with Remphelia igniting into flames before anyone could obtain a genetic sample.

After restoring the power of language and speech post

the perish of Liliana, Damon became, not only the new headmaster of Baylor Orphanage, but the new literacy teacher for Stockbridge, with students young and old flocking to the education center in the orphanage to learn from him. Some of his students still remembered what it was like when speech was dominant in the world, while others were learning how to speak for the first time. Among these students, was Colton Javernick.

Colton Javernick was loved by everyone in the orphanage, including the other students and the children. He had a charismatic personality and an affectionate smile, always well-dressed and polite. No one knew where he came from or who his family was, but they all just assumed he grew up in a respectable household based on how he presented himself. He was extremely intelligent, picking up the English language faster than anyone thought possible. He was a star student.

However, Damon didn't trust him. There was something strange about Colton, from the way he'd always disappear to different sectors of the building without reason as to why to how he constantly read books on past dictators and world domination. He would constantly ask Damon questions about the life of Liliana, his eyes perking up at the darkest of events, almost like he worshipped her.

Even though Damon had set a rule in the orphanage to never mention the name Liliana, Colton would always talk about her in secret, especially to the children, believing that the world needed another leader to keep order and peace, someone to reign supreme over all others. Damon never knew whether Colton was trying to scare the orphans or brainwash them, but either way, he didn't like it.

But no one else believed Damon's suspicions. Colton

was an obedient student and caretaker at the orphanage. He would never even hurt a fly, much less an entire human being.

But he was too busy working with the Secret Service to follow Colton around and make sure he didn't do anything he wasn't supposed to. Ever since Liliana tried to murder his mother, he made it his mission to help track down the next Red Queen, the next child born with Remphelia. It was something that seemed almost impossible. Over seven billion people in the world, and they had to find just one girl with glowing red eyes. She could be anywhere!

And the guards didn't help, so paranoid that every child was *the* child that they just ran around killing thousands of innocent infants, hoping to kill the one with Remphelia before it got old enough to harness its powers. They broke into every maternity ward they could find all over the country, slaughtering baby after baby, with mothers powerless to go against the orders of the government.

Families began living in fear, hiding their newborns from the searches of the soldiers or aborting their pregnancies to avoid the same fate, but babies were hardly ever left unfound. Soon, the soldiers branched out overseas.

"THANK YOU ALL FOR COMING TO THIS MEETING. I know it's late, and many of us have better things to do," Damon announced the night of July 15, 2013 in the conference hall.

He had invited both the FBI and the military to join him in a meeting to plot out a plan to find and capture the successor of Remphelia.

"I'm sure, by now, that we're all well aware of the kinds of threats the world will face under the rule of the next Liliana Watson. It is now 2013, and the child of Remphelia has been alive for nearly two years. We're headed for another major apocalypse if we don't do something to stop this child now."

"But what are we supposed to do?" the head of the military, General Masters, asked. His voice was trembling, and everyone in the room knew why because they were trembling also. "We can't just keep going around killing babies. The towns are beginning to riot, and we can't even be sure if the child we kill is the child we're looking for. We're all becoming monsters, letting our fears dictate our actions. We need a better plan!"

The entire room started to muttered their concerns all at once, distracting the thoughts of the noticeably stressed Damon.

"Listen! Listen! I know this isn't the best solution, but the bottom line is, we need to find this child before she finds us." He walked over to the projector and turned it on. "Here, I have mapped out a list of places in the area where I believe this child is located, based on the patterns of the previous children of Remphelia. Start with these areas and then expand out from there. Keep a close lookout for any girls with red eyes. If you see any sign of red at all, seize the child, and bring her here."

"Why here? We should be killing this child, not giving her a home to live in. What the hell is an orphanage going to do to keep our nation safe from this... this... demon?"

"We have the means we need in the basement to lock her up securely. We need to keep this child alive, so we can extract her DNA and find out exactly what or who she is. We need to know more about Remphelia and figure out exactly how to stop it before it continues for generations and generations. We have everything we need right here in this orphanage, even a high security safe with bulletproof glass to keep her from escaping."

The crowd started up, speaking over each other louder and louder, until Damon saw a hand slowly raise up. He banged loudly on the table, shutting the group up.

"Yes, do you have a question?" Damon pointed to the hand.

"Um... yes... hi. My name's Mason. I think you're making some great points, but isn't there a cure for Remphelia, or at least, a medication to suppress the red eyes and powers? Isn't that what Headmaster Walden used to suppress Liliana's powers?"

Damon sighed. He knew the day would come when people would start asking about the medication. His mind reflected back to two years ago, when he had just killed Liliana, and her worshippers ransacked the state, destroying everything possible that could be used to stop the next successor, including the medication.

He had a chance to stop them. He was there; he could've fought back, and if he knew then what they were up to, he would've. But, with his mother's recent death and his mourning of Remy Kimora, he wasn't in the right mindset to thwart the plans of angry mobs. He watched, helpless, as they burned down the entire medical lab at Elyson, along with everything inside.

"Unfortunately, Mason, no. There is no medication to suppress Remphelia, and the scientist who created it was tragically killed by Liliana in 1952 when he was supposedly caught speaking to his wife in public, instantly killed. And with no documents or records left of his research, no one could figure out how to replicate what he did," Damon explained.

And with those words, the room fell silent, and heads bowed down. They knew they were in for a long and treacherous journey, and if they were to fail, destruction would reign once again.

Years have passed since the military and police set out in search for the child with Remphelia, searching everywhere, from hospitals to homes to abandoned buildings, but she was nowhere to be found. More innocent lives were taken, and more people lived in terror.

Some civilians in Stockbridge even stopped speaking

altogether, for fear that they might say something to make them stand out as guilty. Silence was beginning to loom in the air again, and Stockbridge was starting to become a ghost town. Not before long, the search for the child began to disband, with many either assuming she'd already died or believing she was never born.

The orphanage was no longer the headquarters for the government when they disbanded the search, turning their resources back to catching criminals who actually existed.

IN THE SAME TOWN, ABOUT FIFTY MILES SOUTH OF THE orphanage, Mara ran out into a field of flowers in the backyard of a small cabin home, giggling and spinning around in circles, before collapsing on top of a bed of roses.

"Mara, be careful, dear. You're hurting the flowers," Ella warned her as she walked out with two glasses of iced tea.

Ella *had* planned on putting Mara in the town's orphanage when they arrived home from Jezebel. They all settled in the apartment Ella and Shawn shared while they tried to make arrangements for Mara. But Ella had always wanted a daughter. When she was twenty-one, she found out that she was infertile when she and her fiancé at the time tried to conceive. After years of trying, he eventually walked out on her for someone who could bear him a child.

Ella became devastated after that and swore to focus on herself instead. Until now. Until she experienced what it felt like to be a mother.

She'd even fought with Shawn about it for months before he finally gave up trying to convince her to change her mind about keeping Mara and kicked them both out of the apartment, forcing both Ella and Mara to sleep on the streets. He wasn't about to play father to someone else's child, especially not since that very same child almost got him killed.

For nearly six months, Ella and Mara slept in a tent in the woods just outside of town, foraging for mushrooms and berries to get by. Ella grew up in the forest as a child. Her father was a hunter, and so, Ella knew the ins and outs of surviving in the woods.

Luckily, Ella soon found a job working as a travel agent and was able to live off a steady income. She had more knowledge than all the agents combined, and she knew the best locations to travel for those looking for quiet, remote areas away from tourists. She moved herself and Mara into a cheap cabin and acted as her guardian for the past three years, treating her as her own daughter.

Life together was great. They were each other's best friends. Ella taught Mara how to braid her hair and tie her shoes, while Mara showed Ella the cool tricks she could do with her eyes and hands. Of course, Ella never brought Mara out in public. She couldn't risk anyone seeing her red eyes. It was a cruel world out there, and she didn't trust anyone but herself.

Yes, things were going just great... until they weren't.

A FEW MONTHS LATER, ELLA BECAME EXTREMELY ILL and was diagnosed with terminal cancer, her doctors giving her a maximum of two weeks left to live.

"I'm sorry, Mara. I love you, but I'm afraid I don't have

much time left to live." Ella coughed, blood spilling out onto her white sheets as she remained bed-bound.

"But I need you, Ella. I need you," Mara cried. "I don't want you to die. I love you."

"I know, sweetie. I wish I could stay with you forever, but sometimes, life just doesn't work out the way we planned. It's no one's fault. That's just the way life is sometimes. Remember that, Mara. Remember that, sometimes, it's nobody's fault."

Mara grabbed onto Ella's hand as it brushed against her cheeks. "I'll remember, I promise."

Ella smiled. "Listen, Mara, I don't have much time left. I feel very sick, and I don't think I'm going to make it much longer. Tomorrow morning, Shawn is going to come and take you to the orphanage. I haven't spoken to him in years, but he granted me one last wish. That will be your new home. But don't be scared. You'll love it there. You can make friends and read and even play board games."

She coughed several times before continuing. "But people are going to look at you like you're strange. You're different than the others, special. But sometimes, people don't like different. That's why I need you to wear your special sunglasses, okay? I need you to keep your secret for as long as you can. Do it for me."

Mara nodded, more tears trickling down her face. "I will. I definitely will."

"Good. I also want you to take these," Ella said as she weakly held out a bottle of pills. "Starting tomorrow, I need you to promise me that you'll take one of these a day. These will help you feel better, help you not be so scared."

Mara nodded again, taking the bottle of pills from Ella and putting it in her pocket.

No one ever knew, not even Shawn, that Ella was part of The Order, the group of civilians who worshipped Liliana and what she stood for, and longed to avenge her death. She was there when they broke into Elyson and tore the place down, burning every last evidence of research and pills that the lab had stashed, but not before sneaking one into her own pocket.

She had originally planned on just keeping it as a souvenir, as a reminder of the time period during Liliana's rule. However, soon after she started living with Mara, she began to slowly connect the dots. Mara *was* Liliana's successor. She *was* the child who was prophesied to be the next Red Queen, and her eyes really were due to Remphelia, not a vessel burst like she had originally thought.

And there were enough pills for Mara to conceal her secret until she was old enough for her powers to fully develop. She needed to keep Mara safe, however way she could, so Mara could become the world's new leader.

THE NEXT MORNING, ELLA PASSED AWAY ON HER DEATH bed while Mara packed up her belongings, tucking her pills in between some clothes, and walked outside, where Shawn was standing by his car to take her to Baylor. He helped her put her luggage in his trunk as Mara looked back at the cabin. She had such wonderful memories there, with Ella, and now, they were both gone. She sighed.

"You ready to go?" Shawn asked.

Mara could only nod as she climbed into the car. Her life was changing. An entirely new journey was waiting for her, but deep down, she knew things were only going to get much worse. Without her parents, and without Ella, she knew she was going to have to fight for herself if she wanted to survive.

CHAPTER 24
MARA

"Hi! Welcome to Baylor! My name is Rose. How can I help you?" a woman at the front desk cheerily greeted Shawn and Mara as they walked in through the front door.

"Hi, Rose. I'm Shawn, and this is Mara. I would like to check her in, please." Shawn placed Mara's suitcase down on the floor and leaned over the counter.

"Of course! Hi, Mara! I'm Rose. It's so nice to meet

you."

Mara could only hide behind Shawn, her dark sunglasses over her eyes, and her wide-brim hat on her head. She was never a fan of Shawn, especially not after what he did to Ella, but she'd much rather stay near him than the building full of strangers.

"She's a little shy. I'm sure she'll open up once she's around kids her own age."

"I do hope she does. She'll have a blast here. A lot of kids are scared at first, and now, I can't get them to shut up!" Rose laughed. "So, do you know what happened to her parents or legal guardian?"

"Why does that matter?"

"Oh, it's just for paperwork purposes, but if you don't feel comfortable talking about it or just don't know, that's fine, too." Rose laughed again. "Alright, Mara, you can come with me, and I'll show you to your room."

"Shawn, I'm scared," Mara cried as she grabbed on tighter to him. "I don't want to stay here. I want to be with Ella."

Shawn knelt down and gently gave Mara a hug. "It's okay, Mara. It's okay. You don't have to be scared. You'll be just fine here, I promise. Ella's in a better place now, and you have to be brave, for her, okay? Miss Rose will take good care of you. Soon, you won't even remember why you were so afraid."

"Okay," Mara whispered and followed Rose after giving Shawn one last hug, dragging her favorite blanket and teddy bear behind her.

SHAWN WATCHED, STILL STANDING BY THE FRONT DESK, waving goodbye as his mental confliction fought on whether to change his mind, eventually turning around, and walking out the door.

"ALRIGHT, MARA, HERE IS YOUR ROOM," ROSE gestured inside a small pink room with two twin beds inside. "You're very lucky! You'll be sharing the room with one of the sweetest little girls here at the orphanage. I know you two will get along just great! Dinner will be served at 6pm tonight, and quiet hours are after 10pm. I'll give you some time to unpack and settle in, but I'll be back in about twenty minutes to bring you over to the conference hall. There's a seminar on heroes today!"

Mara could only smile softly as Rose left the room. She sighed as she threw her suitcase onto the bed and sat down next to it. She then unzipped it and took out the bottle of pills, popping one into her mouth.

"What's that?" a voice called out, Mara quickly hiding the bottle behind her back.

"What? Um... nothing," she stuttered, her fingers wrapped tightly around the bottle.

"You must be my new roommate! I'm Stacy!" The girl walked into the room and hopped onto her bed. "What's your name?" she asked.

"Ma... Mara, my name's Mara."

"Hi, Mara! I think you'll really like it here. We get to play board games, go outside to the playground, and we even have snack time! It's great! I think we'll be great friends!"

Before Mara could reply, Rose walked back into the room. "Come on, girls, the seminar's starting. Grab your notebooks, and follow me."

THIS WAS THE FIRST SEMINAR OF THE YEAR, THE FIRST of many. It was a cold and foggy morning. The stage was set with beautiful floral decorations, filling the room with their mesmerizing scent. Mara was given a quick tour of the building as they all walked over to the conference hall.

Standing outside was Colton, greeting and welcoming all the children as they each signed in. Seminars were a requirement for all the orphans. If they were to skip even one, they would have their leisure time taken away for an entire week.

"Welcome, everyone! Thank you all for coming to my seminar today on heroes. I've recently read some interesting articles on what it takes to be a hero. A hero is powerful, strong, and a leader. Can anyone give me some examples of some of their favorite heroes?" Colton asked as he walked around on stage, pointing at the projector toward his presentation.

A couple of kids in the audience all shouted at once.

"My dad!"

"Superman!"

"Batman!"

"Jesus!"

But suddenly, a high-pitched voice screamed out, "Liliana!"

The room turned silent, and Damon nearly fainted after hearing the answer. Everyone looked around the room, trying to figure out who said it, but the perpetrator could not be identified.

"Alright, everyone, let's take a break. We'll continue this seminar at another time." Damon quickly turned off the projector and gestured the staff to lead the children out of the room.

"Colton! Did you plan this?" Damon shouted as the orphans continued to exit.

"What? How can you even accuse me of something like that? I'm not the one who planned this stupid seminar."

"You're always the one reading up on her, telling these kids stories about her," Damon shouted again.

"They're just stories. Just simple stories to scare them straight, that's all," Colton insisted.

Colton Javernick was aware of Damon's suspicions toward him. But it's not like he did a very good job of hiding it, either. Nevertheless, he apologized anyway and walked out of the room, his fingers crossed that he would one day stop.

As he headed toward his office, he spotted Mara in the playground as he walked down the hall. Hundreds of voices were screaming and laughing, enough to make him want to rip his own ears out.

But, for some reason, Mara caught his attention. She wasn't like the other children. She kept to herself, not because she was shy, but because she preferred to be alone. Colton could see that in her. How? Because she reminded him of himself when he was younger. Like him, she didn't yearn for attention or friendship; she yearned to keep them away. There was just something different about her, some-thing special.

"Maybe it's really her," Colton whispered to himself as he noticed her sunglasses.

He walked out onto the playground and introduced himself as the caretaker of the orphanage. She responded that her name was Mara, and how out of place she felt on her first day.

"I get it. It's never easy being the new kid, especially not in a place where you know you can't leave. But you'll get used to it, trust me. Eventually, you'll just learn to realize that all fear and nerves do is hold you back. I never really felt like I fit in anywhere, either."

"Yeah, I guess," Mara whispered.

"Well, I'll tell you what. One week. I promise you that, in one week, you'll start to not feel so alone and isolated anymore. Just stop caring about what other people will think about you just because you're new. And, if you ever need someone to talk to, I'm always here."

"Thanks."

"Don't sweat it! I do want to ask though, why are you wearing those sunglasses? I saw you wearing them inside the building, too. Is everything okay?"

"I'm fine. I just like wearing them so I feel safe. Ella also gave them to me before she died, and I want her with me always." She whispered again, this time, wrapping her arms around her.

"I bet this Ella was a really special person. You know, I had a sister named Ella. We never really spoke. In fact, I don't even know where she is or if she's even still alive. Some families just fade out, I guess."

"She was."

"Can I see them?" Colton asked, trying to get the glasses off so he could take a look at her eyes. He was so sure that Mara was the successor of Liliana, and that after all those years of searching, he had finally found her, the new queen.

"Sure," Mara replied.

However, when she removed her glasses, Colton was shocked by what he saw. Normal eyes. Just normal white eyes, just like every other child on the playground.

"Damn," he muttered. "She's not the one."

"What?"

"Noth... Nothing."

"Can I please have my glasses back? I don't want to lose them."

"Sure, here you go." Colton handed them over and stood up. "I have to go back in now; take care of some grown-up stuff. I'll see you around. If you ever need me, my office number is room forty-four. My door is always open." He smiled and walked away.

IT DIDN'T TAKE LONG FOR COLTON AND MARA TO become friends, Mara seeing Colton as a father figure while Colton felt sorry for Mara because he knew the hardships she was going through. She would come to him for advice whenever she felt isolated from the other children. Plus, he reminded her so much of Ella.

Colton spent the rest of his time locked in his office, still researching on ways to find the next successor of Remphelia. Day after day, he'd ponder through piles and piles of newspapers and magazines that he'd collected before the town decided to incinerate nearly everything to forget about that era.

He felt that it was his duty to find and raise the new queen to who she was destined to be, a totalitarian leader, not just to avenge the death of Liliana, but because he felt like the people deserved law and order.

CHAPTER 25

UNCOVERING HISTORY

The next morning, Colton sprung out of bed to his blaring alarm. Wednesdays were his days off, and he had been meaning to make the trip up to Elyson Library for awhile now. It was the largest library in the entire state, and he was sure it'd contain all the information he needed about Liliana and finding the next child of Remphelia.

The journey to the library was two hours each way, and

he knew he'd have to leave immediately if he wanted to catch the train. Only two trains ever left Stockbridge, one in the morning and one late at night.

The train was equipped with comfortable and spacious seats, with a beautiful interior and all the amenities anyone could ask for, from coffee stations to sleeper cars. The Stocker Line not only took daily trips out to Cambridge, but it also took the scenic route around the entire country, many tourists taking advantage of its cheap prices to sight-see.

Taking in a deep breath of the coffee aroma brewing in the lounge, Colton leaned back against his seat and stared out the window. His eyes were immersed in the ocean, deep thoughts running through his mind of how he would ever find the successor. Growing up, never did he think he'd embark on this journey to find someone so deadly that she could obliterate the entire nation in one single blow.

He wanted to become a marine biologist, sail around the world discovering new aquatic species. Sadly, that dream died when his parents thought a life of reckless gambling and drinking was more important than his future. And the fact that he was arrested for stealing at the age of twelve didn't help either.

He sighed. "Those were the days; those were the days."

Suddenly, the man in front of him turned around. He was an old man, maybe in his seventies, with gray hair and glasses that hung from the brim of his nose. "I haven't seen you around on this train before, and I ride it every day. First time?"

Colton's head popped up from against the window, startled. "Huh? Yeah, first time. I'm headed to Elyson."

"Elyson? That's where I'm headed, too. I'm Raven. I work as a librarian over at the library there. Been riding this train up there every day for the past thirty-two years."

Librarian? Colton's eyes widened. That caught his attention. "Thirty-two years, that's impressive. I bet you know everything in that library inside and out.

"Well, I don't want to brag, but let's just say I know the exact date when Abraham Lincoln took his first trip to the theatre."

"What?"

"Exactly." He smiled.

This intrigued Colton. He wanted to find out what else Raven knew, whether he knew anything about Liliana and Remphelia.

"Raven, is it? What do you know about Liliana Watson?"

Several other passengers on the train gasped and turned around as Raven rubbed his fingers on his chin, unstartled by what Colton had asked.

"Liliana, such a complicated and troubled leader, so little information known about her, yet so many lives were affected."

Soon, the conversation between them flowed, revealing information from when she was born to her first kill to the rule she had over the nation to her eventual death. Colton played off his interest as just a student writing a research paper, but Raven didn't seem to care; he was just excited to have someone to talk to.

"Well, here we are, Colton. It was nice chatting with you, young man. Keep that brain moving. You have a bright future ahead of you." Raven leaned in closer and whispered, "And if you want to know more about Liliana, go see my colleague, Josephine, at the front desk. She'll show you where you can find *everything*."

The time was 11am, and after several blocks from the train station, Colton found himself standing outside Elyson

University, with a flowing river on his left and a colorful garden on his right. He sat down on the bench by the river for a short while, enjoying the beautiful sights before him while he ate his sandwich, freeing his mind from the constant thoughts pounding against his head.

Sometimes he wished he wasn't so invested in this case. Sometimes he wished he could just be... normal. But he could never be normal. If he didn't find the next successor, no one would, and the Earth would perish to free-thinkers who conflicted each other with every word.

The Elyson Library was located in the west part of campus, a fifteen-minute walk away. Upon entering the giant gates, Colton came face-to-face with the most remarkable library he had ever seen, decorated with countless book shelves and numerous desktops. He loved books and saw this as a dream, not just because he needed information on Liliana, but because he found himself in Literary Heaven.

He shook his head. "No, focus, Colton."

He walked up to the front desk, his eyes catching a name tag that said, Josephine. He rang the bell.

"Yes, sir, how can I help you?"

"Are you Josephine?" he asked.

She tapped lightly on her tag. "That's what the tag says. Boy, and I thought *I* needed my eyes checked."

Colton shook his head again. "Right, sorry. I'm looking for any books or documents you have on Remphelia." He looked around before realizing that Josephine was staring at him. "It's... it's for a research paper," he added.

"Alright, then, follow me." She gestured him toward the back of the library, leading him down to the basement.

The basement was old and dirty, covered in nothing but dust and cobwebs. There were several rats scurrying down the hall as they made their way into a tiny room.

"Here, you can find all the resources you need on Remphelia, dating back to 1750, when the first case of Remphelia was discovered. Let me know if you have any questions. I'll be right upstairs." She turned back around as she approached the steps. "And one more thing, young man. I can't allow you to check these out or make copies, so any information you need, it's best you take notes."

"Roger that, thanks."

Sorting through the documents, Colton discovered information that no one had ever known. Back in the early 1700s, a young couple, Trevor Maude and Katherine Sawyer, had fallen in love. Most believed it was love at first sight, any woman's dream come true. However, they lived during a time when those in royalty were able to choose who they wanted as their bride from all the eligible maidens in the country. The high prince, Prince Lile IV, chose Katherine to be his wedded wife.

However, a few days before Katherine and Prince Lile were scheduled to tie the knot, Katherine met Trevor, and they immediately fell in love. Katherine tried to convince her parents to call off the wedding, but it wasn't their choice to make. If Katherine didn't show up to the altar, both her parents would be beheaded.

So, she did. Katherine chose her family over her heart and showed up to the wedding, wearing a beautiful gown and staining her veil with tears. But she wasn't the only unexpected one to show up. Unbeknownst to Katherine, Trevor stood up from the crowd, professing his love to Katherine in front of the entire kingdom before grabbing her hand, running into the woods, and out to sea on his boat.

Katherine's parents were instantly killed, and the kingdom sent out a decade long man-hunt searching for Lile's bride. And they almost gave up, with Lile finding another bride to replace Katherine. Almost. Until they met her. Countess Cordelia, who claimed to be a distant relative of Katherine and promised the royal family that she would bring Katherine back into the arms of Lile.

And she delivered on her word. Eight months later, Katherine was captured and returned to the kingdom, where she was forced to be Prince Lile's bride. Trevor was killed on the spot when the royal guards found him, and Katherine was fed an elixir to make her fall in love with Lile. Everything was going as planned, as it should be.

But what the royal family didn't realize was that Countess Cordelia had put a spell in the elixir that Katherine drank, a spell that cursed one descendant of Katherine's every eighty-seven years with a horrible condition known as Remphelia, a condition that turned their eyes blood red and gave them the ability to obliterate the entire world with the snap of a finger. Lile and Katherine didn't realize this until years down the line, when their first daughter, Helen, was born with bloodshot eyes. The only way to break the curse...

Colton slammed the old book shut; his breath heavy as he tried to register everything he had just read. "So, they're all related. Helen, Francesca, Liliana, whoever this new successor is, they're all related."

SEVERAL HOURS LATER, JOSEPHINE ASKED HIM TO LEAVE and come back another time as they were closing. Reading everything, he actually began feeling sorry for all these children with Remphelia. They weren't evil; they were just cursed.

And he still had his suspicions on Mara. She didn't have the red eyes, but he just couldn't shake the feeling that there was something strange about her, something supernatural. But in order to continue his search and prove his suspicions wrong, he needed to find the source of where Mara came from, starting with the person who brought her to the orphanage. She was the first lead he had gotten in years working at the orphanage, and he was going to follow it.

THE NEXT MORNING, WHILE EVERYONE WAS OFF TO THE dining hall for breakfast, Colton snuck down to the front desk and sifted through the stack of papers, starting with the most recent admissions.

"Mara, got it!" he whispered loudly as he pulled the sheet out, scanning the information for who checked her in. His name was Shawn, and he only lived a couple streets from the orphanage. The hunt for the successor was on, and Colton knew that this was where he needed to start.

Colton lied to Damon that he needed to take the day off to visit his sick grandfather, but Damon wasn't buying it, his face wrinkling in suspicion as Colton told his story. But Colton didn't care. He could care less about his job. The only reason he took the job as the orphanage's caretaker in the first place was to catch the child.

He skipped out the building and followed the address to Shawn's apartment.

"What do you want? I'm busy," Shawn said, aggravated.

Colton could hear the game on behind him. Football fans in Massachusetts were usually pretty hardcore.

"Hi, my name's Colton. Are you Shawn?"

"Yeah, what do you want?" he repeated.

"I work as the caretaker at the orphanage, you know, the one you brought Mara to the other day."

"Okay... Look, man, I'm really busy here. Either tell me what you want or get the fuck out of my apartment."

"I need you to tell me what you know about her, what you know about Ella. There's just something off about her, and I just want to make sure she's not a danger to anyone. It's my duty to protect the children, you know."

Shawn sighed heavily, obviously annoyed. "Come on in." He gestured Colton inside.

Colton looked around the living room when he sat down, his eyes catching a picture of Shawn and a familiar-looking woman together, arms around each other in front of the Eiffel Tower.

"Hey, Shawn, who's that with you in the picture?" he asked.

"Her? Oh, she's just someone I used to know. We used to go traveling together all the time, but then we had a falling out."

"I think I know her. I think that's my sister."

"Ella's your sister? Crazy, dude. She never told me she had siblings. But then again, she never really talked much about her life."

"Yeah! Ella, that's totally my sister. Do you happen to know if that's the same Ella that Mara knew?"

Shawn took a seat, popping open his beer and taking a sip before continuing. "Unfortunately, yes. Long story short, but Ella and I almost got killed rescuing Mara from Jezebel. I wanted to put her in the orphanage years ago, but Ella insisted that she wanted to take care of her instead, and I hadn't heard from her until she contacted me a couple days ago and asked me to drive Mara to Baylor."

"Why? Where's Ella now?"

"Gone, cancer. Sorry, dude. I'm surprised you didn't know, given that you're family and all," Shawn answered.

"Yeah, me too, I guess." Colton looked down at his fidgeting hands. "Hey, did you ever notice anything strange about Mara?"

"You mean other than the fact that she almost got us killed in Jezebel when we found her wandering in the woods alone?"

"I guess that *is* strange, but is there anything else?"

"Oh, yeah, red eyes! Like fucking creepy blood red eyes. Ella always just excused them as a vessel burst, but it's freaky, man. She probably has some kind of disease or something."

"Oh my god, no," Colton whispered, standing up and knocking his chair over.

"What is it?"

"I... I gotta go. Thanks, dude, for everything, but I gotta go."

Colton rushed out of Shawn's apartment and out into the streets, running quickly back toward the orphanage. "It's Mara. It's Mara."

HISTORY REPEATS ITSELF

rowing up in an isolated life, Mara never knew how to make friends. Besides her mother, Mara had only ever been close to Ella, who she also saw as just another parental figure. Her entire life so far, she had been kept under constant supervision, the adults around her too afraid for her to walk outside without either sunglasses or a blindfold. In fact, she never really got to see the world for what it truly was without constantly having a shield in front of her eyes.

Until now. Now, at the age of seven, Mara found herself experiencing the colors and brightness of the world around her, but it wasn't the same as she had imagined. Her entire life, she thought that once she removed the blindfolds from her eyes, she would be welcomed with happiness and joy, the beautiful sights of rainbows and butterflies welcoming her to her new surroundings.

Instead, she was met with disdain, some children on the playground ignoring her while others taunted and laughed at her for being an antisocial loner. In her six months at Baylor, Mara had always been a well-behaved kid, following orders and never causing trouble to anyone. But the other orphans still didn't like her. They still saw her as the "weird newcomer" even as many other orphans were admitted after her.

Among those bullies, was Alyssa, the queen of the orphanage and five years older than Mara. She had been living inside Baylor ever since the orphanage was newly rebuilt, one of the first residents to ever step foot inside. And because of that, she was the one who decided which orphans were part of the "in" crowd and which ones were subjected to insult and injury.

Mara, unfortunately, wasn't one of the lucky ones. Since the first day Mara arrived, Alyssa had it out for her, seeing her as a threat when she saw her getting close to Colton. Alyssa always had a crush on Colton. She thought it was just a funny feeling when she was younger, but as she began to develop into her body, she found herself lusting after him.

But every time Alyssa tried to seduce Colton, claiming him for herself, Colton always seemed distracted, always running off into his office whenever she tried to talk to him. And when he did make time for someone, that person was always Mara.

"What's that? Your crazy meds?" Alyssa taunted one sunny afternoon at the playground.

Mara sat by herself beneath the tree, as she always did, playing with the bottle of pills that Ella had given her. She had been taking one every day for the past six months, just like she had promised. To this day, she still didn't really know why she had to take them. Ella just said the pills would keep her from standing out among unaccepting crowds. She was never allowed to look in a mirror so she never knew whether there was anything wrong with her, if any. She didn't feel any different, with or without the pills.

She looked up at Alyssa, who was now calling the other orphans over. "Hey, everyone! Look! I knew there was something weird about Mara! She's a nutcase! What are those pills for, nutcase Mara? I don't think anything's strong enough to ever make *you* normal." She grabbed the bottle out from Mara's hands. "I'll even take these off your hands. It's not like they're helping you, anyway."

"Hey, give those back! I need them!" Mara insisted, reaching for the bottle.

However, Alyssa was much taller than her.

"Nah, I want to see what you're really like without these, not like you can get even weirder than you are now."

Alyssa ran over to the fountain, Mara and the other children running after her, and she dumped the pills down the sewage drain, laughing as the rapid waves washed over them and into the river.

"No!" Mara screamed, trying to reach her tiny hand in, but with no luck as Alyssa and her crowd gathered around her, laughing at her and calling her names.

Mara didn't know how to handle all that noise coming at her all at once. She usually kept to herself, her mind at peace as she tuned out her surroundings. And that she did try, but the noise around her just kept getting louder and louder and louder.

"Stop it, stop it! Please stop it!"

She threw her palms over her ears to try and quell all the voices, but nothing worked. She felt like her entire world was collapsing down on her. Flashbacks of her mother being taken away and Ella on her death bed forced tears to pour from her eyes. She felt like she wanted to scream, like her head was about to explode at any minute.

Then the bell rang.

THE NEXT MORNING, THE SUN ROSE WITH THE chirping birds. The window was slightly ajar, so Mara could feel the cold breeze of the wind brush against her skin and smell the scent of the blossoming flowers. Sitting up on her bed, Mara reached over to her desk to grab her bottle.

"Oh, right," she whispered.

She had been so used to taking them every morning that it felt strange to not have them there. She didn't feel any different. She felt around her face and ran to the bathroom to look in the mirror for the very first time. Bugs weren't crawling out from her eyes nor was her skin peeling off her face. She was fine.

"Maybe I didn't need the pills after all." Mara shrugged and walked out to the lobby to get in line, leaving her sunglasses on her bed-side table.

The orphans at Baylor had a dress code, a different color

uniform for each class based on their age to easily separate and identify them. Everyone had to stand in their respective lines for a daily head count before they could proceed to the dining hall for breakfast. Mara was in the blue group, along with Stacy, while Alyssa and the older orphans were in purple.

"Hey, Mara, I heard about what Alyssa did yesterday. That was a really nasty thing to do. Are you okay? Are you going to be okay without your meds?" Stacy asked when Mara got in line.

"Don't worry about it. I feel fine, actually. I don't think I even needed my meds to begin with. I feel fine without them."

But Mara wasn't fine. Over the course of the next several days, spots of red began to coat her eyes. This was the first time she was able to look in a mirror without being on her meds, and she was terrified. She didn't know what was happening to her. Stacy tried to help, asking Mara to see the orphanage nurse, but Mara refused. She became hysterical, unsure of how to deal with her newfound change.

On the first day, she thought it was just a bug, or some dust that flew into her eyes that gave her allergies. As the days passed, and as her eyes became painted with a coat of red, she knew she was in trouble. She knew she had to hide it, or else the masked men who took her mom would come chasing after her, too. Grabbing her sunglasses, she threw them onto her face and ran out to the dining hall as the bell sounded for dinner.

However, on her way there, she bumped into Colton, colliding straight into each other, and both of them falling over onto the ground.

"Whoa, there," Colton exclaimed, startled as the pile of

papers flew out of his hands. "There's plenty of pizza to go around. No need to rush."

"Sorry," Mara apologized as she started to gather the papers, looking for her sunglasses.

However, Colton caught a quick glimpse of Mara before she could put her glasses back on. Red. It was red. "It really is you," he whispered.

"What?"

And everything went dark.

MEANWHILE, IN THE DINING HALL, THE STAFF BEGAN taking attendance and calling the students one by one.

"Laura?"

"Here!"

"Lexi?"

"Present."

"Mara?"

Silence. The rest of the room waited impatiently for Mara to respond so they could dig into their meals.

Silence.

"I repeat, Mara. Are you here? Please, speak up if you are."

"Miss Melanie," Stacy spoke up, a squeak prominent in her voice, raising her hand. "I don't think she's here."

The entire room gasped, and alarms began to blare. Ever since the orphanage had been rebuilt, Damon learned to become extra cautious when it came to the orphans, always in constant fear that one missing meant Liliana's successor got a hold of them. That meant that wherever the missing child was, the successor had to be close by.

"Shut down all gates immediately," Damon ordered. "No one in; no one out." He ran into his office upstairs and made an orphanage-wide announcement. "Attention, everyone. This is NOT a drill. I need everyone to listen now and listen carefully. I want everyone to go back to their rooms and stay there until I say otherwise. Staff, please gather in the conference hall, immediately."

"Alright," Damon said as the staff members all gathered together in the same room. "We have a serious situation here. One of the orphans is missing, and she's either dead, or she escaped. Either way, we need to find her before someone, or something, gets to her. We can't have this... this... blemish on our records. Does anyone have any ideas on what we can do?"

"How about we call the cops and file a missing person's report? Maybe they can help us find her," Michael, the groundskeeper, suggested.

"Are you crazy? They're already trying to defund us, especially after we failed to deliver the demon child. How do you think it'll look to them if we just walked up and say we lost a child? They'll shut us down instantly!"

"Colton usually has some good ideas," Rose said, the rest of the room nodding and muttering in agreement.

Damon sighed. He hated Colton and everything about him, from the way he'd look at him to the way he'd sneak around mysteriously and skip out on work with no explanation. "Alright, Colton, you're up. What's your bright idea?"

No one answered back.

"Colton, didn't you hear me?" Damon looked around

the room, trying to spot the stupid orange fedora that Colton never went anywhere without, but all he could see were dark heads of hair. "Has anyone seen Colton?"

"I haven't seen him since this morning," Michael replied.

"Son of a bitch! He always does this. I swear, if I find him at his girlfriend's one more time, he's done, both from this job *and* the school."

Fuming, he pulled out his phone and dialed Josie's number. The last time Colton skipped out on work, Damon pulled her number off his phone when he wasn't looking. He was beginning to grow sick and tired of Colton and his constant excuses.

"Josie?" Damon asked. "Is Colton over there?"

"Who's this? And how'd you get my number?"

"It's Damon, Colton's boss. Never mind how I got your number. Is he with you or not?"

"Um... no, I haven't seen him in weeks. I even broke up with him since he just ghosted me, and I haven't heard anything since then, either." Josie's voice sounded agitated at the mention of Colton.

Finally, someone else who despises Colton as much as I do, Damon thought to himself.

"Damon," Rose interrupted. "You don't think Colton has something to do with Mara missing, do you?"

He froze. He had been so focused on trying to keep everyone safe and coming up with a plan that he didn't even connect the two together.

"No," Damon whispered, dropping his phone.

He bolted out of the conference hall and ran up to Colton's office. Day after day, he'd lock himself in there. If there was any information on what Colton was up to, he'd find it in his office.

"What are we looking for?" Michael asked as the rest of the staff joined Damon in the office.

Damon was frantically pulling open the drawers, throwing pens, erasers, and candy wrappers onto the floor.

Man, for someone so smart, this guy's a slob, Damon thought to himself as he continued throwing trash upon trash. *What's he trying to hide anyway?*

The entire staff, with the exception of Colton, continued to search for any clues as to where he might be or whether he was connected to Mara disappearing. He never trusted Colton, not even once. He'd only hired him because he had proven himself to be the most competent and logical employee out of everyone there. And he was. But Damon never expected him to be crazy.

"Hey, boss, look what I found!" Michael called out, turning Damon's attention away from his memories.

When Damon walked over, he saw that Michael was waving around a diary, Colton's diary, the thickest diary he had ever seen in his life, with hundreds and hundreds of entries dating back an entire decade. He flipped through the pages, reading entry upon entry, recounting his moments from the day he was abandoned by his parents to when he first became obsessed with power and the supernatural, his strong desire to restore a totalitarian leader who could rule the world under one law and banish chaos and free speech.

The entries were frightening, every entry filled with grueling details on how he wished everyone around him would die a painful death to how he'd try to rise Liliana from the dead with a séance every night for seven years to how he'd only applied for a position at the orphanage so he could get close to Damon and kill him to avenge Liliana's death. He worshipped the Red Queen, and he was willing to try anything to find her successor, believing that if he did, maybe he'd become powerful and notorious as well, a true case of grandiose delusion.

And then he came across the entry he needed, the entry about Mara and how Colton had reason to believe that Mara had been a person of interest to Colton for a while now. Beneath it, the newest paragraph documented how Colton was going to take Mara to England, to sacrifice her to the royal family for all the power and riches he could ever want. All this time, Damon just saw Colton as the peculiar asshole who'd undermine his orders and skip out on work to see his girlfriend. Turns out, he had a plan all along.

Mara is the successor of Liliana.

CHAPTER 27

THE NEW DICTATOR

The journey to Stonefall Wilderness was a long one, Colton driving through the entire night with Mara sleeping soundly on the back seat of his car, her hands and feet bound together. Colton prayed no one would come after him, that no one would figure out his plan before he had the chance to enact it. Everything was falling into place. It was just too perfect.

When they finally arrived, so had the sun, bringing a

fresh breath of freedom and opportunity. As Colton reached into the back seat to pick up the child, he smiled to himself as they walked deeper and deeper into the forest. Mara was a fresh start, a brand-new child of Remphelia who hadn't been tarnished yet, someone he could construct to become who he wanted her to be. Together, the two of them would be unstoppable.

"Where am I? What happened?" Mara whispered, rubbing her eyes as she woke up in a small cabin that Colton had found several weeks before while scavenging for a secret hideout to do his research.

Colton gently untied the ropes and placed her on the couch. The room smelled musty, and there was dust coating every surface of the room. It was small, with barely any room to fit a couch, much less anything else. But most shockingly, pinned to the walls were thousands of articles on Liliana, Francesca, and all the events that happened under the rule of the children of Remphelia.

Colton sat down beside Mara and handed her a cup of hot cocoa. "It's okay, Mara. You're safe. No one can hurt you anymore."

Mara stood up; her eyes blinded by the bright sun shining its rays into the dark room. "This... this place looks familiar," she said.

She walked over to one of the walls, running her hand over a crack similar to one she had made two years ago when she kicked her shoe so hard that it collided against the infrastructure. She walked a little farther, and just as she thought, right beside the fireplace, was a carving with the words, Ella & Mara.

Mara fell back, her heart beating faster and faster as she recognized where she was.

"This is my home!" she shouted. "I live here! Where's Ella? Ella! Ella!"

Mara ran to several rooms, calling out Ella's name, but no one responded except for Colton.

"Mara, Mara, calm down!" Colton said as he grabbed her by the shoulders and sat her back down. "You're just imagining things. There's no one named Ella here. You're with me now."

"No! I want Ella. I want Ella!"

Mara jumped up and ran into the bathroom, slamming and locking the door behind her. She leaned her upper body over the sink and heaved heavily, turning on the sink at the same time to splash cold water over her face.

"Calm down, Mara. It's okay, it's okay," she repeated to herself.

But it wasn't working. Her body was still trembling, and she could feel a fountain of sweat pouring down her face. Turning on the sink again, she splashed more water against her face. Then she looked up.

In the mirror, all she could see were bright and blood red eyes staring back at her, with a slight drizzle of blood trickling down her left eye. She screamed and stormed back out into the living room.

"What did you do to me?" she shouted at Colton. "What did you do to me? Why did you bring me here? What did you do to Ella?" She sounded hysterical, picking up the books sitting on the coffee table and hurling them at Colton. Her eyes began to glow, and flames began to rise from the tips of her fingers. "What did you do to Ella?" she screamed again.

"Mara, please, listen to me," Colton tried to speak, dodging the flames and books that Mara continued to throw at him. "I'm here to help you! All those people in your past abandoned you, but I won't. I promise." He bolted behind a chair and used it as a shield against the powers of Mara.

"Shut up! Shut up! You killed Ella! It's all your fault! It's all your fault!"

"No, Mara, I promise! I didn't!" Colton could feel Mara sealing half his lips before he had the chance to mutter, "Ella's my sister!"

And the sealing stopped. Mara's eyes widened, and the look of anger and rage turned into sadness. "What?"

"Ella's my sister," Colton repeated. "I found out about it not too long ago. But not before she died. You see, Mara, sometimes being an orphan because your parents are no longer with you is better than knowing your parents are out there, but they just don't want you. My parents separated Ella and I at a very young age, sending me away to boarding school. I never even got the chance to know who my sister was, other than her name. And you wanna know whose fault that was? Free thinkers, the government full of corrupt people who think they can control the lives of everyone around them, forcing them to give up children and lifestyles just because they don't conform to the norm. I hate that!"

"But you see, Mara, you can change all that," he said as he knelt down beside her, who continued to stare at him without a blink. "You can avenge Ella's death, your parents' death. You can change all that and make this world a better place. And I can help you!"

Emotionlessly, Mara asked, "Can you bring Ella back?"

"No, I'm sorry, I can't, but I can make sure that other people like Ella, other sweet and caring people like Ella, never get hurt again. With your help, you and I can make sure that nothing bad happens ever again. Please, Mara, will you join me, and together, we will restore peace?"

"Okay," Mara replied.

WHEN JOSIE CROIX HUNG UP HER PHONE, SHE KNEW Colton was in trouble. Although she didn't know for certain, she knew that Colton must have gotten a lead; otherwise, he'd never just disappear like that.

Josie had been dating Colton for over six years. They'd met during a rally that supported the cause of Liliana and wanted to see the world under the reign of a new Red Queen. Since then, they had been inseparable, spending day after day plotting out how to find and capture the new child of Remphelia, and promising each other that if one of them ever went missing, it would be because the child was found.

"Son of a gun, he actually did it, didn't he," she whispered as she set her phone down on the table.

In 2011, when the birth of the new child was due, a message was sent out to all of Liliana's supporters, telling them that they needed to conceal their identities, mask themselves as ordinary people who just wanted to live and speak again, so no one would ever catch onto them.

She knew long ago that this day would come, that Colton would one day follow through on his obsession with finding the successor. Out of everyone in The Order, he was the most qualified, the most intelligent and dedicated. If he couldn't do it, no one could. It was that tenacity, that confidence, that made her fall in love with him. That's why she planted that fake diary in his desk, to throw whoever found it off their tracks and go on a wild goose chase while Colton carried out his plan for total dominance.

But that's not all she did. No, Josie was much more

deviant than that. She had always been the rebel growing up, making up her own rules rather than following them. Growing up as a single child, her parents gave her more attention than any child could ever need, and she hated it. She hated being coddled as it made her feel inferior and weak. She wanted to be the one others wanted rather than the other way around, and that's why she felt so attached to Colton.

Colton never really had a family, seeing Josie as the only person he could rely on when he didn't even know where his family was. And Josie loved it. She loved helping Colton, allowing him to come and go as he pleased, as long as he came to her whenever he needed help. It was a love match made in Heaven.

Josie was very well aware of how much Damon treasured the orphanage, passed down from generation to generation and costing him his entire life savings to repair. While he was busy trying to plan a way to hunt Colton down, Josie made a call to another member of The Order, who was also a member of a local newspaper, revealing the secret of the missing child. A potential kidnapping? Maybe. A possible threat to the country? Possibly. Either way, Damon was about to face more than he had expected.

LESS THAN AN HOUR LATER, STONES WERE BEING thrown at the walls of Baylor, and loud voices started shouting outside the windows. Damon stood up from where he sat, surrounded by pages and pages of Colton's diary, and ran over to look outside. There, he saw a crowd of reporters and an angry mob of parents, all curious as to what happened to the missing child.

"Damon Walden, you get your ass out here right now! If you can't manage your orphanage to keep one of your children from escaping, then what's the point of even having an orphanage?"

"Yeah! Who's going to escape next? What happens if fifty escape tomorrow? Or eighty? What are you going to do then? Just let them get away?"

"The children are not safe here with you. We need to get them out and into a better home!"

Soon, everyone started shouting all at once, and Damon felt nothing but a rush of pain stabbing through his head from all the noise. Suddenly, he began missing the days when no one was allowed to speak. It was much more peaceful than this.

He opened the window in his office and tried to address the crowd. "Now, now, I know how this may seem, but we have everything under our control, and..."

"You're a monster!" a woman in the mob shouted as she threw her beer can at him.

Damon quickly slammed the window shut and drew the blinds. He fell onto the hardwood floor and winced. The last time he had experienced a headache like this was when Liliana wailed in his ears during their battle. The pain was unbearable, but he had more important things to focus on, like find Colton and a missing child.

"Attention, staff. Attention, staff. I need everyone to join me in the conference hall. Now!" he shouted over the speakers and grabbed the diary.

"Well, how do we know we can trust whatever shit's written in that diary? For all we know, it could be a trap,"

Sebastian, the chef, shouted as everyone gathered together inside the room.

Damon nodded his head in agreement. "We don't, but England's the only lead we have, and we need to at least try."

"Well, how are we supposed to get there? We can't just abandon the orphanage like this? We can't just leave the kids here by themselves!" Sebastian shouted again.

"I, and a few other volunteers, will go. The rest of you will stay here and watch over the children. Good thing we have a lead, too. Based on my decipher of Colton's journal, he should be in the small village of Bilbury. Something about his grandparents residing there, and he would take Mara there while he waits for his meeting with the queen."

"I'll go, sir," Rose spoke up as she raised her hand.

"Yeah, me too," Michael added.

"Great, then it's settled. Tomorrow morning, we'll..."

Just then, the entire building started to shake, and all Damon could hear were piercing screams coming from inside and outside the building.

"The building's going to collapse!"

"The world is ending!"

"We're gonna die!"

The orphans all poured out of their rooms, screaming and crying as the building continued to shake. Damon ordered the staff to gather up the children and secure them in the basement, the basement surrounded by near-unbreakable walls meant to hold the powerful forces of the next Red Queen if they were to ever find her. Damon rushed outside to see what was going on, hoping it was just construction next door, but what he saw when he walked outside was terrifying.

People were bleeding from their eyes, running up and

down the streets as they clawed at their faces and screamed for salvation. Several dozen were lifeless on the ground, while others started to kill each other to try and escape from an invisible force that was chasing after them. The last time he had seen such a massacre was when The Order took down the protestors who were trying to keep them from raiding the lab. But this was so much worse. People began ripping their own tongues out and sewing together their lips.

When he turned around, Damon saw a group of emotionless bodies marching toward him in unison. "Freedom of speech does not exist. Freedom of speech does not exist. Freedom of speech does not exist," they continued to chant before walking straight into a pit of fire.

"What the fuck is going on?" Damon whispered. "This must be the work of... the Red Queen."

He found himself speaking alongside a female voice. He didn't think anyone else was near him. The rest of the staff were safely locked in the basement of Baylor, and the rest of the townspeople were busy killing themselves. He turned around.

"Josie?" he asked. "Is that you?"

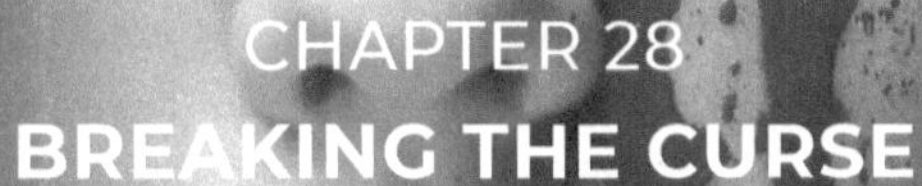

CHAPTER 28

BREAKING THE CURSE

Josie hadn't heard from Colton in weeks. They had made a deal. Once he kidnapped the child, he was supposed to reach out to her so they could rule the world together. Instead, he ghosted her, refusing to answer the hundreds of voicemails she had left for him.

She started panicking, worrying about what would happen to her without Colton by her side. Their plan was to capture the successor and use her powers to dominate and destroy anyone who tried to stand in their way. Colton was supposed to protect her. He knew that once people began figuring out that Josie was actually part of The Order, they would come after her and kill her. She pondered around her apartment, pacing back and forth as she stared intensely at her phone screen. Nothing. She screamed, and just when she was about to call Colton again, the entire apartment began to shake.

Josie lost her balance and collided with the floor. Growing up in California, she had experienced earthquakes before, but this was no earthquake. She rushed to her window and saw cars crashing into each other, people running in flames as they clawed at their eyes, a blood bath coating the streets.

She then looked over to her right and saw the words Freedom of speech does not exist, written in blood in the middle of a busy road. People were going insane, sealing their mouths shut with hot glue and tearing their eyeballs out of the sockets.

Is Colton back? Hopeful, Josie grabbed her keys and sped out of her apartment, running toward the orphanage as she hoped that Colton had brought the successor back to begin their takeover. However, when she arrived, the doors were locked, and Colton was nowhere to be seen.

"Josie? Is that you?"

Josie turned around when she heard a deep voice and saw Damon. She had only seen pictures of him, and he looked much more attractive in person.

"Damon! What happened? What's going on?"

Shaking his head, Damon sighed and looked around at the debris surrounding him. "I don't know for sure, but I've seen something similar to this before. From Liliana. My guess is, the new Red Queen is here, and she's hungry for power and revenge." He turned back to her, "Where's Colton? I swear to God, he better not be the one behind this. He has been a pain in my ass ever since I first met him. I don't know how you stand the guy."

"Honestly, I don't know, but I think I know how to stop him, them." Josie didn't know what started coming over her. Maybe it was the anger and frustration toward Colton, or maybe it was her physical attraction toward Damon, but she suddenly found herself abandoning the mission of The Order and helping Damon. "There's a spell; Colton showed it to me once. It was an old newspaper clipping about the curse of Remphelia. It's a curse. If we can break the curse, we can end this nightmare for good."

"Well, how do we break this... this curse?" Damon sounded confused, his problem now turning into a fantasy story.

"Love," Josie answered.

"What?"

"Love. It's love!" Josie repeated. "The curse of Remphelia was cast upon the first child. It guaranteed that the child will never experience true love, always being neglected and forgotten, taunted and hated. It was a curse that the royal family bestowed upon a peasant centuries ago for finding love, that it guaranteed her offspring a lifetime of loneliness and misery. It's love."

"You're the chosen one, Mara. Look around you. You're the ruler now. No longer can people speak up against you and undermine your power. No longer will you be teased and taunted because you're different. There's order in the world now, people no longer divided, people no longer rebelling. You did it. Your parents would be so proud." Colton smiled as he stood beside Mara on top of a building, whose eyes lit bright red, and her red glowing fingers sealing the mouths of those below them.

The town of Stockbridge had become an army, an army of silenced and emotionless creatures without mouths, without freedom of speech. Everyone was still and robotic, marching to the beat of Mara's drum.

Mara made one more gesture with her hands, and the entire town of Stockbridge all turned toward her, getting down on their knees and bowing to her, to them.

"Success," Colton whispered.

A chill draft ran through the rooftop, drying the droplets of cold sweat that gathered in Mara's brows, in her neck, and her back.

"I did it," Colton whispered by her side, his eyes on the people below, on their sealed mouths and their unseeing eyes. They looked lifeless, purposeless. And she had done it. She had to.

Silence was a welcomed reprieve and in it, Mara let her hands drop, the red light in them dimming now that her deed was done.

What have I done?

Tears were gathering in her eyes, and she wasn't sure if they were for the relief the silence gave or the look of pain on the people down below. Anger still covered her like a warm blanket on a cold night, like the only thing that could keep her safe.

"What now?" she asked Colton.

She had followed his lead, done what he had whispered to her. He'd been a relentless voice in her head, the loudest one of them all. And she had done everything he asked of her so he'd finally shut up. But now, in that silence, she wasn't sure what came next.

"Now we rule the world, Mara. You are the new Red Queen, and people bow to you! Look at them! They are all here for you; they will do everything you ask of them, never question you, never defy us. I've done it... I've found you." The last part he said looking away, looking down at his own hands.

Mirroring him, Mara looked down at her palms. They weren't glowing anymore, but they were shaking. Her whole body shook the same way the building had shook earlier, like a leaf in the wind. There was a rumbling in her mind, in her heart, in her whole being.

"Why me? Why all this? Why does everyone hate me? Why am I so different?"

The words that had lived forever in her mind now spilled out of her lips, and she repeated them over and over again. "Why me? Why this?"

"Because you're our destiny. You are what this world needed, and I've been looking for you since you were born. No one will ever understand you like I do, Mara. I'm all you have. You and I. This is it. And now... now we rule."

Mara opened her mouth to reply, to ask more questions, when the door behind them creaked open. They turned in unison and found two people standing on the threshold, their eyes wide open. The woman looked almost sad, her eyes on Colton. And the man... the man she knew. The man looked at her like he had never seen her before, his eyebrows knit together, his mouth in a tight and unpleasant line.

"Josie!" Colton took a step forward. "How did you find me? How are you here?" He looked over and saw Damon. "Well, well, my love! Why did you bring that man to me? Is he a sacrifice, a gift?" Colton laughed, cold and calculated.

"I am no longer your love, Colton. What you did here... this..." The woman, Josie, swept her arm to point at her, and Mara flinched. "This is not what we planned. I didn't... I didn't think it'd be like this..."

The woman's voice was soft, almost a whisper. She took two steps closer to them, almost making no sound. Mara cocked her head to one side and lifted her hand just in case, red light dancing around her fingertips. She wouldn't let anyone else hurt her.

Josie stopped moving.

"Mara..." It was the man speaking now, Damon. "I'm Damon Walden, do you remember me? I was in the orphanage with you. That man by your side, Colton, he doesn't know what's best for you, but I do, I'm here to help you."

Mara brought her hands to her ears, suddenly over-whelmed. Shaking her head, she screamed, "No, no! You're all liars! None of you care about anything! You don't love me! No one does!"

The building shook under their feet, and Colton's screams got to her despite the roaring in her head.

"Mara, they want to separate us. They want to destroy you; you have to destroy them first!"

The building shook harder, heat pooling in Mara's stomach as her whole face broke down in sweat. Everything anyone ever told her were all lies. No one cared about her; no one ever had. She was alone in this, alone in between all those voices that kept yelling. Her parents were gone. Ella was gone.

"Shut up! Shut up!"

She screamed at the top of her lungs, her eyes burning red as all the contained anger swelled and swelled until she felt like she was a bomb about to go off.

"Mara, kill them! Shut them up! They want to hurt us!"

Colton's voice was a desperate plea, a cry for help. But there, in between all the yelling, there was also a soft voice... a whisper.

"Mara... I'm so sorry." It was Damon's voice. "I'm sorry all of this happened to you; sorry I couldn't look after you enough to keep you from all this pain. You, like every other kid in that orphanage, are like my kids. I think of you as a daughter... And I know I could never replace your parents, who loved you dearly... but I want to be there for you."

They were all lies. All liars.

Opening her eyes, Mara looked at the man in front of her. He was on his knees, his hands extended toward her with his arms open — as if waiting for her to run to him and hug him. Behind Damon, Josie looked at her with pity in her eyes... or was it compassion? Josie smiled at her, a single tear running down her cheek. She didn't know what to think anymore.

"I will do everything in my power to help you, Mara, to find a way to break this curse," he continued.

"Curse?" The word was out of her lips before she could think better of it.

"Shut up, you filthy liar!" Colton stood between them, blocking Mara's view of Josie. He held Mara by the shoulders, shaking her slightly. "Look at me, they're lying to you. I'm the only one who can help you. You and I, we are the same, don't you see it?"

"What curse is he talking about?"

"There's no curse, Mara!"

"What is he talking about?"

"She doesn't know..." It was a whisper again. "He didn't tell you anything, did he?" It was the woman speaking this time, soft as a feather, her voice caressing Mara's mind instead of shattering it.

"Mara, don't listen to them. Seal their mouths!"

With a flick of her finger, they'd both be mute... but for the first time in her life, she was curious about what people had to say.

"What. Curse. Are. They. Talking. About?" She accentuated every word like a child having a tantrum.

Colton kept yelling, his voice rising and rising, but Mara only listened to the whisper past him, to Josie.

"Your family was cursed many, many years ago, Mara. None of this is your fault, and we're only here to help you. We want to help you break the curse so you won't feel like this anymore. I know you don't want to hurt all those people."

Their bloody eyes, sewn up mouths. Empty sockets and blood everywhere. *Was that what she wanted?* She feared it, feared it all, but she didn't know how to stop it.

"How do I stop this?" Her voice was a murmur hidden under the roaring of Colton's screams.

"If you don't kill them, I'll do it myself!"

Colton turned to Josie, hands fisted. Josie took a single step back, and then Damon stood between them.

"I won't let you hurt this woman, or this child, anymore. This has to end, Colton!"

Mara's eyes swept from one to the other, the roaring in her mind making her sweat all over again. The heat had receded from her fingertips, but she could still feel it inside. That anger, that anguish. But also... a small spark, something telling her to let go.

"Mara, I'm sorry you had to go through everything you went through," Damon said. "Please, don't look. You shouldn't experience any more violence than you already have."

At his words, Colton surged forward, his closed fist aiming for Damon's cheek.

But his fist never impacted.

Mara held him in place, the fist barely inches away. Josie was covering her mouth with both hands, looking at the child with deorbited eyes.

"Is this curse true?" the girl asked the woman, still holding Colton in place.

"It is... and I might know how to break it. It might take us some time to figure it out, but if you stop hurting people, we can help you. We will do everything we can."

"You can come back to the orphanage, Mara, back home." Damon's eyes were on her, too, gentle as ever.

"Home?"

She didn't know she had one of those. Not anymore. Her home was an empty and broken house with writing on the walls, with memories too painful to think of. A house where Colton had offered her hot chocolate, one she had trashed in her anger, throwing things around.

"I promise, Mara, we will do everything we can..."

Everything... It was a promise unlike Colton's. Where Colton had offered her power and revenge, Josie and Damon were offering her a chance to work this out, to break something she hadn't known existed. Because Colton hadn't told her about the curse. He'd known, and he hadn't told her.

"You lied to me," she spat in Colton's face.

She twisted him toward her and closed her hand into a fist. Colton grabbed at his throat, choking, gagging. "I didn't... I wanted... to... help..."

"Mara, please, let go of him!" It was an anguished cry

out of the woman's mouth, but Mara couldn't hear it over the roaring in her head.

"You lied to me…"

Colton wanted to hurt Josie and Damon, the only people who had offered her help, offered her the truth. He wanted her to kill them, to… No. She wouldn't. She needed the truth, needed those two people to help her, and Colton was getting in the middle of it. With a snap of her wrist, she threw him across the rooftop and into a wall. Mara collapsed to her knees, her body trembling uncontrollably as something snapped inside her chest, a huge weight lifting off her at the same time. Damon ran to her, whispering her name over and over.

"Are you okay? What can I do to help you?" His voice was soft, too soft… It didn't bother her. Looking up, Mara noticed the murmur of people far away. The birds sang in the distance, and the screams of people reached her.

She hurled herself against Damon's chest, and he held her there, muffling the dissonant noises even if just a little. They no longer hurt, but the screams of pain reminded her of everything she had done.

"Damon… he's…" Josie was crying; she could tell by the tone of her voice.

He pressed Mara harder against his chest. "Shh, it's okay; it'll be okay," he repeated, patting her hair.

But Mara could still hear Josie's sobs. She knew it the moment his skull had cracked against the wall that Colton was dead.

"What happened?" Josie asked after minutes that felt eternal, crouching by their side.

"I think she did it…"

"She did what?"

"I think she broke the curse by choosing us, choosing

family, instead of choosing to help Colton and be manipulated," Damon explained.

"The curse was first put upon someone who chose love over family... maybe by choosing the love for her family instead of something else..."

"Yes, I think that's it." Damon pushed Mara gently by the shoulders, looking down at her. "Are you okay, Mara?"

"I... I don't hear them anymore. The voices in my head..."

Tears slid down both Josie's and Damon's cheeks as they stood with her and headed toward the door to the stairs.

"Let's go back home, it's time we rebuild it one more time..."

Damon holding one of Mara's hands, and Josie holding the other, they led her down the stairs. Their fingers never shaking, their voices never wavering when they told her over and over again that it was done. That they would do everything to keep her safe from now on.

And for the first time, Mara believed them.

Curse of Silence

THE TRAGIC STORY OF REMPHELIA

9 781952 716195